Entirely

Isla K. Mar
Book 1

Book design by
Isla K. Mar
isla.k.mar on Instagram

To my younger self-you did it!

Trigger Warnings

Attempted Rape

Arranged/Forced Marriages

Controlling Behavior

Gore Scene

Guns

Mentions of Killing

Mentions of Murder

Mentions/Thoughts of Suicide

Panic Attack

Prejudice Against Races

Sexual Acts

Violence

Name Pronunciations

Jiho (GE-ho)

Eun-Ya (OO-n-ya)

Nari (NAH-lee)

Iseul (EE-sol)

Min-Jung (MIN-jong)

Yu-Jun (YOU-joon)

Do-Som (DO-sum)

Taeyoung (TAY-young)

Kyong (GE-ong)

Saoirse (SUR-sh-ah)

Allyria (ALLY-re-ah)

Petrov (PE-trof)

Contents

Entirely

Chapter Zero

Nineteen Years Ago

KIM EUN-YA. The first dead body eight-year-old Yoo Jiho saw was that of his classmate and friend, who had been alive only a few hours ago.

Her face was blue, her neck reddened by the cord wrapped around, and her eyes bloodshot from tears. Eun-Ya's yellow horizontal striped shirt was wrinkled by what seemed like a struggle. Her tan brown cargo pants ripped here and there, parts of her skin showing blood-soaked on them. The right shoe was still on, and the left was a few meters away. The young boy was hysterical; screams were heard by his small-town neighbors.

Many ran to the scene to see if he was injured, as Jiho's father and mother had built a good name for them. Incidents like watching children after school, having shelter for families in need, and always having food ready for the students and factory workers after a long day of work out front of the establishment. Because of these honorable deeds, many tried to be as helpful to their son as possible.

A handful of the neighbors looked at the view in horror; Jiho was up against an old tree trunk, his vomit mixed with his tears stained his hoodie; near him, the little girl, her eyes still staring.

It wasn't till Eun-Ya's older sister broke down, repeating to herself that what her eyes saw wasn't true, that everyone else came out of their daze.

The Kim family was raised by their grandfather. Their mother and father in Seoul, South Korea's capital, earn money to send to the mother's father and two daughters. The poor grandfather was approaching his crying granddaughter when a few men stopped him from seeing the youngest dead.

The guardian was confused about what was happening. He wanted to comfort Taeyoung, the oldest. Finally, he broke through the crowd with his cane and hurried over.

Once there, the man pulled Taeyoung close to him, soothing her the best he could. When Jiho came into his line of view, his confusion was at an all-time high. Following the line of sight, the poor man's heart dropped to the depths of Earth.

"Eun-Ya…?" His heartbreak was evident in his voice; the cracks broke his strength as the tears poured out of him. Unfortunately, the little girl would only be the first death of that year.

When the police force came to the scene, most of the spectators had cried themselves out into exhaustion. The majority became mute towards one another that year, not even an exchange of greetings when entering establishments such as classes, workplaces, and homes.

The town had placed a curfew, and many parents started to homeschool in fear of their child being the next to die.

JIHO'S FATHER HAD BEEN more distant from his son since Eun-Ya's death and other killings in the last two months. A boy, Si-Woo, another classmate of Jiho, and a girl, who happened to just be visiting some relatives from another providence.

Many providers within the neighborhood have found it challenging to keep their jobs as businesses went under, moving closer to the capital in hopes of a safer environment where their families can continue their upbringing. The stress had strained their relationship, a tension that had broken the tight-knit Yoo family.

His father, Yu-Jun, felt worthless. He could not shake the disheartening feeling that he was a nothing who couldn't shield himself and his family from the evil the world possessed.

Yu-Jun was, in other words, a self-loathing individual who felt as if he was the killer, all while Jiho's state of mind was tormenting him, and the vivid images he replayed in his head were refusing to let him be at peace. A battle in which all he wanted was to escape. No respectable parent wants to see their child fight off their demons alone. Yu-Jun wished to take some of the pain, but he couldn't.

As the schools around them had shut down until the killer was caught, the teachers would all go door-to-door, leaving the stack of work for that week on the steps of each home before knocking and walking away. All contact with one another outside the breadwinners was zero.

Many had thought this method was the best option to ease the worries of parents, guardians, and other older children who understood the events happening. Most of the time, it was silent in the Yoo household, with occasional pregnancy sickness Jiho's mother, Do-Som, had in the morning when she ate or even smelled, something the child disagreed with.

Jiho's parents, before the death count increased significantly, were the couple everyone was inspired to be. Yu-Jun, a name meaning king or ruler, held the authority in the house-what he said goes. But like any great ruler, he considered what his actions might do to the rest of the household, wanting only the best for them.

Now, a ruler would bow to only his equal, his love.

His Do-Som.

Jiho's mother had been named one out of love, literally. Her parents had wanted to keep to tradition with names, but still, something that their daughter would be happy having, twisting the classic 'love' with the new: Do-Som.

Their relationship was something out of a movie. Growing up next door to each other, having been friends since birth, crushing since their late years of middle school, and finally dating in the middle of high school. The two were textbook examples of what a partnership should be: respectful, communicative, empathetic, and caring. They understood the hardship life can throw at them as individuals, let alone a partnership, causing them to always voice their appreciation and love for one another.

Having Jiho only strengthened their bond; the excitement and nervousness were the most potent emotions during their child's first two years as they settled into confidence, wanting to do everything perfectly, though most of the time, they didn't. Of course, something is bound to go wrong when things seem picture-perfect. In this case, death.

Do-Som wanted to leave. She wanted her son to see the best Korea can offer in therapy, having Jiho overcome his trauma with a professional. Plus, with another child on the way, Do-Som could not risk their life.

Yu-Jun wanted to stay. His family and his wife's family had lived in this small town for generations. The man would not leave their history behind just because of a killer he believed would get caught soon. This caused many fights between the 'perfect' couple, damaging how they perceived each other.

With no contact with anyone else, the two forgot about the volume of yelling, the effect of their debates-staying or going. Yu-Jun and Do-Som may have values that each understood, but neither was going to back down on this subject.

JIHO HAD NOT SPOKEN to anyone since the incident, which clearly has been doing more damage than his family initially thought. It was hard for them to accept such news of Jiho's trauma. Although he had not been very talkative, to begin with, he was still able to say words here and there.

But now he was diagnosed as mute by health doctors, breaking the hearts of his family and neighbors. Though very shy, the boy was kind to those around him: helping with class work, taking the blame for undone class cleaning when others had sports or homework to do, and even helping the elders during the afternoon.

His mother and father often fought over how to approach him, his studies, his safety, and what to do in general, as the killer was still out. Usually, the arguments started at dinner, with a small amount of bickering, keeping it minimal for Jiho's sake.

Once he was in bed, they would escalate to taking harsh words at one another, causing old misunderstandings and previous mistakes to be thrown into the conversation. Both assumed their son was asleep and would not have to hear or see any of their fights. But if they had just turned to look around, often, the little boy was standing right in the doorway, holding on to the stuffed animal that was supposed to be for Eun-Ya's ninth birthday.

Jiho blamed himself for the death of Eun-Ya and the strain on his parent's marriage, knowing that if neither happened, everyone would be happier. He wanted to be the perfect son for his mom and dad, but he couldn't. All he wanted to do was take Eun-Ya's place right now; not knowing what else to do, Jiho stayed quiet.

One night, when the arguments were happening, Jiho had enough of the pinning against each other, wanting them to put their anger on him rather than each other. He approached their smaller lamp on the end table closest to their patio. Picking it up, Jiho took a deep breath before throwing it across the living room, causing some of the glass decorations and cups that were left out to smash. The light bulb shattered to pieces near their feet.

The silence was something the Yoo house had not been welcoming to in some time. It was strange but peaceful to be alone with their thoughts. Dawning in the adults' minds, their child had heard them all this time, fighting against one another, not caring about the damage it was doing to the family.

It was the first time Jiho had done something so drastic and out of character. Unsure of what to do, they had all just gone to bed, waking up with an awkward feeling of misplacement. The adults are unsure of what to do with the consequences of their actions. They had agreed to at least try to be civil for their son's sake, not fighting.

THE YEAR HAD COME around, and the killings just stopped towards the end of January, the last one being five-year-old Seok Yu-Jin. He was found wrapped in plastic, as if mummified, at the bottom of a tree many had passed on the trail around the park.

Jiho's parents did not want him to return to school in fear of the killer still being out there, remaining with homeschooling as the best option for their mental state.

Yu-Jun and Do-Som did not trust the killer had entirely stopped her doings. Some thought it was a man leading the children out of the house with treats until a high heeled print showed itself at one of the crime scenes. A kiss lined in lipstick on a child's forehead solidified they were now looking for a woman. Forcing the authority figures to start at the beginning again.

Some parents returned their children to in-person schooling right where they left off, ignoring that many of their children's classmates had been brutally murdered by a person still free. It was confusing for Do-Som to understand the blind trust they had. The killings just stopped, but the killer was not caught. Yu-Jun had difficulty finding common ground with his wife during this nightmare, but now he was on her side. *How could you send your child out when so much danger still exists?* It was unfathomable.

Being around so many people would do more harm than good for their son; it's already hard for him to be near them. Jiho had taken to staying in bed, unable to leave his room or even eat alone. The couple had also noticed that he had stopped trying to make connections outside their immediate family; hell, it was hard for the poor boy to accept his younger sisters for a while.

The only son of the Yoo family was mute for a few years after the first kill. Those eyes staring at him blamed him for his absence, appearing in nightmares, for not saving her.

His night terrors were the worst the first year and a half; it wasn't until his youngest sister was born that Jiho's terror subsided to an occasional nightmare. Ticks had formed to stabilize the young one; he would pick his skin till it bled on his left arm. Some stayed as minor scars with the depth of his picking; others faded as if he had never touched the area.

The family had thought he was better, not wanting to start from the beginning again. Yu-Jun and Do-Som had decided never to talk about that year. The couple told their parents to never mention the horrible night in front of or around him. Fortunately, they had agreed and ignored the entire thing.

Chapter One

Eighteen Years Ago

"JIHO-YAH, PLEASE eat. Just a little bit." The pleas of the nine-year-old's mother went in one ear and out the other. Her son did not react when her dried thumb smoothed over his right cheek.

Jiho was nothing more than empty, his lungs barely even moving to keep him alive. His mind wanted nothing more than to follow his friend. Greeting death to rid himself of the guilt of not saving Eun-Ya and other classmates.

Jiho reminisced about his last encounter with Eun-Ya every few minutes. They had a science project that required them to gather samples of different dirt around town and test them to see which was best for growing crops and other plants. After collecting two other samples around their homes, they agreed to meet at the park; they lived in different directions, and the park was the best option to go over their find since it was an equal distance from each house.

If he had not stopped to get ice cream with the money he had saved from his new year, she would still be in the class with the others. Or at least he thinks, unsure if the killings would continue without her death.

Lost in his own self-loathing, Jiho did not notice his mother letting visitors in his room. The three newcomers thanked the woman for taking a leap of faith for them to speak with her son, which was appreciated tremendously. Once his mother left them, the three slowly made their way beside the boy who last saw the youngest in the family.

Clearing her throat, the daughter spoke, "I don't know what is going on in your head as all of us grieve over Eun-Ya's death, but you should not blame yourself…"

Taeyoung had known the two children were to meet that day for a school activity. She did not blame him for her sister's death. If anything, she was happy the boy found her sister earlier rather than later, as nature would decompose her too fast for any chance of recognizing her. It hurt her that the image haunted them all, more for Jiho, as he was the one who had to stare directly into her dead eyes. Taeyoung would have taken her life if she were in his position.

Although she, too, had seen the body firsthand, Taeyoung gave the young boy a lot of respect as he was still alive, even if he wasn't living. She wanted to take his pain, but that wasn't possible.

The teenager let a heavily shaken sigh leave her before shifting to lie with him, spooning the poor child and holding him tightly as if Jiho were her younger sibling.

Taeyoung spoke with authority, "You are not the cause of her death, Yoo Jiho. You found her before that…*woman* could do anything else to her. You have nothing to do with the outcome. If you had come when you wished you did, two families might have been mourning their child."

Sentence after sentence, Jiho slowly came back to the emotions he'd been trying to push away. Tears threatened to spill.

"I am happy you got to live, but you must promise me something. You must live for not only yourself but for Eun-Ya, too." Her whispers consoled the screams and shrieks she wished to voice of denial over her sister's death. "We both must."

The two children now faced each other, their tears pooling out. Taeyoung's voice cracked at the end of her sentence. Taking a moment to collect herself, Taeyoung combed through Jiho's hair while his face was in her neck, sobbing. Gently, she held on to Jiho, rubbing his back. After another minute passed, she moved, eye to eye with each other.

"You must live. Eun-Ya always spoke well about you. Saying you helped her with her studies and practice tests. Continue to be kind and caring, Jiho. If it is difficult to return to your old self, become something you believe she would be proud of. You are loved, and we do not blame or hate you for her death."

During the whole interaction, the parents of the Kim family stood there, embracing each other with bloodshot eyes due to their crying. The parents confirmed the statements their living daughter made.

Jiho could only nod in acceptance of their words as his voice had not been used for a year and was too scared to use it now.

His action shocked the three as he exited his bed and bowed formally toward them. It was his last interaction of apology to the family, sending them off and wishing them the best for their future. The family of three now had smiled and bowed slightly towards him before taking their leave.

Once they had left the house, Jiho had yet to stand. A choked cry blew through his lips. He had no strength in standing, so he continued to bow, with his knees on the floor and forehead on top of the back of his two hands, being the divider to him and the wooden ground.

The cry had gotten so loud his mother and newborn sisters heard from outside, as his mother knew it was best to get it out. There was nothing she could do now but allow him to scream and shout to his heart's content over the constant neglect of his sadness, guilt, pain, and anger.

JIHO WAS STILL MUTE towards everyone, but his behavior has improved since the Kim family visited. He has stuck to the promise of becoming something Eun-Ya would be proud of. In doing so, his studies and time spent with his family increased.

The interactions with his new sisters were also a sight to see. Instead of ignoring them further, the boy embraced them, becoming a protector. If he could not protect his first friend, who was like a little sister to him, he would be their protector. He would gladly put his life on the line for them; he would love for them.

His mother and father were happy to see this improvement, as well as his siblings. They had fun together as the three children communicated without words, just gestures.

At first, it was gibberish and pointing gestures, but unsatisfied with the divider placed with their son's silence, the parents had begun using at least some flashcards to get closer to each other.

The two included these teachings to the twins, wanting them to communicate with their brother on another level.

Jiho was intelligent for his age, knowing that his parents did not fully understand how to support their son and build their family again; he placed books and left websites dedicated to mutism and ways to communicate around the house. He loved his family for trying to support him and appreciated the effort they all had made; even his grandparents and family friends learned a little bit for him.

Jiho was not entirely himself and would not be for a relatively long time, but he was progressing. In upholding Eun-Ya, the boy vowed to become someone who would help those in need.

To make those feel safe as he wishes, he could do for himself, her, and her last moments. Jiho would go the path Eun-Ya wanted. He would become the doctor that she always claimed to become. He would uphold that wish.

He would be a safe place for those in need of help.

Chapter Two

Twelve Years Ago

LOOKING AT THE CASTLE-LIKE building, Jiho only wanted to get back on the plane and go home.

In his opinion, the school was much too tall and historical looking. There were large windows and an alarming number of corridors. The only Korean there very much wanted to leave, but his parents had already paid for the remaining share for the year, so going back home was not an option for him.

Slowly, Jiho began his search for his dorm through the sea of new and returning students. Many looked at him with wonder; the school only took those of wealth or an ungodly amount of knowledge, a prodigy. Not having a familiar face or a renowned name, many have concluded that he was a brain, not wealth.

Broduil Academy was the most sought-after school in Ireland. Once a student, you could be categorized into one of the two groups-brains or wealth. The academy had been known for the high marks their students accumulated, but money had to be paid to fund these teachers and staff.

They maintained their reputation by only giving scholarships to a few of the world's top markers. Parents who wanted their children to be attached to that reputation donated their money to gain them a spot on the roaster. Jiho was labeled a brain before he even stepped into a classroom.

Two sections to the right from the front gates, on the third floor, and the last door near the hall's windows, Jiho's surname was placed on a plaque attached to a rustic wooden door. His dorm only housed one, relieving the boy. The room had been modified a bit, with the walls being three-fourths white and newly painted while one wall was brick. A small desk was complimentary, along with a shitty, uncomfortable chair. The mattress was relatively thin. Mental notes about purchasing a mattress topper were made.

Thankfully, he had gotten the corner room, giving him a clear view of the campus yard, mountains, and shores that caught his attention the most when looking at the academy on the flight.

Jiho had put together his living space for the rest of the evening. Putting up photos of his family, hobbies, and one of Eun-Ya. It had been years since that day, yet the boy still had so much anger and guilt lingering. Having Taeyoung's words and letters echo in his mind always helped him keep progressing toward the future that the Kim family would be proud of.

NOT ONE PERSON WAS able to break Jiho's silence. It had been five months since the students 'met' Yoo Jiho; many wanted to know why he attended the school, others wanted help with their studies by copying his work, but the majority wanted to know why he was mute.

They had tried everything: being friendly towards him, asking him to read during class, annoying him daily, trying to anger him, and even physically harming him. They wanted answers, and knowing there was no punishment for their actions, they bullied him.

It was hard for the other brains to see, but they would rather see him go through all the misery than them. He thought it was selfish of the others, but what could they do? They had no money or power to really do anything to help or protect themselves.

It started so small by pushing him around and 'accidentally' bumping into him, resulting in the boy falling. As the months went by, it progressively got worse. Those who bought their way in put tacks on his seat without Jiho seeing them beforehand, beating him, wanting a sound to come out. Until one day, it was known to never bother Jiho.

Typically, the bullies never entered his dorm, allowing him to have his guard down and to be himself. Jiho was almost done with the essay the professor had assigned the class when his door opened. It was common for his door to remain unlocked during the daytime.

At this moment, he wished to have locked it as five boys entered. Jon, Aster, Devon, Nathan, and Gerrit were seen standing at the doorway. They were the main ones who took their bullying to extremes.

The five entered Jiho's haven, looking around, touching everything they could. The target was worried and scared but mostly irritated. Jiho was told to never enter without knocking first and waiting for an indication to join. The boy was silently judging the other five.

They had trashed his room, looking through everything and anything they thought was valuable. Jon had almost called it quits, wanting to leave as there was nothing in the room, but Devon had found it.

The one thing that had kept Jiho at bay was something he could never replace. An old photograph of himself giving a piggyback ride to Eun-Ya during their school's field day; they were smiling, having fun trying to win the contest where they had to keep their partner from touching the ground for as long as they could.

It was one of the last moments that the whole town had fun and happiness before the sadness wrecked it. The last thing the Kim family had gifted him before they left. The grandfather had taken the photo that day.

The terror on Jiho's face only confirmed to Devon that he had found the holy grail of the boy's heart, a simple picture that the five did not know the history of.

"Who's this? Girlfriend back home?" Aster and Gerrit laughed at the idea that Jiho could be dating anyone, "Someone who rejected you? You know it's creepy to keep this if she did." Aster had taken the photo to show the others what she looked like.

"I bet she wouldn't be caught dead with you." All five boys laughed sinisterly in Jiho's mind like they were taunting him for guilt. He was at his breaking point, wanting nothing more than to shut them up. The amount of red clouding his vision was ungodly.

Jiho could calm down, but only after repeating Taeyoung's speech a few years ago; those words had been his anchor for anything that had troubled him. It wasn't until Gerrit, acting impulsively, ripped the photo, swearing to be helping Jiho move on from a waste of space girl in complete mockery.

Jiho's world had slowed. It was like a bad slow-motion shot; Jiho could see every tear and fingerprint smudge in the photo.

The ringing in his ears increased tenfold, unbearable to anyone who would take his place at that moment. Jiho focused only on the picture, which had become even more damaged, as one of the five stomped on the remains, twisting his foot to emphasize the destruction they created.

Jon leaned close, painfully so, to Jiho, whispering towards him, breaking the last wall containing his wrath, "When you see her next, tell her if she wants a fun time to come with you after the break. We are dying to see her." The only thing racing through Jiho's senses was honoring Jon's longing.

Dying.

Without glancing back, Jiho's textbook collided directly with Jon's skull. The impact made the white boy fall, grunting in misery; his glasses splintered on impact, causing some fragments to cut his face. While down, Jiho picked up the durable plastic chair, its legs were made of copper, hurling it at the other four, resulting in the exact same as the first.

Once Jiho's eyes landed on the wood mop located outside his open door, a wicked idea came. Not bothering to step over or around, the emotionally destroyed boy placed his foot on any vulnerable part still accessible.

Jon's hands, Aster's kneecap, Devon's arm socket, Nathan's throat, and Gerrit's balls. Jiho waited a few seconds with each step, adding more weight to the foot. Grabbing the mop, Jiho noticed that the commotion he had caused gained some viewers; he closed his door before locking, only after giving a bone-chilling smile to anyone looking.

The five bullies gathered together, still on the ground, holding their upper bodies up, leaning on each other or the wall. Once they saw Jiho, the regret was too late; his eyes helped nothing but pure hatred, and his smile and aura were traumatizing.

His movement was so painfully slow as he detached the mop head from the stick; even the way he blinked was taunting. Jiho slowly stopped before them, a step away from Gerrit's ankle.

Tapping the end of a long wooden handle on the side of the head, Jiho thought about who to start with first and who to save for last. Thinking about who found the photo first, he pointed toward Devon.

However, he moved to Jon, who he remembered was the one to start the bullying in the first place, thinking again that the brothers, Aster, and Nathan, usually physically harm him. Still, it ends with the one who destroyed his last sentiment of Eun-Ya. Gerrit.

As the realization struck them all, Jiho stomped on his ankle, shattering it with a disheartening crunch. Gerrit's raw scream was enough to have the other students in the hall cringe, even tearing up at the mere thought of their bone breaking.

Grinding the foot placement further into the ground was an extra satisfying moment for Jiho, his own version of the same action the group did a few moments ago. The smell of piss broke his focus on the sobbing brunette. Staring to the left, the sight of Devon was shaken to the bone with a large wet stain on the inner part of his pants. Knowing he wanted to leave Gerrit for last, Jiho straightened out, moving to Devon next.

The indication of rejection of what Jiho would do to Devon was not acknowledged; nothing could save him at this point. Raising the wooden weapon, Jiho swung it down. Over-*wack*-and over-*wack*-and over-*wack*-and over-*wack*-and over again, with the thick object breaking in two after four more hard hits on the boy's head. Once broken, Jiho could see that he was knocked out, blood oozing down his face, mixing on the ground with tears and piss.

Whimpers of frightfulness came from the right side of Jiho; he was still filled with anger, the same anger he had hidden away for years. At the sight of three more sniffling babies, his rage only amplified.

How dare they be the ones to cry after all the suffering I went through? How fucking dare, they.

Those two sentences were replayed in Jiho's head, and he went to Jon while the other two hid behind. Since the mop handle had broken in two, Jiho grabbed his stapler, which was sitting on the table above Devon, before he continued his target route, stepping on the still-broken ankle of Gerrit on the way.

Crying filled his dorm and his hall; the students could hear the impact of the hits without having an ear to the door, sickening, and freezing them from moving.

Pleads were ignored, and the smile that once was seen on Jiho by the less injured three was replaced with a stone of a face. Nothing but relaxed eyes of emptiness and the thoughtfulness placed on his lips, debating on the severity of pain the mute boy wanted to do.

Jiho remembered his torture when Jon placed staples on his skin a few weeks ago. Jon looked at the new weapon with the same recall, shaking his head and begging Jiho not to. The only difference was that it was Jiho doing the torture this time.

Pulling his shirt up, the shortest of the five, begged again for Jiho to stop, and again, he was deaf to words.

Stuffing the end of the shirt in Jon's mouth, he stapled it to his tongue and lips, making the shirt stay in place even when he let go. The cries of pain, almost the same as Gerrits, just slightly muffled.

Jiho wanted them to smile as much as they told him to smile. Being thoughtful, he began to make smiley faces on Jon's upper body; the whole thing covered his chest and stomach.

Jiho was displeased when he saw the beggar closing his eyes; it wasn't nice to shun something pretty in his mind; after all, he did say they were dying to see. He granted, securing Jon's eyes stayed open by stapling the lids for him to see.

Standing up once more to view his art was divine. Jon's drying eyes were red with irritation, his hands swollen, and he could not remove the metal from his face, mouth, chest, and stomach. He threw the object on his bed, picking up the two broken sticks.

The brothers had just cried, choking on air as their oxygen intake surpassed exhaling. Aster and Nathan held each other, asking for them to be spared, again, no use. With one swift motion, Jiho had impaled the sharpened ends in their knees; a future in walking without a limp can be out of the question. Because they had cried so much, the pain not helping, they soon fainted from the pure exhaustion of their bodies.

Slowly, Jiho turned his attention to the person who rid him of the last possible thing of Eun-Ya. He had walked over before squatting down at eye level with Gerrit.

"You aren't worth saving…You took something precious from me and destroyed it. I'm returning the favor."

This was the first and last time the bully would hear the voice of a broken boy, and it was just above a whisper, making him the only one to hear.

Before he could process that the mute wasn't, in fact, a mute, he felt the breeze of Ireland's evening. While in shock, Jiho grabbed him by the back of his collar, pulling him towards the door. The selective mute unlocks to see not only crying students but vomiting and scared ones taking a step back in horror.

They had heard the terrifying screams and acts only to have their imaginations paint what truly happened in the room. Since Jiho lived right by a large window, which was conveniently able to open, the nine students watched and screamed as they saw Jiho push the brunette off a third-story window.

He watched for a moment before walking back into his dorm to move the other four out; all five bullies landed on gravel, two sections to the right from the front gates and only five meters in front of the staffing office.

Before returning to his dorm for the night, Jiho made a zip motion on his lips before smiling and waving goodnight to the others. The next day, the five were found, but no one would say how they arrived. It was also the day people knew not to bother Yoo Jiho from now on.

Yoo Jiho is more of a monster in the students' eyes than the big five, the five most influential families that happened to attend that year, which he demolished within ten minutes.

Chapter Three

Ten Years Ago

JIHO WAS IRRITATED, more so than he thought he could ever be. The primary and only factor was a blond ball of annoying sunshine.

Allyria Turner (though she prefers Ally), his partner for this year's history project, which would be worth around fifty percent of their final grade. To say he was disappointed was an understatement. Jiho had been content for the past two years of being alone during school. No one bothered him after that 'accident,' and he loved it. But here stands the most brutal opponent yet, a sixteen-year-old girl who would not stop talking.

"I told Henry that I would love to watch the rugby game with him, even though I would rather see a book be burned than be alone with him, but I had this project with you. So, thank you for saving an evening with a boy who would only talk about himself." The hyper blond finished her rambling.

Jiho stared at her, unamused with being her scapegoat for a situation he did not even care about in the first place. The boy did not know why she was so keen on talking to him when he told, well, he wrote in a notebook to communicate that he would do all the work if she never tried to speak to him. All his past partners took that chance, knowing it would be up to the school's standards as Jiho was the top student.

"So…I was thinking of doing the project on the Celtics; my dad did a past uni paper on them and read me some facts about them. I thought they were interesting. What do you think? Of course, if there is another topic you want to do, I'm all ears! Although I do hope you know I will be less enthusiastic about it. But-" Jiho shot his hand up, indicating to her to stop talking, before taking out his notebook.

Will you shut up for a second? We will do the project on the Celtics, but you really don't need to be here. I can do all of it if you never talk to me again. Okay?

Sliding the book over, he stood up. Assuming Ally would finally accept his offer, Jiho started packing his things. He saw that she had closed it and begun collecting her things, as well.

Finally, Jiho thought, *I can return to my space and be at peace.* Picking up the remaining stuff on the table, he started to walk away.

Before he could step, the boy's sleeve was tugged gently. He turned back around to see the confusion in Ally's brown eyes, reminding him of a grizzly bear's fur on the summer morning.

"We have a project to do. So, are we going to your dorm?" She had not let go of his sleeve, knowing if she did, the boy would bolt for the door with no hesitation. Jiho was now the one confused with her.

Did she not read what he just wrote? Did she need help understanding the meaning behind his message: Leave me alone.

Before he could fully process what was happening, Ally continued, "I will not allow someone to carry my grades for me. So, we either work together and pass, or we fail together. You pick." Ally had now let go of his button-down sleeve.

Knowing that with a failure on this assignment, his rank would go down, and the money his parents used to help with the remaining balance the scholarship didn't pay for would go down the drain. After a minute of battling back and forth with the pros and cons, Jiho clutched Ally by her wrist and pulled her towards the direction of his dorm. Ally beamed at the action; she had heard about how inhumane and distant Jiho could get. She thought he just needed a friend, and she would be delighted to be that.

The two did not neglect the looks on the other students' faces. Most thought the worst for the little sunshine of the school; they had no idea that Allyria Turner had just threatened Jiho to have their project fail if the boy didn't work with her.

After the short walk from the library to his room, Jiho locked the door and played some soft music from Korea, mainly ballads but some soft pop here and there; he did not want others to listen as he knew they would most likely want to know why after two years he brought someone in his haven. It was the same room as his first year, as all the other students refused to be placed there.

Ally took her time to look around the infamous cursed room. Although hearing about the incident, she was not even there when it occurred. Ally had transferred to this school at the end of the term last year and was still reasonably new to Broduil Academy. She could tell Jiho was a relatively tidy person; there were no dusty areas anywhere, and everything had its own place, but it still looked inviting to the eye. On the desk, hidden poorly by some textbooks, was a photo. It was ripped, being repaired with some scotch tape.

Jiho was preoccupied with setting things up on the floor, as his desk would not be able to fit two people, and he refused to work on his bed with outside clothes. Seizing this opportunity, Ally grabbed the photo, and saw that one of the young children was clearly her quiet partner, but who was the other one? And how could one smile this big in the past but, when grown up, maintain such emotionlessness?

The heiress did not know what to think about the information she had just learned, information that, indeed, few others knew of.

Many around her had spoken vaguely about the boys who were hospitalized, only confirming it when she found out those injured were the sons of business partners of her father. Ally quickly realized who was responsible for such injuries as she spent time talking with the other students. But she would always ask why Jiho went to the extreme with punishment.

Some other girls in her hall told her that Jiho was bullied seriously and snapped one day, but no one knew why or what set the whole thing off. To her belief, Ally had just found out why. The photo. She simply couldn't understand why the image was so meaningful.

A gasp escaped her mouth when Jiho snatched the picture from her hands. Furious, his eyes turned black with anger at the thought of Ally just glancing at it, let alone touching the photo. His strength caused her shoulder distress; the girl knew there would be bruising tomorrow morning. Ally thought she would end up like the five boys at that moment. Jiho was drowning in his anger; he was unbelievably upset and looking at Ally with such hate.

Was this why she wanted to come to his dorm? To mock him about the past, about the photo. Was Ally only here to get even for her 'friends'?

Jiho wasn't stupid; he had the markings to prove it. Just because he won't talk to others doesn't mean he can't hear. A couple of the known gossipers were discussing how Ally was a successor, and her family knew the relatives of the five boys he granted the wish for. Well, partially granted; only one had been left in a coma; the others were still walking. Jiho knew a lot more than others considered.

He was the ears of the academy, and because he wouldn't talk to others, many gossiped in front of him, knowing that he would never repeat it.

In a fluster, Ally started to ramble, "I'm sorry. I…I didn't mean to touch it." She stuttered due to the increase in pain Jiho provided. He was annoyed she had spoken. He wanted her to just shut up for a minute, "I really didn't mean it. I was simply curious. I'm sorry, okay?" The pain was too much for Ally; her eyes welled with tears, unsure of what to do.

Thankfully, after two years here, Jiho had pre-written cards with simple phrases and sentences that he could show without writing them every time. Jiho placed the damaged picture on the top shelf behind Ally and pulled three cards from the bunch.

Here. Why? Boys.

It was a simple question but still heavy for the two. Jiho wanted to know why she was there. *Why did she have such a stick up her ass about being involved?* He wanted her to answer. If the answer did not satisfy him, Jiho would kick her out and 'talk' about being uncomfortable around her to his dean.

Confused with what he asked her, Ally was stuttering and trying to realize his desire. It was like a bullet hit her; he thinks she's friends with them. In a rush of words, Ally clarified any misunderstandings.

"I…I'm not friends with those boys. Really. My dad works with their families, but I don't see them. I even try to keep our talks limited. Please, just sit down, and I will explain."

Ally was not one to plead or clear up misunderstanding as she had been taught that one's perspective is not the fact; it is what you believe is true.

Unsure about the sincerity, Jiho took a chance. He withdrew his hand from her shoulder but stood before her. Nodding his head for her to continue her explanation. Ally took a breath she had been holding.

"As I said, I only know them from my dad, but that's all. I don't know what they did to you or 'who' hurt them."

She paused slightly, and Jiho knew she was lying about being unaware. Still, he waited until she looked away, claiming she was done.

"I just…I saw the photo, and my impulsiveness got the better of me. I am sorry. I didn't mean to touch something that valuable. I didn't come here to hurt you or anything. I just really want to get to know you."

Finally looking away, Jiho watched with calculated eyes. Still not pleased with the answer, he showed her two cards.

Why? Me.

She blinked a little, unsure if Jiho was being serious or not, "Why do I want to know you?"

A short nod was given. Jiho still did not fully trust her and her motives, but nevertheless, he waited for her to answer.

"I honestly think you need a friend. I'm going to be your friend now." It was concise. The sentence was the same as Eun-Ya's.

"I'm going to be your friend now," a five-year-old started.

Her bowl cut and bangs bounced as she hopped to his level. Jiho had been hanging upside down on a bar at the park when he heard her speak. Although the boy had grown up with all his classmates in a small town, he hardly played with them or even tried to get to know them. He was too shy to say hi.

"I'm Kim Eun-Ya."

Getting down from the bar, the small boy rapidly blinks for a second before sticking out his hand, "I'm Yoo Jiho." The two smiled at one another.

"-iho…Jiho…!" The blonde had been calling his name for a few minutes as he stared at her. It wasn't till she had grabbed his forearms and shook them did he returned. "You okay…? You were kind of…gone for a moment."

Jiho looked at her with an unreadable expression. Breathing in and slowly out, he took her by the hand and pulled her to the low table, a standard piece of furniture in Korean households, before pulling his laptop out and starting their history project. Typing and rustling of paper could be heard between the two, the soft music still in the background. Although Jiho wanted to finish the project as fast as possible so Ally could leave, he had been at war with himself to open to her.

She did seem genuine in wanting to be his friend, but there was the possibility it could be a lie. But she had the same look of determination as Eun-Ya did in the past. These two distinct types of thoughts were swarming in his mind. He desperately wanted to have another friend, but he feared losing them like he had before.

It wasn't something he wished to go through again. It was almost dinner after a few hours of getting the general idea for their project and their self-made deadlines for each topic.

THE ROUTINE HAD BEEN the same for the past two months: attending classes, Ally clinging to him at the end, Jiho giving up, doing homework and projects in his dorm, walking to the dining hall together, and separating at the door. It had been something Jiho secretly enjoyed.

Having someone else around was strange, and he was unsure of her intentions initially. The boy was on guard the first month, but now, going into the second, Ally had not changed at all in her personality or shifted to ignore him when he revealed nothing of his past.

It was Friday before the weekend, and they had continued the same routine, but Jiho could not concentrate on his work or the day. An inner battle was happening within him. Weighing the benefits of taking Ally away from the acquaintance relationship to become a friend. Seeing their evening meal was approaching, the two decided to stop for the day, agreeing to continue tomorrow.

After cleaning up things, they made their way down the empty halls and corridors; Jiho had come to a decision, one which he hoped wouldn't come and bite him in the ass at one point.

Before Ally could round the corner where her hallmates were waiting for her, Jiho grabbed the back of her blazer uniform; the dark navy made a pleasing background for his tan complexion.

She had turned to face him, and her eyebrows knitted as she took in his shy demeanor. Ally's head tilted slightly, "Was there something you needed?"

Her voice displayed confusion and curiosity about why the school's well-known ruthless boy was now shy. Taking a paper out that he had pre-written, he had one question.

Did you really just want to be my friend the whole time?

Jiho's hands were shaking just a bit, awaiting her answer to determine the result of his leap of faith. The concern left Ally's face as she finished reading, giving a small, close-mouth smile.

She nodded quickly, "I just want to be friends. Nothing more, nothing less."

He took a deep breath, trying to drown out the dead image of Eun-Ya and replace it with the happy, alive ones, trying to give him the strength to grab the reaching hand Ally was offering. And with that, he went for it. It was crackling at first; doing this was difficult for him. He was proud that he could open a small part of himself. Jiho wanted to start afresh with her, making it seem like they were just now meeting.

"Let's be friends then," he said, sticking his hand out like he did those years ago. He looked nervous, fearing rejection, "I'm Yoo Jiho."

Ally, revealing all her teeth this time, smiled and placed her hand in his, "Agreed, let's be friends. I'm Allyria Bridget Turner."

Chapter Four

Seven Years Ago

"JI, WAIT."

Ally had to stay after the lecture to talk to her professor about a paper due next month. It had been two almost three years since they decided to be friends, and attending the same university helped them tremendously. Jiho and Ally were now at the bottom of the food chain, new in their first years. However, many of the upperclassmen had known about Jiho's incident at Broduil Academy, and there were still unknowing seniors who tried to befriend the young man or even intimidate him.

It did not end well with those who considered Jiho a small prey among predators. They soon learned he was a wolf in sheep's clothes, scaring them psychologically mostly, though in some cases, Jiho did use physical methods when his mind games did not achieve his expectations.

Turning towards the blond, Jiho had taken her features. Ally's hair was cut to a chic bob, giving a more mature look that contrasted the baby face she still held on to her cheeks. She had grown a bit, standing to Jiho's chin; her lean body was toned after the years of tennis her mother insisted on her taking since childhood. His friend had grown into a young woman more than he would have liked, as her changing attracted perverted looks around them.

These eyes did not help Jiho's need to be protective over Ally. She would state that sometimes he was worse than her father and the security he hired, confusing Jiho for being one of the undercovers.

She had always seen Jiho on the slim side of strength as he never wore anything that really fitted him in a showy way, always loose-fitting tops, and some dress pants most of the time. This sight gave her the full belief that her father hadn't hired Jiho as a guard until she saw him in the gym.

The man had been kickboxing on his own after hours when she had trouble sleeping. It was the first time Ally could see how much muscle he had. One would not know just by looking at him, but the man had a fit body once he activated.

His height helped hide the fact and the clothing, but knowing this now, it was hard for Ally not to see the slight flex whenever Jiho had to pick up something or give her piggybacks when she was too drunk or too tired to walk. It made her believe that he truly did put the five boys in hospitals alone, only doubting the rumors a little since she could not understand how a sweet boy could do harm.

"You…walk…too…fast…sometimes." Her breathing had quickened to steady her beating heart. Ally had run from the other end of the building to catch Jiho before he disappeared like usual.

Blankly looking at her poor attempts to catch her breath, Jiho closed his eyes before sighing. Grabbing her arms, he held them above her head, "Keep them up there. It will help with your intake."

Nodding, the woman gave a shining smile. The two presumed to walk to wherever Jiho was initially heading. Ally still had her arms raised and occasionally got confused gazes from passers-by.

After a few moments of silence, mainly so the blond could collect herself, Jiho questioned her, "So, why were you yelling after me?"

"Oh, right, well, I was wondering if you would like to go to a little party with me-"

"No."

"No?"

"No."

Ally had stepped in front of Jiho, arms now crossed over one another, her lips pressed together, creating a fine line, and her brows furrowed into one. To say she was unhappy with the answer was cutting it short.

"What do you mean 'no'? I haven't even told you the details yet."

"No, and I know this may seem surprising to you, but no means no." Matching Ally's stance, Jiho had told her as if it was the most obvious thing. Upon onlookers and passers-by, it had looked as if Jiho was about to hurt the girl, but seeing her match, or at least attempt to match his menacing aura, they all left the two alone.

"Can't you just hear me out before you say no?"

"No."

"Is there any other form of rejection besides 'no' you can respond with?"

"Nope." Jiho gave a shit-eating grin as he popped the 'p,' annoying the woman to no end.

"Please? I won't ask you about it again. And you know I will continuously ask 'till you let me." Ally poked her finger on his chest. Her determination and the compelling bargain of her silence were slowly getting to Jiho.

He thought, *if I just pretend to hear this, she'll never bring this up*, before nodding his head, stuffing his hands in the pockets of the quarter zip pullover.

Her hands came to a clap. The excitement behind convincing her introverted friend to come out with her again. "Yay! Okay, this is a little house party at Harriet's vacation home here."

"Jassin Harriet?" Snapping her head, Ally looked at the man with a questionable look. Jiho just rolled his eyes, "He came up to me last week and this morning asking about you. Wanted to know if we were dating or if you were taken by another."

"And let me guess, you said nothing, huh?"

"Of course. I don't know him, and I'm not wasting my valuable energy to answer the dumbass." Jiho had a slight offended expressed on his face.

Laughing at Jiho, Ally continued, "Anyways, thank you for that." He nodded, "Back to what I was trying to say. The party will only have thirty people there, and most, if not all, are from high-elite families. It will be a small, sophisticated event. But you won't even have to be too dressy."

Opening the door to his dorm, Jiho stood as Ally plopped herself on the small couch she bought for his dorm, giving her a place to lounge with all the time she was over. "Let me see if I heard you correctly. You want me to go to a dumbass party hosted by another dumbass just to be surrounded by other dumbasses?"

"Basically."

"I can't say no, can I?"

"Nope."

Jiho ran his hands up and down his face before going through his hair. The exhaustion he would feel after this conversation and the party was getting to him already.

"Fine. What day?"

"Tonight."

"Al, you waited until the last minute to tell me this. Is that why the jackass asked about you again this morning?" Jiho had wondered why, after he asked a week prior, on the same thing.

"Possibly. Anyways. I'm going to get changed. I'll be back in two hours to get you." Ally had made Jiho accustomed to her greeting and goodbyes, as her kissing his cheek was nothing new now.

ALLY WAS GOING TO DIE tonight. She had lied about the whole thing. It wasn't sophisticated; no, it was an entire party; their whole university was shit-face drunk.

The air was muggy and humid, making it suffocating to be in while sober. The whole event was too much for the man. Jiho wished he had never agreed to come, wanting to just be back in his dorm finishing his work, maybe calling his family, and catching up with each other.

Jiho was rather angry with Ally, not just for the party but because she had vanished from his sight, worried for her safety. Usually, during these occasions, Jiho would take care of Ally, being her guard dog.

It was hard at first, seeing his friend in a completely vulnerable state: physically, emotionally, and mentally, having been in a drunken haze. Jiho had always suspected she was also a partaker of a type of drug, never really knowing if the prediction was true or false, but he also never asked.

That night brought a lot of old memories for Jiho. Carrying back the feeling of weakness, the fear of not being enough to protect those he holds dear.

He had not left her side at all during that first night nor the remaining days that week; the boy Jiho tried to hide away, had not only come back in behavior but also his muteness, bringing the two a step back in their progressive friendship. Much like the first night, those feelings came back.

"Have you seen Allyria Turner?" Although he mostly stuck to his quiet nature, Jiho did conversate with others when needed. At this moment, he had questioned a girl from his biomedical research course, Lisa Nerthan.

Lisa was pretty, giving a sweet girl next door, a look in stark contrast to Ally's. This sweet girl was blind as a bat without her round glasses, fitting well on her elongated face, resting on between her clean-cut eyebrows and her button nose. Lisa's rich, dark skin glowed as she looked at Jiho. It was no secret to many that the girl wanted the boy, never telling him.

Poor Lisa was a mess around him, a constant fidgeter, avoiding eye contact, too nervous to fully meet his brown eyes, the same eyes that made Lisa first take an interest in him.

Pondering, Lisa nodded, "I believe she went upstairs with someone." Jiho gave a small thanks, lightly placing his hand on her shoulder before racing up the stairs. He had thought of what would be waiting once he reached Ally. Whether it was her talking with some of her other friends or partaking in something that would leave her too intoxicated to do anything but lying there.

Annoyed by the number of rooms, Jiho was in a sour mood, his anxiety rising each second, he could not find Ally. Placing one hand on the doorknob and the other on the door frame, opening to find nothing. Jiho repeated this with three additional rooms before coming to the fifth one.

He heard Ally pleading before he could open it, sounding like she was crying. The desperation in her voice was there, hoping to make whoever was in there with her come to their senses and stop what they were doing. Fearing the worst upon her cries of rejection and pleading for help, he pushed the door open.

Unfortunately, his fears came true.

The sight in front of him was gut-wrenching. His friend, someone who he had taken a chance on, was lying there; her dress pulled past her breast, her undergarments had been pulled off forcefully, and red irritation marks showed the struggle.

A boy, visibly more muscular than the other three boys, held Ally's wrist above her head. Two of them had one of her legs locked at her knees, so a slight movement would cause her discomfort and pain.

The last one of this group was hovering over his friend, pants unzipped and his fingers a couple of centimeters away from Ally's naked cunt. The boy was Jassin Harriet. The same dipshit who, only this morning, was asking about her.

"Jiho! Plea-" Her cries were muffled as the bigger one, who he realized was Gabriel–Jassin's older cousin–covered her mouth with his free hand.

Ally's face was covered in black tear lines from her mascara, her eyes bloodshot, just like Eun-Ya's when he saw her all those years ago.

As her voice brought him out of his heartbreak, Jiho replaced the ache with anger. The four assaulters had heard about Jiho. Cameron–the one holding Ally's left leg–was in the dorm hall when Jiho was first labeled a monster. Cameron had let go of Ally, trying to run out the open door only to be stopped by Jiho.

Slamming the only exit shut, Cameron ran right in the door, falling back on his ass; fear filled his body. Shaking his head, he stretched a handout, indicating for Jiho to stay exactly where he was.

"Please, I'm sorry. I didn't know she was your-"

He was cut off when Jiho grabbed his head, sandwiching his skull between his hands, before kneeling his face in, cracking his nose, and breaking some teeth.

The sound alone was sickening to the other three. Once seeing the rumored violent side of the closed-off man, they had all let go and got off Ally, retreating to the farthest corner of the room from Jiho.

Taking his zip-up off, Jiho wrapped it securely around Ally. Not taking his eyes off the boy's, he held her close, feeling just how shaken up she was. Her nails dug deep into his exposed bicep, drawing a little blood from just how sharp they were; sobs escaped her mouth, and Ally buried herself in him. Jiho was her security blanket.

Lifting her head, Jiho quickly glanced into her eyes, "Can you stand by the door-" Ally furiously cried more, not wanting to leave his side, "Please, Al? I won't leave the room, but I do have to finish what I started."

She looked at him again; hiccups left her mouth before she nodded. Jiho lifted her up, setting her down on the chair and turning away from her assaulters. She clung to the jacket as Jiho gave her head a lingering kiss before he turned his attention back to his targets.

With Cameron knocked out from impact and pure terror, his blood oozed out of his nose and mouth, a full display for the others to witness, and with the realization that they would not be leaving here untouched. Taking a step towards them, Jassin and the other one pushed Gabriel forward, hoping he could get Jiho to leave them alone.

Gabriel may look buff, but due to his height and only focus on his upper arms, Jiho could pinpoint his weakened areas. The legs. Before the sacrificial lamb could get into a fighting stance, Jiho kicked his right leg inwards, blowing his kneecap.

Gabriel's curdling screams were only heard in this room as the music from the lower level drowned out any other sound.

While Gabriel's back was fully on the ground, Jiho snatched his hands, the same ones that touched Ally. His dear friend. Knowing that no matter what he did to them, it would never be the same fear they placed on her, Jiho broke one finger at a time. With each finger, the other two began to cry, looking away, closing their eyes, and pressing further into the wall as possible.

Once the last one was broken, Jiho wanted more pain to flow through this one, enjoying at least a small fraction of the forever feeling Ally would always have; he broke the inaudible man's wrist. The popping sound brought joy to Jiho's heart before he knocked his head hard against the ground, rendering Gabriel unconscious like Cameron.

Knowing that the unknown coward was just a follower of Jassin's crime, Jiho grabbed his face with one hand and smashed it against the wall the boy tried to camouflage with.

The impact was enough to crack the head open as a trickle of blood came out, the boy groaning in pain, hazed with his disorienting and throbbing brain. He would be in and out of consciousness for a few hours.

Snapping his glare at Jassin, Jiho saw the same fear Gerrit had in his first year abroad. The uncontrolled emotions and hyperventilating made the boy a mess, tears clouding his vision of the monster he thought Jiho to be.

Taking this time to speak, hoping it would bring some cushion for the blow he will get, "Please. Ally was being flirty. She wanted it!" Jassin's anger increased with the sad excuses dripping off his thin, chapped lips. "She was asking for it!" Coming face to face with Jiho now, somehow gaining some courage, "She was just playing hard to get. I bet she was rather enjoying herself…the thought of taking all of us, like the whore she is-"

Jiho had never felt this anger before in his life. Sure, he had been in an all-time depression, wanting nothing more than to take his own life after the death of Eun-Ya. He had suicidal thoughts coming in and out of his mind even now, though they had just been whispers.

Taking his family into consideration, he never followed through, of course, and having Ally helped him hold on to life a little more, but rage. Rage was always controlled, granted the one time with the photo. Jiho, thinking his action was valid, disciplined those five bullies the way anyone would if they were in his position.

This type of anger was new to him. Jiho was on the way to becoming a doctor, spending his time researching and studying different cases, giving him a basic understanding no matter the subject and trauma he would be treating.

This month he was investigating rape and assault cases, both male and female, old and young. These things sicken him. Thinking of his family possibly being victims and seeing Ally the way he did was too much. When they first met over the summer, he had vowed to her father to take care of his precious daughter, his only daughter.

He shot his hand out, gripping Jassin's throat, cutting his airway from the oxygen the boy desperately needed. Jassin began to scratch the hand, trying to inflict any pain. But Jiho was unfazed.

Giving him a droopy gaze, his rage mixed with disbelief were the only things one could see in the man. Looking down at the disgusting excuse of a human, Jiho bent to his eye level, taking a moment just to stare at him, not blinking, unsettling Jassin to the bone, making his blood run cold.

"You will tell your family what you did. Ally's family, as well. You are going to leave this school." He forced Jassin's head to look at his accomplices. "Your friends, too."

Pulling away, his hand firmly attached to his throat, Jiho looked back down at him, asserting a dominant aura.

"If I hear, even if it's a small whisper, of you or them, I will kill you. And trust me, Mr. Turner will ensure nothing is traced back to me. Understand?"

Jiho loosened his grip slightly to hear a response. Sadly, Jassin gave a nonverbal nod. Not the answer Jiho was looking for, causing him to slap Jassin.

"Understand?"

"Y-Yeah, I understand."

"Good."

He looked over Jassin before pulling away from the scared man. The assaulter thought how lucky he was to leave unharmed, boosting his hurt ego about not doing anything Jiho asked of him.

Midway through his thoughts, Jassin was tasting a metallic liquid before his hands reached for his mouth, again breaking into a hard cry. Jiho knew that his words wouldn't fully get Jassin to do what he asked, thus causing his actions to be necessary. Jiho had punched him in his mouth, shattering his teeth into tiny pieces.

"Do you understand?"

Unable to give a cohesive sentence, Jiho could only assume the soft, harsh grunts as a 'yes' before he turned to Ally.

The girl had wanted to see what her friend was capable of and switched her seat around in time to see the first one fall. It scared her just how violent he could be, but she was relieved it was for her defense.

Freezing at the sight of Ally looking at all the boys on the ground, Jiho thought he had just lost his only friend. It was slowly breaking him that he had failed to keep Eun-Ya's promise and show this side to Ally.

Thinking she wanted nothing more to do with him, Jiho slowly retreated to his former self, the eight-year-old he had locked away inside. Ally smiled when his anxiety was about to get the better of him. It was soft and pure, absent of any hate or disgust. The smile held gratitude and warmth. She stretched out her hand, still covering her body. Her dress had some tear here and there, asking for Jiho to come to her.

Not long after the reassurance from both, he carries her out of the party, only gaining some onlookers, as many race upstairs to find the four boys beaten and bloody.

The two stayed in his dorm, much to Jiho's unwillingness as he wanted Ally to get checked at the hospital, but she refused, panicking at the mere thought of being there. Having her father's phone number, Jiho got the okay from her to explain what had happened and where they were, leaving in the details where he left a trail of blood behind.

Besides the dinging sound of his phone telling him that Mr. Turner would take the rest of the matter into his own hands and thank him for protecting his daughter, the two rest in his bed, ignoring anyone who dared to knock on the door.

Chapter Five

Seven Years Ago

ALLY WAS FRUSTRATED.

Point blank.

Why was she so frustrated? Simple. Her so-called best friend had taken it upon himself to follow her everywhere she went; her classes in place of her guards when he was able to, tennis practice, and even her dorm where he would wait on her bed as she showered and changed–covering his eyes and turning away until she was done.

It was driving her mad.

"Why?"

"Why what?" He tilted his head to the right. It was the same move you would see from a puppy when someone said 'treat.' It was cute, but weird at the same time.

"Why are you sticking onto me like fucking glue?"

"I'm not."

"Then what are you doing?"

"Following you. Protecting you." As if stating the obvious, Jiho continued to be a smartass. "I can't stick to you; that would be impossible unless we are conjoined twins."

His sarcastic smile was not helping his case at all. The two had been studying at her family's small cottage on the outskirts of town, less than sixteen kilometers away, around a twenty-minute drive from the welcome sign. The two of them knew how to drive, but her parents always assigned one of their own to take them places they wished to go, causing a habit of calling Harper, their driver for the year, to get them.

"But why are you doing that? I do have security, you know." Ally had rolled her eyes, fed up with his attitude.

"Because you need more protection."

"I do not need more protection. You sound like my fucking father." Huffing, the young woman slumped onto a nearby reading chair. She was throwing her legs over the armrest while her head was hanging over the other, comfortable seating for Ally.

"Well, he's right."

"He's never right."

Jiho gazed at her, not wanting to talk about it any longer because they had had this conversation more than enough, "Just because you don't agree with his methods doesn't make your father wrong."

"Will you stop being his fucking lap dog!" Ally sprung out of her seat. Ever since that night, the two most important men in her life have acted like she is fragile, like a glass plate—it was getting on her nerves.

Her father and friend have been talking non-stop over text and phone, updating each other on what is happening daily. Ally hated being pitied by those around her, a feeling she never liked from an early age.

"I'm not his lap dog. I'm just helping him be informed of his daughter." Jiho had placed his phone on the glass coffee table that separated them. There was difficulty in understanding the Turner Family's love for breakable things as they had family members- uncles, aunts, nieces, nephews, and in-laws who liked to roughhouse with each other.

"No. You're acting like one of the security details he hires. I want you to be my friend again, not his!"

"I *am* your friend. A friend that cares about you and your well-being!"

They both had gotten up, glaring at one another, not with hate but frustration.

They both had their own views on the matter and could not understand how it was only making sense to one of them and not the other. Jiho was using the resources to protect Ally, who clearly couldn't defend herself, and Ally wanted their relationship to go back to being only them, not with one of her parents also in it.

"You care?" Astonished by the statement he made.

"Yes."

"I couldn't tell. You've recently loved spending more time on your phone than me-"

"Don't act cute, Al. If I recall, I'm still the same as I was before. You made it your mission to be my friend when I didn't want it."

An amused, breathy laugh left Ally, "You are lying to yourself. I know for a fact that you were longing for this, Ji. Whether you want to believe it or not, you are human. Humans need friends or a form of relation to fully function."

Jiho moved his head from side to side, not agreeing with what she was saying, "Nope. I didn't need this. But since I am stuck with you, I must protect you, especially since that night happened."

Letting an aggravated noise of bewilderment, Ally came closer to him. Her shins touching the coffee table, the cold glass giving her goosebumps as her exposed legs hit them.

"Can you not bring that up? It was one night, okay? Just one unfortunate thing that almost happened but didn't, emphasis on the word DIDN'T."

Her hands began to move around as she talked, a habit her nonna had passed down to her since the older woman partially raised her.

"It doesn't matter if it was almost. You would be taken advantage of because you can't protect yourself. You are just some alcoholic party brat who doesn't know the real world. Here's the harsh truth: You cannot make it out there alone. You cannot protect yourself from the dangers and evil minds out there. You can't, so I must."

Jiho's voice began to lower in tone. He did not raise his voice when things went on a more serious route, always keeping it even so the other person stayed calm. But in this case, it didn't work.

It hurt her to know the man's view of her; she was weak and unable to help herself. Ally knows she should have thought twice when Jassin offered her a cup of liquor, but she didn't care since she just wanted a drink.

It wasn't until Ally started feeling a bit fuzzy, unsure of her surroundings, that the realization hit her. She, undoubtedly, had been drugged. Her hope was gone once she could make out three other figures upon entering the room. Of course, Ally was delighted when she saw Jiho, becoming only buzzed when the thought of being raped flowed through her mind.

Having Jiho there to rescue Ally meant the world to her. After that night, she valued his friendship and him as a person but hated herself for being so stupid in accepting things from others without a second thought.

"I am capable of helping myself, you know," Ally confesses. One thing that annoyed Jiho was her stubbornness in admitting others were right. It was something that Ally herself knew as well. "You don't need to feel responsible for my actions, Ji."

"Yes, I do."

"No, you don't."

"Fucking hell, Allyria! Yes, I do! I have to because I can't have another person, I value end up like her!"

Until this point, Jiho kept his calm composure, not wanting to rally them both up with shouting, but it was different. Now, he is terrified, angry, and heartbroken. Thinking back to the helpless feeling of seeing Eun-Ya dead when he looked at Ally that night brought all the emotions back, making him on edge about everything and anything.

Ally's mind was going a hundred before crashing into a wall of confusion, "Like who? Who is 'she'?"

The blond was met with silence; for the first time, there were no emotions in Jiho's eyes. No matter if the man had a stoic facade, his eyes always gave away his feelings until now.

Ally felt like she was staring at an empty person, nothing but a void, terrifying her to the core. Shaking his head, Jiho kept quiet, refusing to speak.

"Like who? Jiho?"

Ally moved around the coffee table, standing beside him at arm's length. If it were anyone else, the young woman would have left them to deal with their emotions, not Jiho. The one person who made her feel safe had now made her suffocate with a feeling of fright.

"Yoo Jiho!"

"What?" Jiho's voice was anything but familiar. It held distance as if she were nothing more than a stranger to him. "What do you want?"

"I want to know who 'she' is. I want to know why you are so hell-bent on protecting me like this. Why are you comparing me to someone I don't even know?"

Placing his hands over his face, Jiho let out a shaky exhale. He knew that no matter what, somewhere along the line in their friendship, he would have to explain Eun-Ya to Ally. He never really wanted to discuss it with her, at least not this soon. Looking up at his friend, Jiho nodded, patting the seat by him, signaling his cooperation to her request.

"I...I don't know where to start, if I'm honest, Al. This happened back when I was small."

"How small? Wh-" Ally stopped.

Seeing Jiho send a warning look about her interruption, she zipped her mouth with an invisible key before throwing it away. This action caused a small chuckle to leave Jiho's mouth at her antics. Sometimes, he really couldn't stay mad at her.

"As I was saying, I was small, maybe around eight. I had this friend, Eun-Ya. She was my only friend really, always including me in activities and when we had breaks during school hours. Eun-Ya was so in tune with her emotions. Sometimes, she was too cheerful, or sad, or worried, or excited. She was always changing her mood. No matter their age, people would tell her she was like a sea, unpredictable but intense."

Jiho let a small smile land on his face, reminiscing how they both would laugh and chase one another around the playground.

Ally could see the pain in his eye but refused to be interrupted again. She sat there waiting for him to continue with his explanation.

"I always saw her wearing something orange, you know."

Playing with the orange bracelet around his wrist, something that the said girl had given him on his seventh birthday.

"I hated the color back then, but she was always so happy when she saw it. I had to lie to her that it was one of the best colors in the world. I mean, you saw the photo; her mood impacts those around her so easily." Letting a small laugh, he let the tears form in his eyes, blurring his vision.

Taking the time to place her hand over his, Ally squeezed. This was the first for Ally saw him so vulnerable. She was taken aback to see the broken state that left Jiho.

"I was late. We had a project due, and I was late meeting her. I really wanted a snack. I also bought her one, her favorite, to compensate for my wasted time. I didn't mean to leave her alone for that long; I didn't."

By now, Jiho had started sobbing but tried keeping them to a minimum so his sentences could still be understood. This was the first time he had told someone what he was feeling outside his therapist from his childhood. Sniffling, Jiho pulled himself together to answer Ally why he was so willing to protect her the way he couldn't with Eun-Ya.

"I…I was the one to find her before anyone else. Eun-Ya…sh-she was just staring at me. She was lying on the ground, staring at me. Her-her face was blue, and her neck was red with the cord around it."

At this, Ally had put together about what he was talking. He had found Eun-Ya dead. An eight-year-old found his friend.

"I didn't mean to be late. Her eyes just asked me, 'Why were you late?,' 'Why did you let this happen to me?' I screamed. I-I didn't know what to do but looked back at her." At this point, he was having a panic attack, breathing heavily, eyes shifting, in a consistent fidget.

Ally took his face between her hands, making them make eye contact. "Hey, hey, Jiho, listen to me, okay? Just follow me. Breathe in, breathe out. Just like that, again." The girl sent encouraging reassurance, taking long, deep breaths and keeping a steady rhythm.

Jiho has never shown Ally one of his panic attacks or even tears. Those were a sign of being weak and close to someone, which was something Jiho wasn't sure he wanted to be this close to his friend. It may seem selfish and a bit distant of him to want Ally at arm's length, but with how much he realized the girl meant to him, Jiho feared her leaving the same way Eun-Ya did.

Taking a few minutes to follow her pace, Ally continued her instructions, "Good. Now, can you tell me three things you can, see?" Darting his eyes everywhere, Jiho was starting to become overwhelmed once more. Hearing his friend call his name, he focused back on Ally, "Take your time, okay? Look to the left and tell me the first thing you see."

"The glass cabinet," he hiccupped.

"Yes, good. A glass cabinet. Now look to the right; what do you see?"

"The armchair you were on."

"Now behind me."

"Double doors."

Ally smiled, glad her three-three-three rule was working for Jiho. "Now, tell me three things you hear."

Jiho closed his eyes to concentrate; his heart had begun to slow down, not by much, but it was still coming down. His ears had picked these three up faster than he could see, "The clock in the hall, the wind chime, and Harper singing."

Pleased with Jiho's progress, Ally let go, placing some space between them. Her last three would hopefully be the latest effort in calming him ultimately, "Now, three things you can touch."

With a longer exhale, Jiho let his hands wander from his lap, his fingers grazing over the wool texture on the sofa. "The blanket your nonna made you." His hand felt a chilling metal in the opposite direction. "A glass of iced tea." Finally, Jiho reached forward, placing his hands over Ally's, "And my best friend, who I view as my sister."

Her eyes began to gloss over, pulling the man into a hug. Jiho's breathing had finally evened out, his head clear, and the images of Eun-Ya's lifeless body had vanished to her smiling and laughing.

Pulling away, Jiho was the first to speak, "Can you promise me that no matter how safe you think you are, no matter how secure you feel, promise me you will always come back unharmed, no matter if life takes us in different directions, we will come back at some point the same way we left. Whether emotional, mental, or physical, we come back together safely. Promise me."

"I promise."

Chapter Six

Three Years Ago

THE SEA OF PEOPLE brought Jiho's anxiety to an all-time high. The man was waiting near the restrooms for his sisters.

Winter break had just started for Jiho, letting him pause his studies during his last year in medical school. Jiho had been able to take extra courses and even tested out in some.

Although this wasn't different from the previous years, this would be his last one till Jiho goes to America to pursue his career. Knowing he could work in a few other countries, Jiho and Ally decided to move across the world after graduation, and America was the mutual ground.

Jiho was so consumed with thoughts of the future he didn't see that Iseul came up from behind, causing him to let out a short, high-pitched scream.

A handful of onlookers gave judgmental looks at the group of four, the two youngest laughing while Nari held a phone up, recording the moment. Feeling embarrassed, Jiho looked away, his face flushed. Luckily, due to the harsh December air, most of his face was covered with a scarf, beanie, and hood, but he was still freezing.

"You three kids done?" He continued his walk towards their original destination, "Halmeoni is waiting for us."

Skipping arm in arm, the three were still giggling here and there; having been the first to calm down, Min-Jung spoke, "We'll get there in time, don't worry. You must admit, we got you good."

Releasing her hold on Iseul, the younger girl ran towards Jiho before jumping on his back, causing a slight stumble. The multiple layers the Yoo children wore caused their weights to be heavier than usual.

Sliding his hand under Min-Jung's leg and holding them in place by interlocking his hands together, the twenty-five-year-old shook his head.

"You love us, no matter what we do."

Letting out a loud hum in agreement, Jiho started running in circles around Nari and Iseul, who recorded the interaction for their own enjoyment. This year, the parents would not be spending time with their children. The couple had gotten a surprise trip for their anniversary gift from the siblings.

Their way of thanking them for raising them in a comfortable home was more for the girls than Jiho. There were times, after the murders, when they ignored the only son or snapped in a fit. They loved Jiho, and Jiho loved them, but that did not erase his pain or the silent screams of his parents, who had no idea how to help as he got older.

The group of four would be spending their time with their mom's parents as they moved in as soon as they left for their schools.

Min-Jung's school was in Switzerland this year, the twins started their first year at Sungkyun Kwan University, and Jiho was finishing his medical degree. Their mom and dad were mostly lonely when the house was only the two; adding to her parents' health, it only made sense to have them move in.

"I'm going to throw up on you…" Min-Jung's head spun as Jiho immediately stopped all movement, not wanting to deal with the smell and feel of the meal that might come back to greet them all.

Their grandma wanted them to spend this night out together as the remaining week and a half would be a lot of housework and preparation for the New Year. Nari held on to her baby sister after being let down. Iseul took the opportunity to speak with her brother, something she missed dearly when he was away.

"How does it feel? Leaving home once again, for longer this time." Her eyes trained on the snow path the two girls ahead were leaving. Much of the time, Iseul felt disconnected from her brother. They were still closer than other siblings, but she felt left out compared to his relationship with the youngest. Sad and jealous thoughts circled in her mind when she saw the two together.

"A little different than all the other times," he shrugged, unsure of how to really put into work what he was feeling, "It saddened me to leave, but I'm happy I can support the three of you with your tuition with the money I will be making."

A hum of understanding was formed; Iseul blew into her hands as the feelings left her body. Seeing the action, Jiho took out his hand warmers and placed them in front of the girl, ushering her to take them and put them in her gloves.

"Thank you."

"Can I ask you something?"

Iseul glanced at him from her peripheral, "Sure..."

Making sure the other two girls were already in the house, Jiho stopped them outside the gates a few meters away, "Why do you think I care or love you any less than the others?"

Iseul's eyes widened. "W-What?"

"I'm not stupid or blind to your feelings."

Although he may be almost ten thousand kilometers away from his family, Jiho knew, based on the tone or facial expressions, that there was something wrong.

"You've been more distant. Not only me but Minnie, too. What's going on?"

She was silent.

How could he pick that up so fast? Iseul thought she did a decent job hiding from everyone. She closed her eyes and sighed.

"It's the truth, right? You love Minnie more than you do Nari-yah and me. Eomma always says that you had a tough time accepting us but loved the idea of her as soon as she announced her pregnancy."

"It's not true." Jiho's face contorted, genuinely confused, upon his younger sister's statement. "I love you and Nari-yah just as much as Minnie. I have no idea why Eomma would tell you that, but you must realize there was a reason why it was so hard for me to accept you two as a kid."

Iseul rolled her eyes, "What reason could you have to hate a baby with the two of us but not the other? How could you have such a perfect connection with her but completely push aside us?"

Taking her hand out of her pockets, the girl pushed her hair out of her face. The anger was building up as Iseul's voice began to rise.

"Even with phone calls, you talk to her in perfect English while Nari-yah and I can only pick up on the basics, and when we ask what's going on, you two state that it is nothing."

Iseul was done keeping things in. She was exploding and not feeling sorry about it. The first-year university student held this resentment for years. And she was hurt.

"I could not protect you both; how could I? How could I stop the torment of a murder from taking not only the life of Eun-Ya but yours as well?"

Jiho had never spoken about these things with the girls, but he knew their parents and grandparents told them how hard his life was and to always be nice to the only son.

"What does she have anything to do with this? Yes, she was your friend, but that was it?"

"I found her."

"What?"

Looking back from the sky, Jiho let out a shaky breath. This was the moment to share the horrors he faced, "I found Eun-Ya's body. I was the one to bring to light there was a killer out there. I was the one who failed to protect someone valuable to me. So how could I protect you? Or Nari-yah? How could I be happy that something so innocent was being brought into a world of hurt and unfathomable pain?"

Iseul was silent.

"I hoped for the life of me to die before and after the two of you were born. I wanted to die. At least then I could try my hardest to pay for my sins in death."

"That…You wanted to die…"

"No one told you?" He laughed dryly, "I had to see a therapist to help fix my broken self. I still see someone from time to time on my own without Eomma or Appa knowing. Ally is there to help most of the time, but even she didn't know about this till recently."

Running his hands up and down his face, Jiho was exhausted from repeatedly explaining himself. To go through the memories of those lonely times. Sometimes, he was so isolated, even with everyone around him.

"I-I'm sorry." Stumbling over her words, Iseul's hands began to tremble.

"Why are you sorry? You felt neglected by me. I understand, but you must realize I never hated you, just hated the thought of you. I hated that you had to be born when a murderer was still out there. Is still out there."

Her lips quivered. Never did she think Jiho had gone through all this. Iseul was only given shared PG versions of those years.

"I love you. And Nari-yah." Taking a step closer, within arm's reach, "The times in which Minnie and I talked in English without telling you two about the topic was because it was for your surprise gifts for your birthdays and graduation. Even times when she wanted to practice her skills in that language. We never intended to make you feel like you were on the outside."

By the end of Jiho's little confession, the two siblings embraced.

Iseul was letting out short cries, sorry for feeling such resentment and jealousy when all she should have done was talk to them.

Turning around, there stood the other sisters, sad smiles on their faces. Nari was the one to brush the snowflakes off Iseul's hair as Min-Jung wiped the tears away.

They both understood what had happened over the past few months when Iseul pushed the oldest and youngest of the Yoo children away. Min-Jung was hurt by her sister's hatred but figured it had to do with their mom's angry ramblings, something even their father had difficulty taming.

"You know I look up to you, right, Unnie. I looked up to Nari Unnie, too. Never did I think I had a better relationship with Oppa. I know he loves us all equally." Min-Jung chuckled at the silly thoughts her older sister had. Laughing out of embarrassment of being heard by them, Iseul muttered an apology.

"You are so dumb sometimes, Iseul-ah. Coming up with these silly little things." Nari voiced that, having been her twin, she knew her sister was an overthinker and wanted to know what was going on as much as she did.

The difference was Nari asked the neighbors around the murders to tell what really happened to Jiho when he was a child. She never thought to tell Iseul, and that might have been a fault on her part, but it was also something she wasn't supposed to have knowledge about.

"I'm sorry." Each syllable was said after inhaling, a result of Iseul's cries.

"Stop crying." Jiho rubbed her back; the smile could be heard in his words, trying to be as lighthearted as possible, "Let's head inside before Hal-Abeoji yells at us for being in the cold too long."

"You're the one who wanted to have this conversation outside." Nari pointed out, "If we catch a cold, I'm blaming you for everything."

"Yeah, yeah. I'm the default." The sarcasm brought the girls together in laughter.

JIHO HAS BEEN DELIVERING briquettes around the neighborhood for the last three days. He was tired, to say the least. The exhausting work was too much for those not used to the load. Every time Jiho was back home, he would help do these little odd jobs no one wanted to do but were necessary for the livelihood of their town.

While he was out doing these, the sisters were scattered here and there, helping with cooking, and moving items from one house to another as the cold was making some lose power, having to stay with friends and family. Their grandma was not lying when she told them there was a lot of work to do after their sibling's outing.

"Ajusshi, what height do you want these to be at?" Jiho shouted to the middle-aged man, who was three rooms away.

"Hold on, Jiho-yah, let me come see." The man hurried over to see where Jiho was trying to drill the shelves. "Ah, a little down...to the left...right there." The man took the right side of the heavily carved wood and allowed Jiho to finish this project in one go. Once he secured the left side and middle, Jiho took over the right side, allowing the owner to step back and see the finished product.

"All done. Is there anything else I can help you with?"

Shaking his head, the man clapped Jiho's back, "No, you did well. Thank you for your hard work, Jiho-yah. Rest well and tell your family they have a good son. They should be proud."

Bowing, repeatedly saying 'thank you,' and smiling at the owner, Jiho left, heading home as the sun set a few hours ago. The day was longer than usual; his muscles were aching, and he felt a cold coming.

He made a note to head to the pharmacy to grab some medicine and ask his grandparents to make some rice porridge. Having this be one of his last times back home till his life started in the States, Jiho reminisced over the past: the good, evil, beauty, and ugly.

The times when he stood watch for danger as the girls played in the kitty pool during the hot summer's home when they were still young. The sunburnt skin starts to peel as their mom and grandmas' fuss over their skin conditions and the long-term damage this might cause.

The family meals the siblings cooked for their elders' received pointers and compliments when each dish was tasted.

These were the things Jiho would miss once he moved, knowing it would be challenging to visit with the busy schedule he would have. The snow had stopped falling a day ago, causing the sidewalk to be shoveled with leftover slush; the soaked, wet feeling was seeping through his boots and into his socks.

These boots had been last year's gift from the girls, as he was only wearing sneakers in the snow that winter. Having worn them till they had holes in them, Jiho needed new ones.

Reaching his home after another fifteen minutes, Jiho took off both layers covering his feet before placing them in his designated slippers.

Yelling out his arrival, many voices greeted him, one being unfamiliar. A puzzled look was on his face before he continued walking till, he reached their family room divided by doors.

His world stopped. Undoubtedly stopped. Jiho had frozen over; there were no thoughts in his brain or even sounds in his ears. The silence was the only thing to welcome him. Recognition was present in his eyes.

Jiho pointed at the woman in the middle of the room and looked at his grandparents. The two grandmas and grandpa nodded, confirming his question. The sisters had all been wondering who this person was, why their elders were being so secretive, and now they were wondering why their brother knew of this person.

"Taeyoung Nuna...?" Crooking the name out. She was here. She still looked the same as he remembered, with only a few differences.

The crow's feet around her eyes, the cut hair that now reached her chin instead of her mid-back, the ring around her finger on her left hand, and the more cheerful, soft color palette in clothing and make-up she had on.

Giving a once-over nod, the woman's body was slammed into by him, who had become the vulnerable young boy she once held all those years ago before she moved with her family.

"Jiho-yah, it's been a while. You've grown so well."

She was just as tender as Jiho remembered. Clinging on tighter, Taeyoung shushed the young man, gently rubbing his back. The only person who understood his hurt. She also saw the body of her younger sister, Eun-Ya. It was a pain they could only know together as the grandfather of the Kim girls passed away a few months after Eun-Ya's death.

All this time, all the work Jiho had put into forgetting the pain and torment he felt for being a failure has all crashed down. He was always sorry, even more guilty for the Kim family. He wishes to return and take Eun-Ya's place, but Jiho knows he can do nothing. The only thing in his control was to make good on the promise the two made when he was nine.

"I'm…s-so s-sorry…I-I'm s-" The words became mushed together with the painful wails coming from Jiho.

Taeyoung's hands cradled his face, lifting their eyes to meet, "You have nothing to be sorry about, Jiho-yah. I do not blame you, never had or ever will."

Jiho tried to protest her claims but was silenced by a quick hush.

"Do not try to say otherwise. What happened to my little sister had nothing to do with you. It had everything to do with that monster. You were the best friend she could have. You were all she talked about during our dinners."

It was true.

When the little girl was still alive, Jiho was the topic of conversation. The two were best friends. They did everything together, always. It was not uncommon for the grandfather and sister to be a little irritated, but they were glad to know the youngest was making happy memories with the boy.

"I could not ask for a better person to make her feel so much joy in the short time Eun-Ya had."

During all this, the sister put the pieces together. Nari was the first to understand who this woman was due to the digging she did on her own time. Min-Jung was the second, hearing her brother speak in his sleep around the anniversary of Eun-Ya's death. Iseul was the last, though she did not fully understand at this point and time.

Taking a second to collect themselves, Jiho straightened up. He wanted to introduce the woman officially to his family, "Um, this is Kim Taeyoung. She's Eun-Ya's older sister. She used to live here before that incident happened…"

The look of realization came over Iseul's features. She had no idea who this person was and why she was in their home. In the middle of her rude thoughts, Iseul judged Taeyoung due to her closeness to the Yoo grandparents.

Getting up, the three sisters greeted their elders respectfully, wanting to make a good impression, at least in front of everyone else.

"I remember seeing you two before I left. Nari-yah and Iseul-ah, right? You two were just born when I visited for the last time."

"You met us before?" Nari question. This was new information to her.

"Of course. You two were the first twins born here in the last twenty years. It was a celebration for the town."

Nari and Iseul looked gob smacked at this. All their life, they were always left out as they didn't have their own birthday or identity. Their mom only talked about how Jiho wasn't happy with their birth, stating the negative times it was back then. The thought of being celebrated was out of the ordinary for them.

"Now you, Min-Jung-ah, this is my first time seeing you." Giving the shy girl a look over, Taeyoung smiled, "You are beautiful, just like your sisters. I know you will become a great person like your Oppa."

"Why did you come back after all this time?" Iseul's judgment was peeking through her question. The others were thinking the same but knew better than to ask.

"You are a straightforward person, I see. Eun-Ya was like that too." Taking out an envelope, she handed it to Jiho, who was sitting right next to her, "I wanted to invite you to my wedding…and I also want you to be a part of the ceremony during the wedding. What do you say?"

Jiho was speechless over the whole thing. He had not spoken to her during those years, occasionally writing to each other around the anniversary date.

He had read about the man she was marrying and was excited this person was always caring and tender with her. Jiho was stunned she had asked him the question, knowing that it was one of the essential parts of a traditional Korean wedding.

The groom had to get approval from him and her mother before he could marry Taeyoung. Being seen as necessary and recognized as a family member was an honor.

"Close your mouth. You look like a fish." Taeyoung laughed. She knew this announcement would shock him, but she wanted him there and valued him at the same level as Eun-Ya.

"But…why me?"

"Because you were and still are someone we talk about during the dinners." She joked. Scooting closer so her arm was over Jiho's shoulders, "You are important. You make us remember the joy in life. The letters you write and the pictures of you and Eun-Ya are hung everywhere. Kyong-ah wants to meet you because we can't stop talking about you and how proud you make us. How proud you've made Eun-Ya."

Over the last few days, Jiho felt like all he had done was cry. These emotions had made him go into overdrive. The level of hiding them, pushing them down full force, was overwhelming for Jiho, "Are you sure…?"

"Yes." Taeyoung rolled her eyes, "I'm sure!"

"Okay. Thank you."

"Oh, you all are invited too. As well as your Eomma and Appa." The girls started to get excited. This would be their first wedding.

"When is it?" Iseul was giddy about this information.

"We decided to have it in May," Glancing at Jiho, "You should already be graduated by then."

Happiness was coursing through his veins. Knowing, after years, that the Kim family was still so caring about Jiho and never blamed him was heartwarming. His relationship with them as a child still stood even after Eun-Ya.

They were like second parents to him, an older sister, something that was a comfortable haven. Writing over the years only did so much to reassure him, and the guilt Jiho had still had a hold on him. Though they did everything they could to help these negative thoughts and sometimes felt repetitive, they never gave up.

"Thank you, Nuna." Pulling her into another embrace.

Chapter Seven

Three Months Ago

JIHO WAS NERVOUSLY PACING next to Taeyoung. The woman was beautiful. There was no denying that.

Her traditional red Hanbok fit so well that Taeyoung was beaming excitedly and joyfully. Jiho could not pinpoint why he was on edge, but seeing her like this, all set and ready to go, amplified the feeling.

"Jiho-yah." Gently, the bride called, "Stop pacing around. You're making a hole in the rug, and I don't think the staff would appreciate that." Giggles around the two were caused by the rest of the Kim family and the present Yoo family.

Upon returning from their getaway, Jiho's parents heard of the news, calling Taeyoung to congratulate them on the big event. Yu-Jun and Do-Som had not been to a wedding in some time, as many getting married opted for the Western style over traditional ones.

Jiho had been talking nonstop about the wedding to Ally. It was to the point where Ally placed earplugs when the rant took longer than ten minutes. It was hard for Jiho to tell Ally she could not come as the invitation was only extended to his immediate family, crushing her little party of new dress shopping.

After a few days of pouting, Ally realized it wasn't her call and could not persuade them with her words, especially if they didn't speak the same language. That did not stop the girl from making Jiho try on many different outfits.

Ally was compensating for not being able to go herself by buying Jiho all these things, and he knew it, but it brought the girl joy to spend the money even if he tried to protest it.

Jiho was grateful nonetheless because of his friend; the compliments had been coming to him left and right, from Taeyoung, the Kim family, and some of their friends.

Coming out of his little daydream, Jiho sat beside the bride. "How can you be so calm, Nuna? I would have fainted in your position." Taking the handheld fan, he began to fan both aggressively, making Taeyoung laugh even more.

"It looks like you might now." Iseul mocks. Her mother sends a warning look as she passes her, handing a handkerchief to Jiho, "What? I'm only telling the truth. He's sweating through his clothes and looks sick."

"That does not mean you have to speak your mind." Do-Sum whips, "Who will marry you with that smart mouth?" Iseul's lips are pressured into a thin line with the uncalled question, swallowing her remarks. There was an underlying tension between the parent and child, for which reason Jiho had no idea, but it was there and stayed there all his life.

"Aein, leave her be." Yu-Jun says, "She's just trying to make light of Jiho's nervousness, nothing in poor taste."

A small huff was heard as Taeyoung hid her smile behind the long sleeves. It was amusing to see the family bicker after all these years. Remembering all the time, she would poke fun at Eun-Ya made her miss these unseeingly fond moments.

"Let's not fight; it's almost time for the ceremony to start." Nodding at the slight lie, Jiho was happy to stop all this chaos. He wanted this to be perfect for her, not wanting anything to mess with this day.

There was some difficulty getting Taeyoung up, as her foot was caught in the Hanbok, but after the little mishap, they took their places. Jiho was the one to greet the groom and approve of him first, outside the bride's 'house' where he guided him to the next step: the geese exchange. They were carved sculptures, a symbol of everlasting love, an unbreakable bond the bride and groom had with one another.

Taeyoung's mother was the next to be greeted. The woman wore a delicate pink Hanbok and bowed her head only at Kyong-ah, who had done a full bow.

This was the last greeting and approval for the ceremony. From this point on, Taeyoung's friends would help with the rest of the process as the couple consumes the same items: alcohol and food as a sign of unity-two halves of a whole. The rest of the ceremony came and went. Jiho was ecstatic to have witnessed something so important. An event that would have been a core memory if Eun-Ya were here.

"Jiho-yah, when we grow up, I will marry you!" Eun-Ya yelled. The two six-year-olds were running around the playground.

"Why?"

"Eonni told me that you should marry your best friend. You are my best friend, so we are going to marry." Eun-Ya rubbed her hands on her shirt while climbing up the steps. Jiho was not too far behind, ready to catch the multi-tasking girl in case.

The children were within the view of Do-Som, who was talking to the little girl's grandfather, laughing, and swapping tips on how to deal with more children. The woman was a first-time mother and wanted another one soon.

There was a conversation about the best time to go through with pregnancy again as the grandfather helped raise Eun-Ya and her teenage sister, Taeyoung.

Taking one last big step, the children semi-ran toward the newly placed slide. They wanted to be the first ones down it, crying and complaining throughout the day just to get ten minutes on the playground. "Does that mean she's going to marry Chul Nuna?"

Sitting down between his legs, Eun-Ya looked back, "Maybe? Eonni said she likes her, and Chul Eonni always sleeps over like you. So, I think so."

"Jiho-yah." The two children snapped their heads, "Appa wants us home early. We need to leave."

Jiho answered a short, loud 'yes' before he pushed them both down the slide. Patting off the dust-off Eun-Ya and himself, they walked over to their guardians, hands out, reaching for them to pick the children up. Saying goodbye to each other, the grown-ups walked in opposite directions to their homes.

"Did you have fun playing with Eun-Ya?" Switching which side Jiho was sitting on, Do-Som brushed through his hair. Combing out the tangles he got while playing, "What did you two talks about?"

"We're getting married like Taeyoung Nuna and Chul Nuna."

"What?" Do-Som was shocked. Her little baby was still afraid of the dark yet was planning to marry already. "What do you mean?"

"Eun-Ya said that Taeyoung Nuna told her to marry your best friend. Like you and Appa. Best friends marry each other, right?"

Letting out a nervous chuckle, what in the heavens is Taeyoung-ah telling these kids? Moving her hair to the side, Do-Som spoke, "When you are older, you can marry. But don't marry just because your best friends."

"Why?"

"Because you want to marry someone who's your best friend but also someone you love differently than best friends or family." He takes his shoes off as they enter the house.

"I don't get it..."

Patting his hair, Do-Som kneels to come face-to-face with her son. "You know how you love Eomma and Appa?"

Jiho nodded.

"And how you love Eun-Ya and her family?"

Once again, he nodded.

"There is a different type of love. A love where you think about them all the time. Not just to go play with them or to show them something cool. But just sit there and be near them." Yu-Jun stood not too far, hiding behind the divider between the entrance and living space.

He loved seeing and hearing his wife explain things to their son. In Yu-Jun's opinion, Do-Som had a better grasp of explaining things to people than he had ever done.

The times when he explained why they couldn't wear outside shoes in the house but only slippers ended with Jiho being more confused than he was at the start. Do-Som saved the day and kept the messy boy from walking with outdoor shoes in their home.

"Why do we just sit there? Does that mean Eun-Ya and I won't marry?"

"If you feel like Eun-Ya is the one for you, you can marry her after you finish your studies and get a good job. But if you don't want to marry her, that's okay too. She'll stay your best friend forever. Okay?" She poked his stomach.

"Okay!" Jiho laughed.

"So, you're the best friend and pen pal?"

Time had passed, dinner was over, and the bride and groom wanted a more intimate and exclusive celebration-having a nice dinner with the in-laws and close friends. Jiho had taken a moment to breathe in the fresh air. After this wedding, there was going to be a last adventure with Jiho and his siblings-something they will never forget and always cherish.

Turning only his head, Jiho's eyes set on the devil himself, Kyong, the new husband, and an older relative figure. Jiho would never voice his thoughts out loud, but Kyong was average-looking. Nothing too special, but from his knowledge, the man was talented in the cooking department, a personal chef for the higher class.

"Nice to meet you, Seonbae." Before Jiho could bow politely, Kyong started to protest, stopping the man mid-way.

"No need to do all that. We are family now, as Taeyoung-ah sees you as a little brother."

A pleased smile stood on the groom's face. Jiho had to admit the gentle, soft-spoken way the older man used was nice. Most of the time, Jiho had to hear yelling, harsh and, at times, hurtful tones.

It was when he would walk around the neighborhood or go into the city where there would be scolding of some sort happening. Even at home, the yelling did not stop. But Kyong was being sweet with his voice, like a lullaby his mom used to sing.

"I've been wanting to meet you for a while now, but never had the time. It's nice to see you in person, even though you've grown from the pictures I've seen."

"I was only a kid back then."

"Still a kid now." He sipped the liquor in his cup, "I don't mean that in a bad way…You have a lot of years left to have fun. To take chances in life."

Jiho held his gaze on Kyong. This man was new to him, physically but not mentally or visually; Jiho had known him through the letters. Jiho had seen photos of the man when Taeyoung first started seeing him, asking, and answering questions through her to get to know him. Still, he felt weary of Kyong, unsure if he could fully trust him.

"I plan on making the most of my life to make people proud. Especially Eun-Ya…"

Kyong agreed, "You have the right to live however you want. But do me a favor; think of it as a wedding gift from you to me."

"And what's that?" Jiho questions, he was intrigued.

Setting his drink on the rail near them, Kyong laid his hands on Jiho's shoulders. "Don't forget this is one lifetime. You have every right to make peace with Eun-Yu's death. I know how much it has affected you. Just don't let that defy your own wants and needs. Find more friendships, make mistakes, and take a chance on people. Most of all, find love."

Each sentence was more potent than the last. Decreasing the doubt in his heart.

"If it doesn't work out, that's okay. Sometimes, you need different types of heartache to grow as a person. Don't let it define you."

"...What if I can't let myself do all those things? What if I fail everyone?" Jiho's voice was barely above a whisper, scared and timid.

"Are you going to try?"

He hesitantly nodded.

"Then you can't fail us. You can't fail yourself, either. If you are trying your best, letting yourself be driven by your feelings and intuition instead of always thinking the worst, you will always make us proud. You understand?" Jiho had been sniffling since the confirmation that he could not fail them.

It's difficult for him to understand why people can't see the failure he is. How he failed to protect Eun-Ya, to protect his classmates. He failed to save his parents' relationship with each other and the one with him.

Jiho could not make his sisters feel equal love from him and only felt like he loved one above the other. It hurt. But to hear this person, who is so vital to his Nuna, to say he's not failing, that he is loved and can make mistakes made him grateful for the man in front of him. Knowing Taeyoung is in good, caring hands.

"Jiho-yah." Kyong called out, gaining his attention, "You understand that we will never be ashamed, unappreciated, or blame you, right? We will be grateful for your efforts to make

Eun-Ya's dreams come true; we will support and cheer for you no matter what you want in life for yourself. You are loved by people, okay?"

Breaking into a sad, grateful smile, Jiho muttered, "I understand; thank you, Hyeong." As he motioned for a hug.

A clicking sound broke their moment; seeing a flash go off, the two looked to find the source. Standing there with a camera in hand, Taeyoung giggled, "Awe, look at my two men, having a moment."

"Really, Aein?"

She kissed Kyong's cheek and gave an innocent smile, "I want to capture a moment that won't happen in person after today for a while." The husband looked confused, "Our little Jiho-yah is going to the States."

"Really? Why?"

She motioned for Jiho to answer the question. Scratching the back of his head, he said, "Umm, I got my medical degree. I already moved into my place, started my job and after this summer, I'll be back over there."

Letting a small chuckle at the shocked face. Kyong knew the younger man was going to school abroad with a scholarship but never thought he would work overseas, let alone with a medical career.

"Wow…"

"Yep, our little Jiho-yah has made everyone proud," She teased the man before placing her hand in his, "He's made Eun-Ya extremely proud."

"Thank you, Nuna, Hyeong. Thank you."

Chapter Eight

Just Saoirse

THE RELIEF SET INTO JIHO.

After a thirty-six-hour shift at the hospital, he was free to sleep fully tonight. Jiho did not fully account for the strain or stress his job would have on him, thinking it would be a little more complicated than his studies.

Not that it bothered him. Lately, there have been more and more patients coming in with injuries. Those hurt did not tell him how they came to have such damage, including broken bones and heavily bruised areas.

It wasn't till the smell of his body odor that Jiho pulled himself from his thoughts. The young doctor made his way inside his house. After a shower, his head was about to hit the pillow when his phone rang. Immediately, he knew who it was. She's been trying to get him to accompany her on a night out for ages.

"Hello, my great demon from hell. What do I have the pleasure of getting your call on this special night?"

His voice was sarcastic; he could sense she was rolling her eyes. He loved her, but sometimes, he wanted her not to call or bother him. But sadly, he was cursed with such a lovable-annoying and, at times, a bitch of a best friend, who he loved with all his heart.

"Get ready. You are coming with me to a bar. And you can't say no because I already told the press that someone was coming with me, so get dressed. Love you!"

She made a kissing sound as the line went dead. Jiho knew he couldn't get through to her, so instead of arguing, knowing he would lose, he got dressed. After fifteen minutes, the doorbell rang before someone burst through the door.

"Honey, I'm home!" A chuckle left his mouth as he heard her walk in. No matter how often he took her key away, it was as if she had another one on standby.

However, they had only met when they partnered up for a history project in their fifth year; they became the other half of each other. Many thought they were dating, which was no surprise. They acted as they did.

Kisses on the cheek and head. They wore similar clothes sometimes and spent holidays and vacations together. It was all spiritual, never romantically perceiving each other. It did help with the unwanted flirtations that came their way. They were more soul sisters than anything else.

Quickly putting on his jacket, Jiho yelled to the hyper girl that he had just got done. Once Jiho reached the last step, Ally gave him a 'serious' look as he came down.

"You are always wearing this style. When are you going to change it up a bit?"

Looking over his choice in the mirror, Jiho sighed before shrugging off the jacket, rolling the sleeves of his fitted dress shirt till they reached just below his elbows. Ally had made it a point to make more of a difference by unbuttoning the top two buttons.

In turn of doing this, some of his old scars were on display for the world to see.

"Happy?" Jiho made some jazz hands while still looking defeated.

"Who knew you had a great fashion sense?"

An eye roll came from him. Jiho loved his friend; he indeed did, but her shit-eating grin was annoying. Jiho didn't have the best fashion taste, but it wasn't the worst. He loved his time capsule clothing items, knowing he would never have to worry about being on trend with those their age. He had more of a posh look in his attire.

Walking out the door, knowing Ally would lock up, Jiho turned around.

"You're the one wearing designer shit." Jiho looks at her in the porch light. She wore a white Swarovski dress designed by Alexandre Vauthier, a designer she usually works with. It did look very stunning and complimented her fair skin tone.

"Don't start. We both know the reasoning behind this stunt."

He nodded as he jumped into the car. After twenty minutes, Ally was singing her heart out, he exited the vehicle, saving himself from the tone-deaf girl. Walking through the front door, they were instantly welcomed by music.

"I'm going to the bathroom. I'll meet you at the bar." Jiho nods in agreement. He settled down next to a girl who looked a bit younger than those around them. Sitting on the stool, he asked the bartender to get him water–being the designated driver that night.

The venue had been over its capacity, the music loud, and people's bodies were close to each other.

If Jiho had not been hauled out tonight, he would have left as soon as he walked in. The bar never a place where you would find him.

Often, you could spot the man at the library, reading up a storm or even walking around the park trails. He could read any and everything as well as go for hours, admiring nature. It was his way of escaping reality, not wanting to face some of the harsh truths the world gave him.

"You come to a bar and only get water. Interesting."

The woman next to him speaks after a couple of minutes. Jiho turned his head and saw her writing on some documents he could not fully view. Her eyes focused on her work.

The accent did not pass him, knowing she was not an American, maybe France or Ireland, as there had been a mix of the two. Her hair pulled back, helping her line of vision.

"You bring work to a bar. That's interesting." Jiho replied, causing her to curve the corner of her lips up. He did not know what came over him to engage in the conversation; Jiho was not one to speak unless it was more than ten times meeting someone.

"Good point."

She puts the papers in a neat pile, the pen on top, and turns to face him. Once he saw those green eyes, the poor man to lose his train of thought. He found himself seeing the mountains of his homeland and the green fields through her eyes. Jiho did not know how homesick he was. Time was unknown to him, not knowing what to say. The woman smiled at the man's daydreaming.

"What's your name?"

Shaking his head at her voice, he retrieves his composure with a slight cough. Embarrassed by the awkwardness he created, "What's yours?"

"I asked first." Not skipping a beat to his reply, the smile turned into a confident smirk. She enjoyed the effect she had on the older male.

With a sigh, he nods, introducing himself by first name then last–the way he's realized most people do outside his customs, "Jiho. Jiho Yoo."

He sticks his hand out. She nods and shakes his hand. She had slowly taken her hand back, not wanting to leave his.

"Saoirse." She replied, sipping the drink he had not seen.

"No last name?" He cocks an eyebrow. Saoirse chuckled.

"My first name should give you my last name if you've lived here long enough." There was mischief in her eyes, the knowledge that she would toy with him, and he would not have a second thought in stopping her and her bittersweet enjoyment, "Especially if you come to this place often."

Pinching his brows together, he continued, "Well, I just moved here from Ireland eight months ago. Though I did stop in Korea for a short while to see family over the summer."

He thought his accent was the dead giveaway to where he was from and where he studied, as sometimes intermixing happened. Though he spent most of his childhood in South Korea with his family, the young man had lived in Ireland since he graduated.

Saoirse's eyes turned into slits at the news, "If you're from Ireland, then you should know who I am."

"What do you mean?" Confusion laced his comforting voice, a bit rough from the strong accent but still intriguing.

Saoirse turned her body facing him. "You look adorable when you are confused." She said with a hint of amusement.

Jiho blushed, shocked at her bluntness towards him, "You didn't answer my question." The excitement grows when Saoirse sees him affected by her comment.

Wanting to see how long it would take him to assemble the pieces was all too much fun, "How old are you?" Still holding amusement in her expression.

He felt a little mad at her unwillingness to answer his questions; he gave in to hers, "Twenty-eight; how old are *you*?" He emphasized the word 'you.' His time spent with Ally developed an attitude in his personality.

The amusement left her face, placing a bored and annoyed emotion, "I'm twenty." She shrugged as he looked at her with wide eyes.

He leaned towards her and whispered, "How'd you get in?!" Not wanting to get her kicked out, he looked side to side. Praying those around were not listening to their conversation.

"You really don't know me, do you?" She leaned in closer. Their faces were just a few centimeters apart. He blushed even more, astounded at the young woman's confidence. He was about to say something when a man came from a different direction.

Saoirse's playful demeanor switched to a cold appearance, like she had built a wall. The man whispered something into Saoirse's ear; her face showed anger and annoyance. Turning back to Jiho and smiling, "Seems I must go. I do hope to see you later, *mon amour*."

Once Saoirse and the man were gone, Ally finally returned, "Ji. Please tell me you ordered me my usual." She sat in the now empty seat, eyes pleading. He shook his head no.

"Sorry Al, I was…," unsure if he should tell his best friend about the young woman he just encountered, the up-and-coming model interrupted.

"Well, I'll just get my own; no biggie." She smiled.

THE NIGHT SOON TURNED to early morning as the two slumped on Jiho's guest bed. Although the two friends had a close relationship, they held each other's privacy to a high standard, never allowing them to get too close in personal space regarding bedrooms and connections with others if not asked to. It was their safety net between them; she had her secrets, and so did he. They loved one another in a family way but still wanted things for themselves, which they both understood.

Jiho was the only sober one of the two, while the blonde was on better terms-shitfaced drunk, "My wonderful friend Ji…," she announced in slurs and stutters. "Can I ask you a question, and you can't be mad."

A soft chuckle came out as he agreed to her terms.

"How can one tell another they have feelings for them? I mean, I've given them hint after hint. They don't see it."

Jiho was a bit taken aback. For the first time, Allyria Turner had spoken aloud that she had feelings for someone in a romantic sense. He remembered her having many of the boys admire her in their school years, but Ally never showed any interest in them or even spoke out to them in a passing tone.

Ally never cared about the idea of dating; she stated so during the summer before their third year of university at one of her family homes.

Her family's position in the social clubs of the world's elite had gained her a lot of attention when she had invited him. Still, the rumors of them dating were put to a close when her father denied that sort of relationship happening.

Having a bit of a complex past with men, Jiho understood and never pushed for her to get out there and date. But now she's asking for advice on pursuing someone he's never heard about.

Jiho knew it was serious, too, as Ally only got this drunk if she tried to run or hide from something bothering her. He didn't fail to notice it tonight, as well.

The last time she had gotten like this was during the end of their third year at the academy during their winter break. She had been on edge on one of their vacations at her family's small cottage nearby. The thought of introducing Jiho to her family so early in their friendship weighed heavily on her.

She had a couple of bottles of wine stored away from when she stole them from her father's cellar. After drinking until she was on the edge of blacking out, she poured her heart out about the issue, stating that she didn't want to lose their friendship if her family thought he wasn't good enough.

Ally shared about all these outrageous rules her past friends had to follow, causing them to distance themselves. He had felt horrible knowing this information without her being sober. So, the next afternoon, they talked about it, allowing them to become even closer than before.

"Well…"

Taking a breath as he debated if he should answer her question now and bring it up the following day or just ignore it all till, she asked him again when she was sober. Although it would be a fifty-fifty chance of her doing the latter. He decided on the first just so he knew what to say the next day.

"I guess just tell them straightforwardly. Nothing compares to saying what you desperately want than dancing around it for a while." he said, tucking her in. Sitting at the edge, he continued. "Having a clear understanding of what you expect from someone is the only true line in which both parties know. It's-" A snore interrupted his sentence.

Looking at the messy drunk fast asleep, a ghost smile appeared on the man's face. Jiho stood up, kissing her head before leaving for his own.

As he changed, Jiho rethought his advice. It was strange that he spoke about something he had no experience with. Being antisocial, he didn't date at all.

In university, some asked, but he was so focused on his education and his promise to Eun-Ya to entertain the idea. The Yoo family did want him to settle down soon, expecting a grandchild-either through adoption or birthing-but understood the reason behind his ambitions.

He loved his family; indeed, he did, but sometimes, he wanted them to stop nagging and allow him to move at his speed. He promised them a grandchild later in life with the intent of being a single father. Even with his thoughts on his family, Jiho couldn't help but let his mind wander.

The young woman he met; her name echoed in his head. How she could take the spotlight without even knowing was bewildering to him.

Even when they had a small conversation, he never let his attention move from her and her movements. He only saw her in that room. It was strange for him to even look at another person so close for a few seconds before being pulled back into his shell. But with her, he was ready to forsake his comfortable box and engage.

Jiho would never confirm, but he was a romantic at heart. Often daydreaming about a happy life, a significant other, their little one running around them. It was a dream that would stay a dream. Or at least that's what he had thought until he saw her.

The way the dress clung to her body was enjoyable; it was also the first time he was genuinely interested in a person that way. He never thought about what his partner would identify as or anything.

He knew they had to keep his attention just by their playfulness, which this woman did without a second thought. He enjoyed the little game she played with him. Jiho felt his lips tug into a small smile at how many times he was flustered with her.

Though Jiho himself never pursued people, that did not mean those around him did not try. People try to calculate what he wants in a partner as his cold demeanor screams dominance, leaving them to play a little damsel act or go over the top and play a more aggressive one.

The man had more masculine features, was wealthy from his achievements, and came from a good traditional family background with his parents and three younger sisters.

Having that woman run him in circles with humiliation in a way where he did not feel anxious or unsafe was new to him. The opposite of what he is used to. He had hoped she enjoyed his company as he did hers.

She didn't seem to mind the age. But Jiho wasn't sure if he had overstepped and made her uncomfortable. He was captivated. That woman would be his undoing, and he was perfectly fine with that. Hoping that he can meet her again soon, even if only in his dreams.

Chapter Nine

Honey Dog

THE FOLLOWING AFTERNOON, the two friends were lounging around the living room as an episode of *The Real Housewives* was playing, though neither knew which one it was as they were chatting about last night's events.

"Wait…I asked you for advice in my love life?"

Ally asked in horror, only to be met with a short nod of confirmation. Her face burned red as she threw herself back, pulling a pillow over her face, screaming.

"I cannot believe I got that drunk. Off a Havana Beach no less!"

"To be fair, you had fourteen of those and some Cranberry Kicks.' I was surprised when you woke up before noon." His grin did not help her feel better as he asked the question of who she was talking about. A battle of who would crack began—a smile on one's face versus a blank look on the other.

Jiho was proud that he had broken her not too long in the battle and was now sitting up, his legs crossed and pillow in his lap, ready to hear how Ally had figured out she liked someone.

With a deep breath and a moment to collect the events that accrued, Ally thought *fuck it, might as well tell him everything.*

"Well, we both know I'm a bit of a clutz when I'm late to things, right?" He nodded in agreement, recalling past events; a small snort left him. Ally glared at him briefly before continuing. "Right, well, I was going to the photoshoot that Jennie, one of my agents, got me."

"The one for a clothing ad, right? Like a commercial?"

"Yeah, a commercial. Since the bus broke down a few blocks away, I got off and booked it. It didn't help that I had to bring some of my stuff to the shoot, but what can you do on a short notice gig? I made it into the building and accidentally ran into this handsome guy. Like Johnny Depp in the nineties when he was dating Winona Ryder. And spilled his drink all over him."

"Wait, he was Johnny in the nineties?" Jiho was shocked.

Ally adored the man more than anything and has always been a massive fan of his work and characters. She never compared anyone to him, not even Johnny himself in his later years, though she still loved him no matter which era he was in.

"How is that possible?"

She excitedly nodded, "I know; I was so surprised. I told him I would make up for the accident." Ally sat up straighter, taking a sip of her smoothie the two had ordered, "After the shoot, he approached me, asking if I was serious about my promise of running into him. Which, of course, I was. So, we got coffee."

Ally excitedly went on to say how they hit it off and went on more outings together, becoming friends.

"Eric is wonderful. Going out was tricky; it's over as soon as our friendship gets out."

It always amazed Jiho how far-fetched the media would go to make anything become a story. He remembered the first time the two friends went out in public: pure chaos.

"Are you having a good time with him? Does he treat you with respect?" Jiho had asked, worried. This wouldn't be the first time a man tried to use his best friend for gain.

Placing her hand on her worried friend, Ally nodded, "Yes, he does. I would be denying his existence if he weren't respectful."

"That doesn't help my nerves, Al."

"Can you not act so serious?" She laughed.

"Not happening. With you, I lose not only my sleep but also my sanity."

"Don't be like that." Ally pouted, "Would you calm down if I told you more about him?"

After a moment of delay, Jiho nodded. The woman recalled everything she could about Eric.

They went to the park with his dog, cooked and baked together. Eric had bought some of her favorite products from beauty brands, clothing vendors, and bathroom essentials; he wanted to be prepared for anything and make her comfortable.

"Okay, okay. What was the moment you realized you liked Eric?"

Don't get Jiho wrong, the two friends will always be in each other's lives, but they both know they have different dreams.

Ally smiled in contentment; her demeanor came to a stillness of calm. "We were sitting on his couch, his dog, Honey, resting on us. The windows were open, some nice soulful music was playing, and we just sat there. Enjoying each other's company. I never really felt comfortable around any man besides you and father. I honestly didn't even think about being with him romantically. I was just trying to be his friend, but…I really like him, Jiho."

"I'm so happy for you, Ally-Bear; I know how much you wanted this connection." The pair smiled at one another with pure happiness. Each is grateful for the other.

Slowly, Ally's face showed worry, "I just don't know if he likes me back or not."

"And why do you think that? Is there any reason?"

"Well, not that I can think of." She sighed, "But, I mean, look at me. I'm just some blonde bimbo when people first look at me. I'm not someone else's wish as a girlfriend unless it's arm candy-"

"You are not just a blond bimbo or an arm candy." Jiho sternly said, seriously pissed at her for thinking such thoughts, "You got into the top school in Ireland based on your grades. Ally, you are smarter than most people; you weren't at the top of the class because of me, but you were still in the top ten." Jiho chuckled at the last part; it was his way of lightening the situation.

Ally gave a sad smile, "Thank you, Jiho. I really mean it, but I still am unsure."

"Based on what you've told me, he does. Some guys would lead on a beautiful woman like yourself, but Eric? I don't think he would do that. If this man has spent so much time and effort with you, allowing you to meet his pride and joy of a puppy, and ticking the press, making them run around like headless chickens just to spend maybe an hour with you, I think he's feeling the same or will feel the same at some point. But it's better to ask than not. Even if it's not something you want to hear, at least you'll know the truth and be free from worry."

Jiho shrugged his shoulders at the end as if his answer were the most obvious thing to do. Which to him it was.

"You're right. I just need to ask Eric. But I think I'll do that tomorrow; my head is still killing me." They both laughed at Ally's expense. They lounged the whole day, ordering takeout when they got hungry.

At around eight, she went home to prepare for tomorrow's confession with a little self-care night.

After she left, Jiho thought of a particular lady who piqued his interest. He wondered how she was doing.

Thought about how their conversation was something he enjoyed, even if he made an absolute fool of himself. He hoped to see her soon and wondered if he could go to the bar, hoping she would be there again when he arrived later that week.

Chapter Ten

Bethany Keith

"THE NEXT PATIENT TO QUESTION my knowledge is going to get my foot up their ass."

With her wild language, Jiho couldn't help but let the snort leave him as they ate their lunch and took refuge in his office.

Usually, he wouldn't have taken to another person, but Bethany Keith was different. The mid-forty-year-old woman had become an aunt figure to him, constantly checking on him and bringing him to quiet rooms when he felt overwhelmed. She was ultimately a caregiver to him when needed, for which he was thankful.

Honestly, her approach caused her to be different from all the other women around him during work. Instead of the constant flirty comments or desire to know every little thing of his personal life, Beth only wanted to know how he was doing in the present time and if there was anything she could do to help him feel more comfortable and safer.

"I don't think Mrs. Keith would appreciate a call from me telling her that her wife has a foot up someone's ass." He mused, taking another bite of his food, "No matter how hilarious that would be."

"How many times have I told you to call her, Darlene? She rather hates it when you don't."

Blushing at the scolding, he meekly spoke, "Sorry-"

"There is no need to be sorry. I'm just reminding you. No harm in what you did." She sweetly smiled, taking her time to explain. "But between you and me, Lene would only put a sex ban for a day before she gave in." Sending a wink to the embarrassed man, she giggled.

"Beth!?"

"What? Even old people like me need a little sex in their life. Especially when they have a stunning wife such as mine. If you had met us when we were still in our twenties, you would have fainted from the stories."

"Good lord, please stop," Jiho muttered, burying his face in his hands. His cheeks burned, and he felt uncomfortable, so he avoided her eyes.

"I'm just teasing…sort of. But what is going on in your life? Has that girl…um…" Struggling to remember the person, placing her finger on her chin.

"Ally?"

"Yes!" Beth smiles, "Has Ally taking you out recently?"

"She has…"

Just as he answered, memories of that night came back, the way the mystery woman captured his attention. Truth be told, he was somehow coming back to her. It only started with her eyes, but it was her mannerism and constant toying that kept him thinking of her.

Jiho felt conflicted. Part of him wanted to see Saoirse, but the other wanted to forget her, as he knew they would never meet again.

"Something happened." She stated.

"What?"

"Something happened when you went out with Ally."

"N-No. Why would you say that?" Jiho chuckled nervously.

Humming at his state of being, Beth watched her words carefully, "Because you look the same way I did when I met my wife for the first time."

"And that was?" He hesitated in asking.

"Being entirely consumed by her enchanting aura." Taking the last bite of her lunch, she sighed in delight. Leaning back in her seat, Beth crossed her arms, "So what happened? Was it a woman? Man?"

"Beth-"

"Hey, I don't judge." Raising her hands in surrender, she continued, "So what happened?"

Biting his lip, Jiho contemplated. He hadn't even mentioned this to Ally, but Beth was someone he could get advice from.

"Well, Ally took me to a bar of sorts. While she left me alone for a few, there was this woman-"

"You talked to a woman?" Pressing her lips into a fine line, Jiho could tell she was holding in laughter.

"Will you let me talk? Anyways, yes. I did talk to her, but she had to leave before I could know more about her."

"Name?"

"Only a first. Didn't want to give me her last."

"She's cautious. Smart woman. What else? Did you see her again? I heard you telling Viktor of going out to a bar by yourself to too long ago."

Blushing at the sudden call out, he frowned, "I went back, staying till they did last call, but she never showed. I asked the barters about her, but they just said they have no idea who she was…"

"What are you going to do?"

"What am I going to so? Nothing. That's what. I won't see her again, so…"

"So, you just give up and move on?" Beth frowned, "Jiho. I will speak of this once with you and never bring it back up unless you do. Is that okay?"

Nodding his head, Jiho leaned forward giving all his attention to the woman.

"From knowing you over these months and what you've told me in confidence, you don't give random strangers the time of day. For this…mystery woman to swoop in and take your attention without giving you a discomfort…you didn't feel uncomfortable with her right?"

Taking his time to express just how Saoirse made him feel, Jiho took a breath: "No I don't feel uncomfortable. I felt just as I do with you, Al, Viktor, and my family."

Eagerly, she rushed to continue, "To have a stranger makes you feel this way. It's hard for you to come by again."

Nodding along as Beth spoke, Jiho contemplated. If that were the case, he could only act on his own will instead of overthinking, but that in itself was hard, let alone with a stranger.

"So, what do I do?" He frowned, tapping his finger against his head, "I don't know if I will ever see her again."

Sighing at the truth of the matter, Beth shrugged, gathering her things as their mealtime was almost up, and her rounds were next on the agenda.

"You can only rely on faith and hope. But if you don't try your best to get to know this woman, you could possibly lose a friendship or even more."

"And if that's not what she wants?"

"Then you have to respect that."

TAKING THE TABLET from the male nurse, Andrew, Jiho looked over the scan, "How's the kid?"

"Better now we put some fluids in her. Fever has gone down but still working up a sweat."

"Scans?"

"CT shows what we originally thought." He pointed out the areas before continuing, "Kidney stones."

Glancing in the area, Jiho hummed, "What did radiology say about it?"

"That after so more fluids it should pass on its own in a few days…"

Raising his brow, Jiho turned his attention from the screen to Andrew, "If you feel the need to say more, speak. It's better to be heard then keep your lips locked in this line of work."

"Well, with how bad the pain was for her; I think we should keep them here." He cautiously voiced.

Andrew had been scheduled at different times then Jiho, and today was the first time he had worked with the doctor. As a new nurse to the staffing he was scared to work with the man. There was some gossip among the staff of the newcomer; how closed off he was and the cold outer appearance. But to him, Jiho was just a straightforward man, who doesn't come to work and give anything half-ass.

"I agree." Handing the tablet back to the nurse, he smiled softly, "Nicely done. See that they get a room."

With a blush, Andrew swiftly nodded, walking away. Although there was an unspoken rule of guys complementing guys for him, even he could admit the Korean was handsome, especially when he smiled, and knowing that he rarely did that made his own face flush.

Seeing him walk away, Jiho stood their confused at the reaction. His hand combing through his hair as he tilled his head to the side.

"Even with your oblivious social skills you can still make others blush." Beth giggled. Stepping in toe with her, the two began to walk in whatever direction she was heading.

"And what does that mean?" he nervously asked, tensed at the statement.

"Jiho." She couldn't help the grin widening on her face as the panic appeared so strongly on his face, "I, beside Viktor, know you more than anyone here...There is a lot you don't see even with your glasses."

"What does that mean?"

"It means you need to start thinking in a different way then you're used to. Then you are comfortable with."

His face contorted more, a huff escaping his lips, "And what does *that* mean?"

"That my dear boy is for you to find out." Spinning, she came face to face with the pouting man. Ruffling his hair Beth pushed him at arm's length, "And this is where I leave you."

"Wh-" The words abruptly stopped at the woman's bathroom sign. In a moment of embarrassment, Jiho sped away hearing his coworker laugh.

Chapter Eleven

Familiar Faces

USUALLY, JIHO WOULD BE at home under some blankets or in warm pajamas, lying around on his days off.

Usually.

For the first time since he's been in America, things had not gone the usual way. First, Jiho's alarm woke him up, even after shutting it off the night prior, and then it was his water temperature.

Jiho used lukewarm water for daily showers, but the ice-cold water surprised him. The morning could have been saved, but the power shut off during his cooking. Looking to see if others around him also lost power, Jiho saw the reason. A tree had hit their neighborhood's power box and some power lines, causing a blackout.

So here the overworked man was, walking out of a nearby cafe, each hand occupied with either a cold Americano or a half-eaten bagel sandwich. Jiho did not take long to eat the small meal as he was starving from the previous few days at work. The food itself was divine, in his opinion.

The runny, sunny side egg complemented the crispy, perfectly cooked bacon bits. Melted with the help of the stringy cheese blended in Jiho's mouth, coming together with the stove-top grilled onions and steamed greens. A wonderfully crunchy, seasoned-packed, savory meal for Jiho.

He was in absolute heaven as he took his bites.

With one last bite of his sandwich left he heard some men yelling. Now, he was not one to look into other people's business, but as he was about to continue his walk, he heard it was a woman responding back.

Changing his direction towards the little commotion behind a building, Jiho was surprised to see a familiar face in the group. Though he did not remember her name off the top of his head, he knew it was someone from his school days, and if he remembered correctly, it was someone who had helped him on occasion, feeling compelled to help her in return.

As he got closer to them, Jiho was able to pick up bits of the conversation. "-Why don't you just leave me alone? I told you why we can't be in the same line of work as you."

"I really don't appreciate the reasoning, sweetheart. So why don't you be a good little lapdog and ask your owner–I mean boss," the man quickly corrected as the woman glared, "to come out and speak with me? We can clear up this whole misunderstanding." His shoulders were pulled back as the two men around him had acted as a wall of protection from the woman.

Jiho did not undervalue the power of women, as he placed them on a high platform. Seeing their struggles daily with mundane things and having three sisters, Jiho knew the strength they could have once angered, something he never wanted to do again after the last time.

But to see these men standing a few meters away from the woman in a cautious position while she was seemingly vexed with this conversation was mirthful.

With no verbal response from her, one of the two *guards* had stepped forward, reaching his hand out in pursuit to grab her. Before either could register what was happening, the man was hit by a cold drink.

It soaked his face, hair, and shirt, an unpleasant sensation as the wind dried into stickiness. They all looked over to see who could have done something like this; the three were furious, while the woman was satisfied.

Giving off his best smile, Jiho chuckled, "Oops. Sorry, I thought I saw a fly. Didn't mean to make a mess." He took the last bite of his breakfast.

"Jiho?"

He knitted his eyebrows together at the familiar person's immediate recognition of him, feeling bad for not remembering them. "And you are…?"

The woman deflated a bit at his answer, saddened by the fact he didn't recognize her. "It's me, Lisa. Lisa Nerthan from BioMed."

Scratching her head, she was a bit nervous as she was face-to-face with her school sweetheart, who wasn't really her school sweetheart.

Thinking back to the name, Jiho had connected the dots; although relatively slowly, he still did remember her.

She wasn't the girl next door who was so sweet and shy; she changed. Her hair was no longer pulled back into a bun or ponytail. Instead, Lisa was wearing her natural hair out, embracing the tight coils with pride.

There was no oversized sweater hanging off her body but a tailored one. She kept her skin still covered but flattered her body more. Her glasses are still there but swapped for more up-to-date styling.

"Oh god. I'm sorry I didn't recognize you. You just look different." Jiho widened his eyes as he tried to backpedal, "Not that that's bad. You looked good, just not like before. I mean, you looked good then and now, but just-"

Lisa let out an amused snort as she watched the previously closed-off man ramble in an attempt to save himself. "I know what you mean. Don't worry."

The two stood there not knowing what to say as Jiho didn't know her too well even when they were in the same courses, and Lisa still held some feelings towards him, regressing to her former shy demeanor and finger fidgeting.

They turned their attention back to the omitted three as the one in the middle coughed noisily to gain their attention.

"That was lovely, but I was in the middle of talking with our dear Lisa here. So, if you don't mind, fuck off. Thanks."

Jiho cocked an eyebrow before ignoring his request, "Do you want to talk to this man, Lisa?"

"I told you to leave, so lea-"

"Lisa." Jiho stepped in her line of view, completely blocking the others, "Do you want to talk to this man, or do you want them to leave?"

Chewing at her bottom lip, Lisa let out a small mutter, "I want them to leave."

She knew how to protect herself, truly. But she also wanted Jiho around longer, so she did what anyone would do. Indirectly ask him to get rid of them.

"You heard the lady." Jiho turned back around, "Bye."

Scoffing at him, the man who had done all the talking finally stepped forward, toe-to-toe with Jiho.

"I still need to talk about *business* with Lisa, so I think you should go."

"You leave now. I don't like when people feel entitled to things, especially dumbasses like you. So, leave." Jiho stressed, in a hushed tone, not waiting for Lisa to hear.

Huffing at the name-calling, the man's face turned red. "Just because you fucked this bit-"

He didn't even finish the word as Jiho laid a back hand slap. The impact had made the receiver fall to the ground, holding a hand over his mouth as blood seeped between his fingers.

It was a good day for Jiho to wear some of his rings. He silently thanked Ally for buying them during New Years.

"I do hate when others degrade women just because of rejection." Jiho sighed, fixing his sleeves as they had splatters of blood on them. "Now. Are you going to leave?" Scrambling to his feet, Jiho rolled his eyes, "I really hoped you were at least somewhat smart." Looking at Lisa over his shoulder, he requested, "You mind holding this jacket for me?"

"Sure…" She blushed at the muscles that indirectly flexed in his movements of taking the layer off, brushing her fingers over his.

As soon as she felt his skin, Jiho was pulled away; the one who had initially tried to reach Lisa gripped his shirt.

Moving his hand on top of the taller man's, Jiho used the weight difference to his advantage, tossing the attacker over his shoulder before twisting the other's out of its arm socket.

The groans of pain were muffled as Jiho pushed him away with his foot, swinging his back leg back into the second's stomach. Jiho's new target had been the shortest of the three, but he was faster than them, quickly recovering from the impact.

The two had tried to get the upper hand while throwing punches, only to be blocked by one another; Jiho stayed closed in, refusing to let an opening be seen as he continued to block the high kicks the other was giving.

It wasn't till Jiho hit the wall that he sprang into action, ducking into a squat before swiping his leg and taking the man out by his ankles. Jiho rushed on top of him, blowing open-handed slaps, one after the other, till the bloody man was unconscious.

Still hearing the groans and cries from the taller one, Jiho walked over, knocking him unconscious.

Not wanting to have the injured choke on their throw-up, he turned both to their side.

"I hate violence."

He breathes out as he walks towards the one who started this all. He still held his mouth as the blood subsided from the cuts.

"It makes it hard for me to keep my promise, you know?" He taunted, "Now, I'll ask you once more. Will you leave here yourself, or will I make you leave?"

Shaking his head, the man lisped, "I'll leave."

Taking his answer, Jiho returned to Lisa, slipping his jacket back on before straightening himself out.

"You, okay?"

She nodded, not verbally answering him, as she had millions of thoughts swirling around her head.

Lisa had heard of how violent the man could get in the past, but Jiho had always been so closed off and respectful towards her, so there was no real reason for her to believe them. But now witnessing it firsthand, the woman was shaken up but also viewed Jiho in a new awe.

She had always liked him for some reason. It didn't matter to her that the man had never gotten close to anyone but Allyria Turner. It showed her that Jiho valued close relations rather than the amount, something she loved. Seeing him help her when they had not seen each other in years made her hope that he had finally let the wall he had crumble.

"Good."

Jiho smiled before checking his phone, where he was notified about a missed call from work. Opening the message from one of his co-workers, Jiho saw that there was an emergency and they needed him there as soon as possible.

"Damn…Are you okay getting to wherever you were going by yourself? I need to get to work…" Jiho trailed off, sending a pleading look.

"Yeah." Lisa blurted, "I can get back myself. No problem."

"Good. Well, bye." He waved before taking off on a jog.

"Wait!" Lisa shouted. Unfortunately, he was gone, "…You want to swap numbers?" Mumbling her question. Curing herself for missing another opportunity to get close to the man.

While she looked at the injured, Lisa turned around before entering the building through the back entrance.

Unknowns to them, three people watched, two women and one man, from the second-floor window as it all took place.

The youngest was smirking at the new entertainment, excited to see what it would bring.

The man was confused about the friendly conversation between the two people.

And the last only gave a soft smile with an impressed look.

Chapter Twelve

Invite

"JAY, HOW ARE YOU?"

The man had been sitting in the cafeteria looking over one of his many folders as he prepared for a briefing.

His patient was a seven-year-old boy who desperately needed a spot on a liver transplant list. Jiho hoped to give the family some good news soon.

As his name was called, he looked up to see one of his colleagues, forty-eight-year-old Dr. Viktor Petrov, who mentored him when he first started working at the hospital.

When people first look at Viktor, many would double-take once told he was a doctor, let alone a neurosurgeon. Viktor looked only in his thirties; some even assumed he was the same age as Jiho.

He was around the same height as the younger, standing at five-eleven, but looked slightly leaner, giving off the illusion of a similar build as Jiho.

"Viktor!" He beamed, "I'm doing the same as I was last week, I suppose. How about yourself?" He closes the folder to give the other his attention, offering a seat.

"Same as you, I believe. Although I did spend the majority of my day off with two growing children constantly wanting my attention, Anya's sixth birthday was rather extravagant than last year. The kid wanted to watch all the *Harry Potter* movies again, and you know Lia." A chuckle emitted as a soft smile on the latter.

"She made you all dress up in your house?"

Viktor rolled his eyes before giving a look that confirmed his question, "I swear those two love those movies more than me sometimes." A small pout formed.

"Doubtful. Wasn't Emilia and Anya not here earlier today to bring over the lunch they 'forgot' to give you this morning?" The tip of his brow rose slightly at the question.

A huge smile came over Viktors face, "That they did. Of course, the morning was so busy getting everything ready that they forgot and had to come here." The two men scoffed in a short amusement.

Both knew Viktor's family adored him; even after only nine months, Jiho had gotten relatively close to the mentor and his family. He was welcomed as an uncle to the kids and a younger brother to both parents, becoming very grateful to the Petrov family.

He was rather homesick while overseas. Knowing the long flight was too much for his parents to visit. His three sisters, Nari, Iseul, and Min-Jung were so consumed in their lives that they never saw him.

"I wanted to talk to you about something." Viktor had taken the man out of his thoughts. With a slight nod, the Russian continued, "Well, the wife was wondering if you would like to come over and have dinner with the family. Anya has been asking for you. Nikolia as well."

Jiho was happy to be invited to dinner. This would be the first time he had entered the older one's home as they would eat at a restaurant or have lunch at a lovely little cafe around the children's school.

"I would love to. Would Sunday work? It's only three days away, so I can bring some food, so Emilia doesn't have to cook too much." Remembering that she had shoulder surgery not too long ago and was now allowed to pick up lightweight things around the house for physical therapy.

"That would be wonderful. Lia can't do too much as of right now." Nodding in understanding, Jiho looked at his watch and excused himself as the meeting was soon. Both men bid each other goodbye.

DRIVING HOME, Jiho thought back to his family and how much has changed since childhood. His days wake up to the rustling of his mother and father getting ready for the day and cooking breakfast before trying to get him to eat some of it.

The smell of meat, kimchi, egg, and rice was simple but comforting, yet he had no energy. He was doted on, constantly having the attention of both parents out of guilt; at least, that is how Jiho remembered it, as their sunken faces did not hold any love in them during those hard times.

Once his sisters were born a new routine was made. Jiho would get up and ready, then get them up, helping them change.

Feeding them when asked to by either of his parents. Jiho's mother and sisters would see the two males off for the day.

The father going to work, and the son running errands as both men feared the other three would be dead if they ventured out by themselves. Jiho did attend schooling before he went abroad, though it was online and at his own pace; although he was smart enough to skip grades, Jiho did not want to leave his younger sisters behind too early.

At eleven years old, they welcomed the last of the family. He did not hate her as he did with the twins. He loved her instantly as he was now old enough to know that he would protect his sisters without fail.

Nari and Iseul were now nineteen years old, in the second year of their university life; the two had skipped a grade during their high school days as both girls attended an art school early on in life. The two were very talented, earning recognition in their art community.

Nari was the fashionable one. Her skills were seen as she made clothing from nothing. Hosting her own runways during the school fairs.

Iseul, too, was talented, but her skills were around painting; her work could be seen in galleries for up-and-coming artists. The two were already business savvy with their side income from their work.

Min-Jung, now seventeen years old, is finishing her last year of high school. She was currently studying abroad, as Jiho had done in the past. Though her school was in Italy, she had always been in different places in the previous years. Luckily for her, Min-Jung could pick up languages easily, so there was no barrier.

Once inside, the man opened his phone to call his younger sisters, as it should be afternoon for the twins and morning for the baby. It took four rings before he saw their faces. Nari was mainly in view, with Iseul in the background.

They were walking around the neighborhood that Jiho missed so much, visiting family. The area now had CCTV in place and was inhabited more by people and streetlights, allowing the boy to be at ease.

Min-Jung was still in bed but was more awake than he thought she would be. Her schooling was mainly online, with the occasional in-person lecture. She had the freedom to take her classes at night in the safety of her dorm upon Jiho's request to go out only during the day and with a group of people to hang out and explore.

The four conversed about their day and what they planned to do for the rest of it. The girls knew how much their brother missed them and their family, but they also knew that his being in the States was the best opportunity for him.

The conversation lasted well into the night for Jiho, but he didn't mind it as they enjoyed the time they could spend together, even over the phone.

Chapter Thirteen

Photo of Four

THREE DAYS HAVE PASSED by fast for Jiho. The amount of work he could knock out was unbelievable to the nurses.

Although some of the younger nurses have tried to get their hands on the young, attractive doctor, they all ran out of luck. The only conversations he would entertain were topics on the patients.

But the older nurses or those who did not try to cross such boundaries had been able to peel a few of his layers in terms of personal questions, such as Jiho asking about their day-to-day lives and how their families were doing.

Viktor and Beth were the only ones within the building who knew a little of the terror his neighborhood went through. Having the honor of knowing this information, the two agreed that one would always be with him during large groups and introductions with new staff.

In the days leading up to his dinner with the mentor's family, Jiho had been thinking of what to bring. His mind was endless with the food he wished to make for the family he held dear. One thing was sure: the dish would be from his home country.

Settling on one of his favorites: samgyetang, a chicken ginseng soup. The dish was to be made slowly so the chicken could be as tender as possible, with the broth being a bit bitter yet tasty.

The night before, Jiho grabbed the ingredients he needed for the dish. Making sure to soak the chicken in water overnight before going to bed. The next day, he spent the afternoon making the dish, finishing just in time to leave.

Being careful on his drive, Jiho was excited to give this to Emilia; the other woman he saw as a sister.

ONCE ALL FIVE OF them sat at the table, Jiho explained why he made his dish, especially for tonight.

"It should help restore energy, helping with your appetite. Viktor did tell me the medication has made it hard to keep food down. Hopefully, this helps a bit."

Emilia was very touched that the younger had thought of her condition; it was a burden she had not wanted him to see. She was only two years younger than Viktor, her brown hair pulled into a loose braid as she tried to look a bit put together without wasting much energy.

"I appreciate this, Jiho; I really do." The kind woman spoke. Her soft demeanor was the thing to break the poor doctor's hesitation when they first met.

Emilia had gotten lost trying to find her husband four months ago; she wanted to drop off a meal as the doctor would stay at work an extra night. Though his office had been changed, Emilia had yet to learn where his new location was.

Her thoughts had been silenced when a soft cry was heard a few meters away. Thinking it was a child, Emilia rushed over, finding Jiho having a panic attack. The man before her was backed into a corner of a boardroom, hyperventilating, shaken.

His eyes moved from place to place, hyper-aware of the possible dangers to come. It took around ten minutes to get close to him, but her soft, gentle nature allowed Emilia to cradle him safely.

Jiho was confused, thinking the woman was of Eun-Ya; he held her protectively, refusing to let up even for a moment. Of course, Jiho's stronghold was causing Emilia pain, but she did not want to scare him any further than his mind had.

He was thankful for her willingness to stay with him an extra hour, his emotions too high to let her go. Once he was removed from the illusion of her being his old friend, Jiho let her go, thanking her and apologizing. The man had asked for her name and where she was needed once her visitor's badge and the extra bag were in sight.

Thus, he found that his mentor, someone he trusted, was married to a wonderful woman. It was a pleasant meal, as Emilia had packed more than enough for the three when the two younger ones found Viktor and explained their closeness.

"Dyadya, how come you make Mama something but not the rest of us?" Anya interfered with the conversation the three adults were having.

The newly turned six-year-old had been hounding her parents to get her uncle-like figure to come over and seeing that he only brought something for her mother upset her.

The three looked amazed before the latter chuckled. Jiho had come to love the child's clinging to attention; it made him think of his sisters when they were around the same age. Seeing her older brother, Nikolia, nodding in agreement with a slight frown on his face was too adorable for him to handle.

"Well," the adults looked at each other smiling, "your mama has had a tough time keeping up with you two, and to show that we can see her efforts, I made a dish for her, but also for the family."

The two children were disinterested in his answer, poking, and moving around their dinner. Jiho understood that the six and eight-year-olds were only saddened by his showing favor in their minds.

Sighing, Jiho put his utensils down. The children were still throwing a minor tantrum about the whole thing.

"I was planning to spend time with only you two after dinner to make up for the lack of food, but since you two are mad at me, I guess I'll just go home soon."

Viktor and Emilia enjoy the little lie Jiho made for the kids. It was comforting to see the man slowly become social with others. A giggle escaped the woman's mouth as her children stared wide-eyed, back peddling their statement, trying to make him stay as long as possible with them.

Viktor adored moments like this. The love of his life, happy as she possibly can be, his children laughing at the jokes they made up, all together at a table enjoying one another. He had dreamt of this his whole life: peace within his household.

Not brought into this world of love, he was very confident that his dream would only remain as such. That was until he met Emilia.

His light.

The only thing to keep his sanity in his world of madness, Viktor was grateful to her. This woman had given him everything beyond dreams. She had accepted Jiho into their lives, someone who had become Viktor's little brother of sorts.

He was glad the two got along, afraid Jiho would not open up, and Emilia, skeptical over his cold facade, would have caused tension. But to see the younger lean on his wife as an older sister warmed his soul.

The evening came and went as the five got lost in conversations ranging from the talk of work between the two doctors, the creative ideas of life living as a witch with Anya, having discussions of Nikolia's next violin recital, and Emilia's paintings.

As promised, Jiho and two small children went off to the backyard for a quick game of football, Jiho, of course, being the goalie.

It had been close to ten when Nikolia and Anya started to yawn; the two denied being tired, hoping to spend more time with their uncle. But soft snores could be heard as soon as Jiho put them to bed.

Coming into the kitchen, the ones left awake had started to clean, Emilia collecting the dishes, Jiho washing them while Viktor dried and put them away.

With Emilia's condition, the men told her goodnight, waiting till the bedroom door was closed, and shuffled their way to the front as quietly as possible.

For Jiho's first time at his mentor's home, he was pleased with his improvement toward unknown spaces. Granted, it was with those he trusted, but he was still happy with his progress.

He was not even two steps toward the front when a photo grabbed his attention. The picture was of Emilia, a boy, and two other girls, seeming either siblings or relatively close friends, with the body language happening.

Emilia had been placed on the inner left of the group, then the boy with dark, almost black hair, to the far-left end. The man, who looked about ten years younger, had his arm around Emilia's shoulders, leaning towards the middle of the group, both laughing as if the world's funniest joke had just been told to them.

On her right, directly next to her, was a redhead who was relatively the same age as Emilia. She was a bit taller than the rest; her curls told Jiho she was at least mixed, and her smile was bright as all of her teeth were showing.

The last was a lighter shade brunette; she looked younger than the rest. The girl balanced her height nicely with the group, her arms hugged around the redhead leaning against the taller; only a tiny smile was seen, her eyes not even looking at the camera but at the other three.

Jiho could tell she was at peace around them, and though her eyes were not shown toward the camera, he could tell she cared for them deeply.

"That was after we announced our pregnancy with Anya."

Jiho almost dropped the picture frame he held when Viktor leaned close to whisper, not wanting to wake anyone in the house with his voice. He glanced now fondly.

"Her family and friends were so happy that day."

"Are these her family members or friends?" Jiho had now returned to the photo as Viktor pointed out which was which.

"That one is her younger brother; he was around twenty." He said pointing out to the dark-haired boy standing close to Emilia. "We call him Okean."

The older man recalled the memories of chasing the boy on the beach when he was just starting to date his wife in their earlier years. Continuing with the others, Viktor pointed towards the redhead.

"This is Jessica; she was Emilia's first friend when they moved to Michigan. They've been thick as thieves; madness happens if they are left alone. We once got a call that they had been arrested for trying to steal a bunch of stuffed animals from a store when they were drunk, claiming that they were saving the animals from being in cages."

The two chuckled at the thought, though Jiho had a hard time believing she could be drunk, let alone arrested.

Viktor hesitated with the last one; he wasn't too sure about talking about the younger one, and Jiho could tell.

He noticed Viktor was having a disagreement in his head. After a few seconds of debating, he exhaled deeply.

"This is Lia and Okean's cousin; we call her Irse or her middle name Erin. She never liked to go by her full name with family and is very private with her information. She's about eleven or twelve here. Irse had just flown in for the holidays. Lia wanted her there since she would be Nikolia's godmother and Anya's, too."

Jiho was shocked that the two wanted someone so young to be the godparent to their children. He had just been told that Jessica had been the woman's friend since childhood, thinking she was already the godmother, not a child.

"Hey, don't look at me like that." The latter scoffed in fake offense, "Irse may look like she's a child, but they both talked about it beforehand. I have no problems with it since she's in her twenties now and in charge of…well, she can easily care for herself and our children."

Jiho caught his pause in the middle of the explanation.

"Well, they are your kids, so I have no say, but I'm glad you are confident in their godmother."

As he was about to open his door, Viktor touched his shoulder. Jiho was confused by the sudden stop of the older man.

"I wanted to ask if you could attend a function with me?"

He relaxed at the question, but he was now confused with asking him? *Didn't Emilia usually go*? Upon the look, Viktor explained.

"I was going to bring Lia, but Jessica wants her and the children to fly out to visit the same week and won't be able to make it. I've wanted to ask you, but unfortunately, I could only get one plus one every time. But seeing as she can't go this time, why not you?"

Jiho understood why the man chose his wife all those times; hell, he would too, but to be thought of was touching for him.

"What kind of function?"

Even with the knowledge of these little dinners the couple would attend, he did not know what they were for or what happened to them.

He was terrified of being in the crowd and having so many strangers near him all at once, but it wouldn't be too much trouble if he had stuck to Viktor's side the whole time.

"Well, it's for a family *friend*. They tend to throw these formal banquets for all their close and distant friends to come and mingle with each other."

The word, *friends*, held such distance in it that it wasn't the correct way to describe the relationship.

"It's really just to show off who you know and how much influence you have, as many are from good families, but I have to maintain appearances and go to each one."

Over his time working with him, Jiho had gained little knowledge of how well off his family was. Viktor had told him of all the trips they had gone on when he was still a child, the tutors he had, and all the extra activities he could do.

It was one of privilege, but Jiho always figured he was hiding something due to the avoidance of talking about his parents.

"I suppose it would be fine if I went with you. When is it?"

"Friday night. Don't worry; I checked the work schedule before asking."

A nod confirmed his attendance. Viktor gave a small pat on the younger's back, thanking him for attending.

"I'll pick you up around six that night. Thank you for agreeing. I would have been chewed out for being the only one to attend."

He let out a half-hearted scoff.

They said their goodnights before once again parting. Jiho was somewhat stunned by his agreeing to go at the last minute.

Usually, when he was invited to a social outing, he would have to be asked a month in advance to mentally prepare himself for what could happen that outing.

A deep breath soothed his overthinking; he would have to count on Viktor not to leave him alone that night. And for the first time, outside of his family and Ally, Jiho was okay with trusting the man so much.

Chapter Fourteen

Injured Laughs

WEDNESDAYS HAD BECOME HIS FAVORITES. It was the only day in the week when things were relatively normal. Though he did work in a hospital where anything could happen, Wednesdays held the most consistent workflow.

Rounding around the nurses' station, Jiho was handed a new chart. Once a week, employed doctors were required to dedicate their time to the ER. Beth was the head charge nurse scheduled this day, briefing him on the number of visits they had recently had.

"Kids these days are just getting too rowdy for me." She huffed, "I don't know how you turned out so good." Patting Jiho's cheek at the last statement before walking away.

With a subtle chuckle, Jiho walked to room four, where his patient was waiting. Their curtain closed, but he could still discern what was being said.

"Did we have to come here? Aren't you the doctor, *Zajchik*?"

A man with a gruff voice whined before he let out a small moan of pain, to what Jiho believed was a result of a quick slap over the head.

"Shut up, Dima. It was your stupidity that landed you outside my help." The woman had all but scolded the man.

Knocking on the wall before pulling the curtain back a bit, Jiho entered without looking up as he scanned the floor for any misplaced wires or belongings and checked the chart once more to get the name.

Seeing a familiar name, he could not help his curiosity, "Hello, Mr. Petrov? I'm Dr. Yoo. Are you perhaps related to-"

"Jiho?"

Snapping his eyes up, he was surprised, "Lisa? What are you doing here?" Looking over at the man lying on the hospital bed.

He was tall.

So tall that Jiho didn't need to look down at him while standing. The injured was at eye level just by sitting. Looking at the handholding, Jiho continued with his assumption.

"I didn't know you had a boyfriend. Congrats."

Lisa's eyes widened before forcefully dropping Dmitry's hand, hitting the metal bar on the side of the bed. While Dmitry held no outer pain to the hit, Jiho winced at the sudden impact.

"He is not my boyfriend." Crossing her arms, Lisa looked down, "He's just my boss's stupid distant cousin-in-law that I've been made to babysit."

"Awe, *Zajchik*. You're breaking my heart." Dmitry placed his hand over the figuratively wounded area, pouting, "You know I like you. I don't know why you are denying me so much."

"Because I don't like annoying little boys." Forgetting Jiho was in the room, Lisa focused on Dmitry, "I like men."

"I'm all man, *Zajchik*." He smirked, looking over Lisa through hooded eyes.

Jiho felt uncomfortable with the tension created, forgetting about the question he wanted to ask the man. Letting out a small cough, he got the attention back to him. Lisa was mortified that she had played Dmitry's little game.

"Anyways. As I said, I'm Dr. Yoo, and I'll look after you today."

Jiho was puzzled over the reasoning behind the visit as he looked at the chart once more.

"It says you got two broken ribs, a couple of gashes that you will need stitches for, and a sprained wrist…" tilting his head, he was baffled and unconvinced by the reasoning, "from a fall?"

"What can I say, Doc," Dmitry grinned while Lisa hid her face, "I'm a bit of a clutz."

"Right…" Jiho hesitantly nodded.

Turning to Lisa, he could not help but ask the more reliable person in the room.

"Is that what really happened, Lisa? Because this looks like a fight gone wrong." Thinking back to their first reunion, Jiho couldn't help but ask, "You didn't have those guys come back, right?"

Shaking her head, Lisa sighed, "No, Jiho. He really is just a clutz for '*falling*' down the stairs."

Straining the word as if there was more to it than she could tell. Looking at both, Jiho gave in to the excuse before heading over to wash his hands, putting his gloves on, and gathering his equipment to stitch over the large gashes that had dried blood around them.

"You are lucky these aren't deep. Otherwise, you could have been in surgery and not the ER." He announces after a moment of silence.

Still not knowing how this man knew Lisa, Dmitry kept the conversation alive for his benefit.

"How do you know my *Zajchik*?"

"I don't think that's an appropriate question, as I don't think she's comfortable with me announcing that." Jiho stressed as he applied extra pressure with the alcohol wipes, gaining a hiss from the man.

Lisa held back a small smile at Jiho's unwillingness to give up their relationship even when they had only spoken once since their reunion.

"Weren't you going to ask me a personal question too?" He countered.

Jiho sat quietly, wanting to ask the question he had just remembered but unwilling to give in to what Dmitry wanted without Lisa's consent.

"Come on. I know you want to know something about me, and I don't think *Zajchik* would mind too much with me knowing this, right?"

Looking over at the woman, Jiho pleaded with his eyes, wanting to know if it was okay. Gaining a nod, he sent her a smile.

"You answer mine first, okay?"

"Sure, Doc." He smiled at the victory.

"Are you related to Viktor Petrov?"

Crinkling his eyebrows together, Dmitry became apprehensive at the question, and Jiho saw Lisa shaken by it as well out of the corner of his eye.

"How do you know my brother?" The man suddenly spat with aggression.

Not like the tone he was using, Jiho matched with the same hardness, "That wasn't the agreement. You only want to know about Lisa, not your brother."

Staring down at one another, Dmitry backed down once Lisa mouthed for him to stop. He turned away from them, taking that as a sign Jiho answered the man.

"We used to go to school together back in Ireland. Lisa and I had the same BioMed courses throughout the years."

Lisa was nervous about what could happen. Jiho knew of Viktor; she had to report it to her employer, making her crush known within the families she worked for. Thinking of the worst outcome, the crumbling emotions and overthinking overtook her demeanor, which Dmitry saw.

Reaching over, he gave her a small squeeze as their pinkies hooked on to each other, reassuring her that he would not say anything unless Lisa did.

Finishing up the last stitches, Jiho saw the comfort happen before him, placing a bit of guilt for creating such tension. Putting his equipment down, he looked directly at Dmitry.

"Look, I'm sorry I can't tell you how I know your brother, but I can't just give information about someone else without their say. You understand, right?"

Dmitry did not like that this doctor was right about not giving information out to people, but it was his brother. Nevertheless, he nodded, accepting the reasoning for withholding.

"Yeah…I get it."

"Good." Jiho stood.

Opening a drawer that held a brace and some numbing cream. He gives brief teachings.

"You'll need these for a while. I'll have the nurses print out the instructions for these, but I need you to keep the brace on for two to six weeks, depending on if you feel any more pain."

Reciting the instructions for the rest of the injuries, "I also need you to take it easy for at least six weeks with your ribs. Your stitches can come out in a week. Any nurses here can take them out for you if you refuse me as your doctor. Any questions?"

Standing by the door, Jiho waited a minute as Dmitry shook his head, denying any hint of confusion. Smiling at the two, he informed them it would be a minute before someone came in to hand them the papers and have a good day.

As he finished talking with Beth, Jiho turned to find Lisa standing before him. Raising his eyebrow, he could see she was nervous about something.

"Yes?"

Fidgeting with her fingers, Lisa looked anywhere but the man as she asked him, "Do you want to maybe…catch up on Friday?"

In the background, he could see Dmitry looking at the scene, a bit sad and confused about the state of the two's relationship. "Um, this Friday?"

"Yeah."

Jiho rubbed his neck and sucked his teeth in. "I'm sorry, Lisa, but I already have planned that day with someone else." Intentionally leaving out precisely who the person was. As she deflated, it was hard for Jiho to see, wanting the woman to not be so affected by his answer.

"Oh. Okay, that's fine. No worries." She recovered, wanting to save herself from the embarrassment. Lisa tried to devise a way to leave, which, for her luck, was saved by her phone ringing.

Taking out her device, Jiho could see a name on the caller ID. A name which had not left his mind since the night they met.

Saoirse.

Taking the call-in front of him, Jiho could hear some of the conversation from both ends. Lisa updated her on the condition of Dmitry and Saoirse, asking her to do something before heading back to her.

Hanging up the call, Lisa could see the curiosity swirling in Jiho's eyes, "That was just my boss, if you were wondering."

"What exactly do you do for work?"

"What?"

Flustered at the question, he blurted out, and with a stunned expression on her face, Jiho tried to save himself. "I mean…are you really a babysitter for a man?"

Laughing at his confusion, Lisa shook her head.

"No." Placing a hand over her mouth to stop the snorts that could come out. "No, I'm not a babysitter for him. I'm a personal doctor for his family and another, mainly for evaluations to see if they need to come to a hospital or if I can help them myself."

Jiho scratched his head, nodding in understanding, "Sorry for the weird question."

Lisa waved him off, dismissing it. Before he could open his mouth again, Jiho's pager went off, alerting him of a code in effect.

"I have to go. It was good seeing you." Before he left, jogging away like last time.

"I still didn't get your number…" Lisa mutters before walking to Dmitry, helping him out of the building and into the waiting car.

Chapter Fifteen

Saved

VIKTOR WAS GOING TO DIE tonight as soon as Jiho found him.

It was the evening of the banquet, and he had left his plus-one as soon as they walked in over thirty minutes ago. In fairness, a group of men saw Viktor and blatantly ignoring Jiho before disappearing with his mentor. Jiho was wondering why he had stuck around this long.

He was in a place unknown and surrounded by strangers, becoming one with the walls, a mere decoration to the already beautiful, detailed room.

The whole place was something out of a story; with its ceiling-to-floor crimson drapes, the green background wallpaper complemented the golden detailing and art that seemingly reached out for you.

It was simply magnificent in the doctor's eyes. The ability to admire such beauty was only provided by the seven crystal chandeliers hanging over their heads, accompanied by candles on every pillar sectioning off each full-length window.

Throughout the thirty minutes of being alone, Jiho had spent some time by people-watching. Nothing that was out of the ordinary for him as it was a habit he had picked up during his abroad years, even after meeting Ally.

Many of the attendings had been older than him, around their early thirties to late seventies. Some twenty-year-olds here and there, along with smaller children that he presumed were cared for by nannies-whose' appearance were in less expensive tastes.

Everyone had dressed in their formal best from what he could tell, even the youngest of the children-nothing with being held back. Necklaces, wristwear, rings, and the fabric used to make their attire were not short of money. Jiho was not used to it; the exception would be that of the Turner family, but even then, it was never to this extent.

Being pulled out of his observation, he felt a hand delicately slide from his left upper arm to his shoulder.

"You seem out of place." A nasal voice spoke. An older woman had made him cringe at the batting lashes and her suggestive eyes. Her touch sending Jiho in a newly founded ick, wanting desperately to take a shower and change his clothing.

The heavy perfume hit his nose, a far too sweet scent, causing his eyes to tear up. The woman tried to push herself on Jiho, distressing the man. She wasn't unattractive by today's standards; she had a seduction in her aura. Flocks of men and women would easily bend to her will in pursuing lust.

But to Jiho she was nothing more than an unwanted intruder in his personal space, and not that of his type either. The way her attire showed too much of her skin made him feel discomfort as to him she was almost naked. It was in no way an act of controlling the woman's outfit, he had just not been brought up to view so much of a woman unless they were in a relationship with each other.

Quickly removing her from himself, Jiho answered, "Not out of place…Thank you for your concern. Have a nice night."

He had tried to leave, but the woman gripped his arm roughly. Seeing the look on her face told Jiho she was not used to this treatment, and no one denied her.

"Don't be like that. Stay and chat with me."

The grit in her words and forced smile only distressed him even more. It wasn't helpful that he was near the back corner of the room, away from the people's eyes, when this older woman approached him. He could do nothing, not wanting to cause a scene at such a place, especially being a plus-one; fear struck him harshly.

She started to lean forward to kiss him, much to his horror. Before she could touch the corner of his lips, the assaulter was pulled back with his savior's hand covering the seductress's mouth.

Bewildered by the interruption, the older woman turns to see who dared to stop her, only to be cowardly at sight.

"Come now, Mrs. Granger. I don't think your husband would take kindly to your *'activities'* yet again. Would he?" That voice, taunting Mrs. Granger, filled with a fake concern over her marriage.

Gulping in fear, the adulteress woman shakily answered, "Well, you may be right, Miss. Welsh. I did not mean anything by this, but you must believe me; this man was luring me to act this way."

Her lies piled after another in excuses, putting the poor man in a bad situation. If another were to tell him of a similar situation he would believe the woman till the man. No one would blame him for such, but in this incident, he was being wrongfully accused.

The fear instilled in him caused his frozen state. Silently wishing for any and everything that he had just canceled the invitation, opting to stay a night in with Ally, watching some shitty reality show. Though he was glad to be saved in the nick of time. Finally escaping his shock, Jiho moved away from Mrs. Granger, his savior coming into light.

She was breathtaking.

Her hair is pinned up in a crown-like style, with only a few strands framing her face. Scanning over her, Jiho was again met with the green fields. He had missed those eyes, wanting nothing more than to get lost in them once more and never return.

"And why do I have the feeling of anything that comes out of your mouth regarding this gentleman-" moving towards Jiho, Saoirse clung onto his arm; in a way, claiming him, "-would be nothing but a lie. You see, this man here is nothing more than a sweetheart. Right, *mon amour*?"

At this point, Jiho had not taken his eyes off the siren that had tormented his mind every night since their brief encounter. Zoning out during the interaction between the two, a soft grunt of confusion left him.

"You are a sweetheart, aren't you, *mon amour*?"

Blinded by her smile, a little nod and some breathy in-and-out words were released. His lopsided smile was there for everyone to witness and beam in amusement as he spoke, "Sweetheart…yours…amour…me…."

Saoirse turned her head back towards the married woman. "See, he couldn't hurt a fly, much less pull you away from the *'faithful'* marriage you have."

A couple of snickers could be heard around the group once she spoke. Mrs. Granger was in disbelief with her behavior as a scoff left the married woman's mouth, twisting into a sneer as she countered.

"Don't you think this man is a bit too old for you? Or perhaps not of the same status as yourself? I don't think it's very becoming for a young girl of your importance; what would your father think of this?"

By this point, some bystanders had stopped watching the scene play out. As if luck were on their side, most did not want to upset the host by giving their full attention to the group, especially knowing that one of them was highly admired within their banquet and could handle the interesting game happening.

Besides, most will know of the gossip later that evening or week, as the event staff and security came from many different attending guests.

"I don't really think that's any of your concern." Loosening her grip on his arm, Saoirse leaned forward, her mouth just next to Mrs. Granger's ear. "But I will let you know; I don't intend to let this man be taken advantage of. Exceptionally by someone like you." Straightening up, she placed her head on Jiho's shoulder, "Now run back to one of your lovers; I'm sure you will be satisfied."

The woman ran off with a huff, doing just as Saoirse instructed. Until now, Jiho had not let his eyes wander from the siren who enchanted his very existence; even if he wanted to, Jiho simply could not. His control over his own body had disappeared. He could only look at the extraordinary woman.

Her figure was shown nicely with her formal attire of a fitted top half, covering all but her toned arms, including half of her neck. While the bottom flowed effortlessly around her in an elegant fashion.

Again, Jiho had become speechless; Saoirse also took in the man's appearance, wondering what he was doing here. She was stunned when she spotted him walking-in with Viktor and had a watchful eye until now.

Seeing him, almost in a matching shade of navy-blue suit, looking, in Saoirse's mind, undoubtedly handsome, was very pleasing to her. She had thought of him whenever she had free time to allow her mind to wander.

In truth, it was the young woman's first time really thinking of someone to this degree. Usually, things regarding her work, family, and subordinates occupied her mind.

But as of that night when she met the foreigner, all she could do was think of him. How his narrow eyes had shown her all the emotions without cautiousness, unable to thoroughly look away from his full lips.

"It seems we meet again, *mon amour*." Much to both of their demise, she was the first to pull away, creating an invisible wall in Jiho's mind.

As his thoughts cleared from their fogged state, he ran through hundreds of scenarios to see the best possible reply.

"Thank you. I don't know what I would have done if you did not show up in time." Jiho gave a soft smile, adoration behind his eyes. As Saoirse nodded at him, he continued, "I was wondering if we would meet again. I had wanted to continue our conversation if that's alright…."

He started off fully confidently, but towards the end, it slowly dwindled due to the number of listeners silently ridiculing his attempts.

Noticing the man's self-esteem drop, Saoirse discreetly glared at those around, quickly shutting them up with their petty envy of the man in front of her.

Taking his hand, she promptly dragged him towards the outside bar, which Jiho had not known was there. Unnoticed by him, Saoirse had signaled to those outside to leave.

The woman leaned against the cocktail tables and began, "How do you know about the event? Did Dr. Petrov invite you? You both seemed rather close walking in. Well, till those vultures took him away."

Smirking at the vivid memory of the older man, having to put on a fake smile but pleading with his eyes to be saved.

Laughing at their shared memory, Jiho answered her questions, "Well, we work together."

Taking a sip of his drink, the burning of his throat caused him to make a sour face. Saoirse giggled at the expression. Warming his heart that he was the reason for the heavenly sound.

"He has taken me under his wing, which I am forever grateful for, but I never had imagined being invited to his world in this way."

"Viktor would not have brought you here unless you are important to him." Cutting into Jiho's obvious doubt, "Which makes me think that your relationship is more than you have told, right?"

Becoming flustered with the sudden call out, Jiho flushed in embarrassment, his ears turning pink, "I guess you can say I see him as an older brother."

Looking away when he answered gave Saoirse a view of his side profile. If Jiho had not told her his occupation was in the medical field, she would have guessed he was a model. The proportions were uncannily perfect to her. After a pause in their conversation, a thought struck him.

"You know Viktor on a first-name basis?"

He was surprised and a tad jealous. How does a twenty-year-old know a man in their late forties? Regardless of their likely past encounters that may have occurred, as they both apparently attended the same events, it was too weird for his mind to register.

Although Jiho had no room to think such things as he was almost ten years her senior, he was putty in her presence.

Saoirse was not stupid; she could tell Jiho disliked the possible relationship that she might have with Viktor.

But both adults knew there wasn't a sexual relationship going on as Viktor was madly in love with his wife; it was just the thought of someone else being close to her by a first name that bothered Jiho.

Due to his customs and culture, addressing others by their surname or their first name with the attachment to a title were ways to avoid any unwanted misunderstandings between relationships. Often, addressing others by their job occupation and rank within that field rather than their name was more common.

To stop the overthinking and possessive tendency radiating off him, Saoirse gently laid her hand on Jiho's, gaining his attention.

"He is a dear friend to the family. At this point, he is family, like my older cousin."

She presumed that Jiho still needed to be conditioned to other countries in some way with the reaction to her informal talk of another.

But Saoirse was flattered when she saw that he was already infatuated with her, not caring if it was a crush or lust as she was also interested in the man.

Bashfully, Jiho rubbed the back of his neck, uncomfortable with being caught in a possessive state, which he had not known to have previously. The inner battle was undeniable to him.

The good in him realizing that he had no right to be this way about a woman who wasn't his, even if she was, the reaction was terrible.

But on the other side, Jiho had not been able to get the woman out of his mind; of course, he had a right to react this way. Saoirse is his. To spoil and do whatever she asks. But she was his at the end of the day.

While taking this time to battle between his reasonable and unreasonable thinking, Jiho noticed that the outside bar area was now empty, except for the bartender and security, of which a minimum of two were stationed at every entrance Jiho counted.

The realization had dawned on him. This event was much more than Jiho thought with all the security, more than the hospital, and how many vital figures were here: senators, political parties, CEOs, and COOs of well-known establishments as well as some individuals he's only ever heard of-important people.

Just what did he really get himself into by attending with his mentor.

How did Saoirse know of this, and how could she stand against Mrs. Granger? What family did she belong to? These thoughts were swirling in his mind.

Clearing his throat, Jiho turned to face her again. "So, what exactly does your family do?" Pulling his hand from hers, nursing his still-full drink nervously.

"My family?" Saoirse placed her chin on her palm, her polished nails leaning against her cheek. Her pointer finger lightly tapped against it, thinking. "Why the sudden interest?"

"I'm just curious…" he paused, "are they in the medical field? Is that how you know Viktor?"

Letting out an understanding hum, the woman answered, "We are a family business. My grandfather helped Viktor when he first came to the States to study. Giving him an apartment, an allowance, those kinds of things. If Viktor works for him for some time." She used the small sip straw to stir her drink, "Vik used to tutor my aunt back in the day, so it was a favor from father and daughter."

"Ah, that makes sense."

"What about you?"

Saoirse was rounding the table, so they were now face to face, with no object between them. She had fixed his collar, an excuse to touch him, leaving them around his neck.

"How do you know Viktor on a personal level? I hardly believe it was just from being a mentor."

Jiho was a bit dense in some fields of flirting, and it did not help that Saoirse was around him. With her around, his brain was mushy, unable to use its full potential. This frustrated Jiho to no end; he wanted to kick himself for not taking his sister's advice for wooing women, wishing he had been paying attention rather than zoning out.

Hesitantly he rested his hand on her hips, afraid that he had read her wrong, giving it a few seconds for her to correct him. When she made no indication of moving from him, he was relieved.

"I admit the relationship was just a professional one, but he was hell-bent on knowing my personal life. Don't know why, but I'm glad. I've met his family, which was also a big step for him and his wife."

Smiling at the memory, he said, "It wasn't like they thought I had bad intentions, but I know there was another reason behind not wanting me to be fully in their private lives. Which, of course, I respect. I at first didn't want anyone in mine."

"Why is that? Don't seem to have any trouble from what I can tell."

Saoirse closed the gap a bit more. Jiho's hands caressed her open back, surprising him; he had thought the top of the dress was fully covered at first.

Running his fingers up and down, leaving a ghost trail from the touch, gave Saoirse goosebumps. Jiho was very gentle with her, as if he were afraid of marking her in a harmful way.

"I don't know, to tell you the truth. You just enchant me to do so...Although I'm not complaining."

Chapter Sixteen

Nosey Little Sister

WHEN JIHO WOKE THE following day, the events of last night ran through his mind.

Before continuing their conversation after that little confession, Jiho recognized the man approaching them from the bar. It was evident that Jiho was developing an increasing hatred for the poor worker.

When the worker had gotten to them, all he could feel was the intense glare coming from Jiho. It was uncommon for another to give the same glare as his boss, yet Jiho did.

Saoirse was also displeased with the sudden interruption, wanting nothing more than to continue whatever this conversation was.

Looking back at Jiho one last time. She had grown to enjoy his small, flushed face, how the tips of his ears turned pink with embarrassment when he heard a compliment or even when she touched him.

She was in pure bliss with the effects it had on him. Before Saoirse left, the bold woman gave Jiho a peck, their lips only touching for a second, leaving him frozen with a lopped-sided smile.

It did not take long for Jiho to be once again accompanied. Viktor had finally gotten away from the group of self-obsessed, narcissistic men and women.

The duo only stayed another hour before leaving; within that time frame, Jiho had been introduced to others by Viktor.

Getting up and out of bed, Jiho wanted to be lazy today. His sudden social life was too much for the poor introvert; his battery was dangerously low.

Just these past few months alone, the man had been out more than he had his whole life. His thoughts were cut short when his phone started to ring a familiar song.

His family had been overseas, causing the phone bill to increase, leading them to use an app, doing everything their phone already does but without the cost. Giving them access to change and dedicating ringtones or songs to specific people.

Seeing it was his younger sister, Jiho quickly picked it up. It was nice to have another family member who could speak more than one language, giving him a partner in crime with secrets.

They mix English with their Korean often when it's just the two of them. It helped when one could not think of the term in the native language but could in the other and vice versa.

Jiho picked up the video call and did not anticipate the greeting, "Oppa! You are dating someone?"

He could see his younger sister's excitement, a smile plastered on her face, threatening to fall off with the size of the grin. Jiho had not seen her like this since he announced that he was paying for her studies.

Even with the hyper girl on the other end of the screen, he could only respond with his own bewilderment, "What do you mean dating? I'm not dating anyone. Who told you that?"

To his knowledge, the only person in his life that his family personally met and knows about is Ally. He was asked if they were dating by the rest of the family and close family friends. After denying it and witnessing the interactions between the two friends, everyone had given up, accepting their platonic relationship.

"Don't play stupid; it doesn't suit you." Min-Jung glared at her older brother.

"I'm not trying to, Minnie, but I have no clue what you are talking about." Question after question, Jiho was starting to think the worst of his baby sister wanting to know if she had hit her head, or perhaps she was ill. Slowly, his questions mixed between the two known languages as his worry increased.

Rolling her eyes at the overprotective man, Min-Jung shouted at him, like their mother did to get their attention when they argued.

"Shut up! Please, I have Eomma up my ass. I don't need you there either. Don't switch this on me."

"Wow…you are something else." Jiho rapidly blinked his eyes in astonishment. Here, his little sister shrieked at him, addressing him in such a way most wouldn't unless they wanted to get beaten the shit out of.

"This isn't why I called you, so please just listen." Waiting for confirmation, Min-Jung continued, "I usually wake up this early to go on a little walk with some friends before classes, but to my surprise, my phone was blowing up before I could even figure out where I was." Her hands move every which way, "I open Alessia's messages first. You remember Alessia, right?"

Taking a minute before realization hit Jiho, "The one who was trying to get 'close' to me when I came to visit you?"

"Yes! Still creeps me out that she tried to sleep with you." The two shivered in disgust, "Anyways, she was blowing up my phone crying about you being 'claimed' by someone else."

Her air quotes did not go unnoticed, as the man knew his sister hated the idea of being owned by someone.

"I still don't understand what you are talking about. I'm not dating anyone."

"Didn't I say to be quiet?"

"No, you said, and this is a direct quote; shut up."

Min-Jung scowled at her brother. With an amused scoff, Jiho raised his hands in surrender at his baby sister.

"Honestly, I don't know how I put up with you." Opening his mouth to answer, he snapped it shut at the glaring eyes, "Don't."

Even though Min-Jung is the youngest of the four Yoo children, she is intimidating once angered. The twins usually were safe from the baby's wrath.

Still, Jiho loved to push her buttons, trying all his might to uphold the annoying, protective older brother persona the world had envisioned. He gestured his right hand out while his left grabbed a water bottle from the fridge for her to continue.

"Okay, so, as I was saying before, I was rudely interrupted." Giving a harsher glare, Min-Jung waited a moment. As Jiho was still quiet, she continued. "I was confused and honestly creeped out that she was keeping tabs on you, but I wanted to know what she was talking about. So, I asked her to show me where she got that information."

Grabbing her tablet, Min-Jung showed the front page of a blog that had Jiho's heart drop to his ass.

"Headline reads *Who Is the Mystery Man That Captured the Heart of Ireland and France's Young Heiress of Welsh Enterprise, Saoirse Welsh, Within A Single Evening?*" Moving the tablet away, Min-Jung had a smirk plastered on her smug face, "Mind telling what this is all about."

She only squealed at the sight of her brother. Pointing at his facial expression, Min-Jung giggled, "Look, you're even smiling at her all goofy. You never do that!"

Seeing the photo made Jiho nervous; he had not known someone was taking pictures of them, but here it was. When the photo was taken, Saoirse had her arms around his neck and his around her waist, caressing the exposed back.

At that moment, Jiho saw the large tattoo. It was a rather beautiful, abstract piece, almost resembling smoke, running from top to bottom, directly on her spine. He thought it was odd for her skin to slightly rise in different parts but never thought of a tattoo being there.

The man liked the art on Saoirse's body; it suited her and made him wonder where else another might have touched her. Soon, dark thoughts of someone besides him being honored to feel her skin on theirs swirled in his mind.

"...ppa...Jiho Oppa!" Min-Jung yelled once more, gaining his attention, "You alright...? You never get lost in thought for that long..." Although the younger scowled at her brother, she was somewhat worried about him all the time, "Did I overstep..."

Min-Jung was afraid her little outburst had made her brother uncomfortable, provoking him to hang up on her.

Giving the concerned sister a soft smile, Jiho shook his head, "I'm okay. I'm just a bit overwhelmed; I didn't know we were being watched like that."

"So, you do know her?"

"No."

"No?"

Laughing at the confused girl, Jiho thought it best to explain briefly, leaving some details to himself, "I mean, I don't really know her. I only met Miss. Welsh at a bar. Ally dragged me one night. And we met again at the banquet. My co-worker took me as his plus one. So, no, I don't know her like I should."

Kinda understanding the situation, Min-Jung nodded before a crafty smile made it onto her face.

"But you want to know her, right?"

Jiho blushed at his sister's wiggling eyebrows, indicating how he wanted to 'know' her.

"I'm right!" She gasped, "Look at your face."

Breaking into a fit of giggles, the poor man only deepened in color. For the first time, Min-Jung can make fun of her brother for liking a girl, and he can't deny it.

"Yoo Min-Jung, stop talking about things you don't know."

Every other word stumbled over as the embarrassment was too much for Jiho. Here, his baby sister was teasing him over a girl, only laughing harder as the words came out.

"Fine, fine, I'll stop." Wheezing in between each word. Taking a few deep breaths to contain herself, the smile never fading, "So what do you know about her?"

"Why the sudden interest in my love life?"

"So now you love the girl?"

"I didn't mean it like that."

"Then what did you mean because you've never indicated feelings for someone. But here," pulling back the blog in the frame, "you are giving one of those K-drama looks."

"K-drama looks?" He raised an eyebrow.

The deadpan from her was enough for Jiho to know he was an idiot.

"The look all male leads give the female leads once they acknowledge their feelings for them. God, how do you not know that? I think the amount Eomma watches would teach you a thing or two."

"I do not look at Saoirse like that-"

"Saoirse? I thought she was Miss. Welsh to you. How personal did you two get?"

"I…Well…"

Jiho never meant to slip up, but he did and had no way of getting out of this interrogation.

"You must promise not a word of this will get back to the others, okay? Even Ally doesn't know of this."

"Allyria doesn't know. I thought you two were the best of friends. Did you fall out?" Tilting her head, Min-Jung was confused about how much she was out of the loop.

"No, we still are. We just don't talk about this kind of thing till it gets serious, you know, a little privacy and some boundaries."

Sighing, Jiho was in a whirlwind; the speed of their conversation hurt his head, "I will always love Ally as a friend, but we both understand that, eventually, we will have to part and go down different paths before meeting again."

Min-Jung nods with a new understanding of the depth of their friendship.

"Fine. I promise I won't let anyone know. So…tell me." The girl egged on, wanting to know more about who had made her stoic brother so flustered.

"Fucking hell," he muttered, "calm down."

Although Jiho was not one to curse in front of the family, he made the exception due to Min-Jung causing a pounding headache.

He loved her. Indeed, he did, but he prayed to any god out there that his little sister would gain the skill of patience.

Returning to her famous glare, the younger came closer to the screen, "Cuss at me again, and I will not hesitate to shave your hair clean off."

He gulped at her threat. He had given a weak smile, nodding at her, muttering a small apology. To his regret, Min-Jung smiled.

"Great, now, tell me everything about your 'love life' you keep denying."

"I don't know where to start, honestly."

"The beginning is always a good place. What did you think when you first saw her?"

"When I first saw her…" Jiho had looked a in a daze, softening his demeanor, "I thought she was the most beautiful thing in this life. Her eyes really got me at first. You remember the summer days the four of us would go hiking, and once we reached the top, all we saw was the green fields?"

"Of course, it's always my favorite part of the summer."

"She reminded me of those times, how her eyes just brought me peace, a sense of calm without even knowing her effects."

"So, her face and eyes are the only thing that keeps you wanting her?"

Shaking his head in dismissal, he was shocked that his sister would think lowly of him to only want someone for their physical appearance.

"No, those things are what caught my attention. Saoirse being…well, Saoirse is what makes me want her."

The confusion was evident.

Min-Jung was only seventeen, she had only known things from dramas and books but knew they were over-exaggerated, not fully believing they could be a realistic standard. Seeing this expression, Jiho was not surprised about her lack of understanding or the question.

"I don't understand. How can you want someone who is just being themselves? Usually, at least from what my classmates tell me, it's because they have something the other wants."

"That's not totally wrong, but not right either."

"How? One of the couples at school is together because it's expected. He's popular, and so is she. Their parents are friends, so it only makes sense. Right?"

"Just because it makes sense to you doesn't mean it's the right choice. You can't force a relationship if there is no desire."

"You're not making any sense." Min-Jung was still totally confused with the whole love thing. The unfamiliar and unspoken subject was giving her a headache. "How can something that feels right to everyone be wrong?"

During the conversation, Jiho moved from the kitchen to his living room, placing his screen on the coffee table in front of him, leaning forward; he rested his elbows on his knees.

Taking a brief second to think of a way to make this simple enough for her to understand without playing down his feelings for Saoirse.

"From my understanding, feelings for someone or something so strong can't be categorized in a right or wrong way; it's beyond a human's understanding most of the time." Seeing Min-Jung spaced out, Jiho chuckled at her expression, "Are you with me still?"

"Yeah. I kind of understand, but not fully."

"Take this as an example: I know I love you, the twins, and our parents, but that's because we are family; we love each other because of a pre-existing bond and title. Although that love and bond are not given to everyone, we have it. You can love someone like family, like your friends or even mentors, but-" Jiho smiles as he recalled his mother's words all those years ago, "when you meet that one person, it's different."

"Different? How? Wouldn't it still be the same love as others?"

"It's like-" taking a small breath, "knowing you can't wait to see them. Wanting them to be close to you without fully understanding why. You constantly think of them when you can, wondering if they are safe and healthy. You wonder if you are thinking logically or not, and half the time, you don't care if it is logical."

Jiho thought of his encounters with Saoirse. His feelings when she was near him ran through his veins.

"You feel at home and comfortable when they are around, but being with them makes your brain flat line." Jiho tried his best to get things across to his sister, to make her understand what he was talking about.

A memory popped into his head about the stories of mythology he would read to her when they were younger, knowing these following few sentences would make her see what he truly meant.

"It's like a siren calling out. Being enchanted with their being and way of words. Not given a chance to leave their grasp, but when you finally know what is happening, you don't care about it...You only want them, even if it is the end for you."

She was astounded.

Here, her older brother, a man with no life outside of work and family, is giving her a lesson on love even when he has no clue what love really is.

She has seen many dramas and read many books in her life, knowing the classic tropes and how they ended, rooting for the second lead most of the time but still enjoying the main female lead getting the happy ending.

It was her little escape and delusional way of knowing what love was without ever having that experience. Hearing it from a man almost in his thirties, speaking passionately, was new for Min-Jung.

Her brother was a new person from the last time she talked to him, someone who grew. Giving a small smile, she looked back at the blog photo, seeing the pure adoration was clear to her. She was joking at first, trying to tease Jiho a bit, not thinking much of his feelings for the stranger in his arms but hearing his explanation of the difference between what she thought it was and the reality of it.

She could tell he enormously liked this woman; whether he knew it or not, she had a sneaky suspicion the woman would be the person to help her brother or break him.

Turning back to him, Min-Jung smirked, a glimpse of mischievousness seen in her eyes. He saw this, a bit nervous about his sister's antics.

"Why are you staring at me like that…"

Crackling a bit, she brought her face closer to the screen, with nothing but a smug look in view, "So you love the girl, huh?"

Jiho rolled his eyes before he rambled into a lecture fully in their first language; seeing her brother blushing at her claims.

Chapter Seventeen

A Brother's Threat

"CAN WE JUST TELL people we're sick?"

Jiho gave an unamused look to the anxious woman, "We both know if we did that, not only would Mac come here, but so would this new boyfriend of yours. And I, for one, don't want them to know where I live, let alone in my house. I've just gotten over the fact that Alex has that information."

Ally gave a sheepish smile, knowing fully well that it was her fault her father's secretary knew where their haven was.

Walking out of his pantry with a handful of snacks, she stopped before him. He grabbed them from her with a soft chuckle before placing them in a tote bag.

"What is it that is worrying you, Allyria? This is just a regular company party for you."

He had no idea what was making her so skittish; if anything, he should act like this. True to his word, Jiho stayed home for the last two weeks. Only leaving for work and grocery shopping.

The two had been texting through those weeks but had not seen each other physically till now. Jiho did not attempt to talk about Saoirse to Ally during that time as he did not want to get his hopes up. He was still determining if he would ever see her again.

Jiho thought it might be a burden placed on Viktor's shoulders, as debating on asking Viktor about her, seeing as they had the same social group.

Through the last two weeks, he took the time to re-evaluate his fixation on the woman. He would never deny his attraction for Saoirse or the fact that he enjoyed her mere presence. Quickly, he had come to terms with the fact that he was indeed crushing on the woman, but that is what it will only ever be.

A crush.

It had taken almost a full two years for Jiho to let Ally in his shielded heart after becoming friends and an extra year to reveal Eun-Ya, which at the time was a slip-up on his part.

Beth was someone who understood his fear of closeness and did not intrude in his personal life unless he was willing to tell her himself. That being said they only spoke at work, never outside, causing his fear to be lessened as Beth reassured him that she would always be there for him regardless of her limited contact.

Now, Viktor was a different story, as Jiho knew the man could hold his own in a dire situation.

That did not mean Jiho cared or worried for the man any less; on the contrary. He had always been scared that with each of their encounters, would be their last, but the Russian was very reassuring.

He always handles the more minor oncoming panic attacks with care and patience. With every new person that had entered Jiho's life, more weight had been placed on his shoulders.

The pressure affected him more than he would have liked. His sisters, head nurse, and mentor picked up the subtle change in mood. He couldn't hide this from the five of them, but with Ally, he could.

The model had always been too busy for phone calls, preferring texting above all. They had agreed that the phone calls were for emergencies and the occasional must be said now.

Min-Jung knew the behavior change was due to his hesitation to open and take a chance on this Saoirse woman. True to her promise, the young girl did not say anything, no matter how hard Nari and Iseul tried to pry it out of her.

The twins had a feeling the baby had some insight as Alessia contacted them; no one understood how she had their number, asking if the blogs were genuine since Min-Jung never confirmed or denied the gossip.

Although the two English-speaking siblings talked about Saoirse, Jiho closed off the topic, not wanting to reopen it after their call.

"It's not just a regular company party, Ji. This is the night when you, my brother meets my boyfriend. Something I know neither of us thought would happen this soon."

Ally had run her hand through her hair in frustration, pulling at the roots softly. Taking her hand, Jiho hugged the woman, rubbing her exposed back, gently soothing her worries.

"Hey, breathe for me."

Taking a deep breath, she held it before exhaling, relaxing her shoulders. Lifting her face with his free hand, Jiho saw just how nervous she was,

"Can you tell me exactly what you think will go so wrong?"

"What if you two don't get along? What if you hate each other? What would happen to our relationship? Would I have to pick between the two-"

Covering her mouth with his hand, Jiho laughed at the silly questions, "Ally, I'm going to tell you something, okay?"

Nodding, her eyes plead for him to speak.

"Eric and I will not hate each other. We will get along and never make you pick between us. You want to know why?"

"Why?"

"Because we both care too much for you and your happiness."

Ally scrunched up her nose, frowning her eyebrows. In other words, her face contorted into confusion, "What?"

He leaned back against the island, letting her go, "Well, from what you describe, he cares deeply for you, never raised a hand towards you, or made you feel less than. To me, that's where the standard starts. A good start, but the bare minimum. That was till I heard everything about him risking his reputation and career for you."

"I'm still slightly confused about the 'risking' part."

Jiho hummed, "So you don't know."

"Know what?"

Smiling at her before pulling out his phone, Jiho searched for the video he referenced. Clicking the play button, he turned the phone to her, allowing Ally to take it into her own hands.

The video was a press conference with Eric front and center. This was from the shoot he did in Paris five days ago. The reporters had been asking decent questions regarding his life as a model and what work he was doing for the future.

Just as Ally was about to ask what the point of this was, someone asked him about his dating life.

Throwing the fact that he was seen with, in the reporter's words, *a socialite and heiress of the Turner Family, the known party girl, and alcoholic model, Allyria Turner.*

To say she was outraged by this description was an understatement.

Ally had come a long way from how she used to party due to Jiho's worry, but she occasionally got drunk when allowed. She was ashamed that Eric was forced to listen to how she used to party and there had been photos all over the internet of her being blacked out.

What surprised her was the defensive tone Eric had when given his answer. The man had told the idiotic reporter that he was proudly dating Ally. True that occasionally, a person is allowed to let loose after a stressful day, and what Ally did before their relationship was none of his business until Ally told him directly.

If he had questions, they could talk about it like adults they are, something the reporter had no idea what that was like.

"He cares for you much more than I think you know, Al." Taking his phone back, Jiho smirked, "I was a little skeptical of his intentions, but after seeing this video and his other comments to the paparazzi, I just figured I had nothing to worry about as of now."

Grabbing his coat, he continued, "That being said, I still get to scare him a little bit as your brother. Let's go."

With a satisfied smile, Ally began to skip to the passenger side door, as the plan was for the two friends to drive together, and she would leave with Eric.

THEY ARRIVED AFTER AN hour of driving. Not to say they left late, but Ally and Jiho had gotten stuck in traffic, which was familiar in their living and work areas.

The party that was being held tonight was a monthly event. A way to celebrate milestones for their workers and welcome the rookies of the company. Ally dragged Jiho towards the food spread to the side of the balcony, stress eating while she waited for Eric to arrive.

"*Mo Stór Beag!*" Ally's pause and giggles told Jiho all he needed to know; the boyfriend was here.

"Ricky!"

The couple had given a quick peck before pulling each other into an embrace; the two had been away from each other for the last week and a half due to their conflicting schedules.

Eric was very handsome in Jiho's eyes, nothing less than what he was expecting from the male runway model.

The brunette had looked down at Ally with pure joy; the warming smile showed his one dimple above his squared jawline.

She moved the small strand of hair that fell in front of their view of each other, running her fingers through his shortened hair quickly. Jiho *gracefully* clears his throat, clearly stating the need for an introduction.

"Right! Um, Ji, this is Eric, my boyfriend. Ricky, this is Jiho, my brother in all but blood."

The two men shook hands, Jiho giving a bit more pressure than needed to assert a little foreshadowing of his strength if the fair-skinned man ever hurt Ally.

"Pleasure to meet you. *Mo Stór Beag* has told me so much about you." Eric smiled, not looking hurt or in discomfort at Jiho's grip.

"I hope it was all good things."

Eric confirmed Jiho's question with a nod.

Smiling at the news, Jiho let some tension off his shoulders before raising his eyebrows.

"Is that Gaelic? If you don't mind me asking. What does '*Mo Stór Beag*' mean?"

After saying the unfamiliar phrase, he knew he had butchered it based on Eric's face. Both men let out a chuckle, indicating no misunderstanding about what he was asking for.

"She did say you two studied in Ireland, good ears. The translation is 'my little darling' although there are many ways of saying it, that's one of the ways."

Jiho looked over to the blushing woman, tucking her face into the man's neck, trying to hide her embarrassment, "Cute. Never seen her blush like this sin-"

"Finish that sentence, and I'll tell Jennie where you live."

A flash of horror took Jiho's face, "You would sacrifice me so easily?"

"For that story, yes. No questions asked."

Her face had not moved a single bit of the frown she had. The two had been in a silent battle while Eric watched them in amusement, thinking how similar he acts with his older sister and, at times, brother-in-law.

After another second, they all began to break into a smile, fully knowing there was some truth to that seemingly empty threat.

Jiho raised his eyebrow towards the woman, asking if this was the right time for a one-on-one conversation with the new man in her life.

"I'm gonna go speak with Holly for a quick second. Do you think you two will be okay 'mingling' with each other during that time?"

"Of course, *Mo Stór Beag*. Take your time."

Both men gave Ally a quick hug and kiss on the head, waiting till she was out of earshot.

"I'm going to guess this is the talk brothers have with their sister's partners?"

"You've been through this before?"

"Never on the receiving side, but yeah."

"Older or younger sister?"

"Nineteen years older." The shocked look gave Eric a giddy feeling. Jiho, on the other hand, was processing this new information.

"I know it's a little strange to have another kid when the only one just left the nest, but even they didn't know I was coming. I'm just the surprise baby."

"So…you sort of know what I'm going to tell you?"

"Pretty much, though I'll still listen if you want. I know how important this is for you to say."

Taking a breath to calm his nerves, Jiho was ready to speak, "I'm going to be completely honest with you; I didn't know how

I would feel about you once we met. If I found even a little bit of a flaw in you I was planning to threaten and even inflicting some pain towards you."

The look of hurt was placed on the other's face. Eric didn't think Jiho would be so straightforward with physical violence.

Ally had told him about their school days and the two times her brother figure had 'harmed' some people, but he thought it was exaggerated to an extent.

"But," rubbing the back of his neck, "I saw how happy she was when you were brought up in conversation, as well as the videos of your interviews. Not to mention, I called in a favor to get some information about your past relationships…"

There was a pause.

Silence.

Unbreakable by the music and chatter around them.

"Um…I don't know how to respond to that. No one has ever done this before."

"Well, that's why I wanted to talk with you. I wanted the air to be cleared. Let you know what you're getting yourself into if you were to hurt Ally. I can destroy you if you ever make her cry. I don't mean figuratively, either. So, take good care of her, and I'll respect your relationship and not overstep my boundaries. Agreed?"

Eric smiled, snorting at the utterly unexpected mood shift, "Agreed."

Chapter Eighteen

Liquid Courage

BY THE END OF their conversation, Ally had returned just to pull Eric towards some of the new hires in the makeup department to help them learn the ropes. Jiho's social battery had run out after being left alone.

Taking this perfect opportunity, he slipped through the empty halls, going to the other side of the building, where the additional balcony was.

Unlike the event, this area was bare of all the expensive flower arrangements. No pops of color were spotted in their brown-tone furniture. The potted plants had all been empty from any festivity, and the silence around him brought peace.

The cool, fruity-tasting Pinot Noir slid down his throat. Jiho was not one to drink a lighter-bodied red wine, but with this evening's food choices, he had no alternative but to humor the selected drink.

Leaning against the black railings, his mind drifted again. After those two weeks of going back and forth, Saoirse could not leave his head. Chuckling at the fact, the description he told Min-Jung was so fitting; she was a siren.

Lost in thought, Jiho felt his wine glass being plucked from his hand. Turning, ready to scold whoever broke his peace, he was surprised to find the devil herself.

She sipped slowly, giving him a pleasant smile afterward. Placing the glass on the table nearby, her voice sent tiny chills down his spine.

"How have you been, *mon amour*? It's been a while, hasn't it?"

Jiho's recollection of her beauty had done no justice once Saoirse stood before him. He was blinded by pure marvel. She was seen with a different look than in the last two encounters, where the young woman was caught in dark colors.

Though the darker style suited her well, Jiho was delighted to witness her in a softer and lighter tone.

One that gave her a sense of freedom, not only in her demeanor but her movement, as if she didn't have to constantly look over her shoulder. She seemed more welcoming to herself.

"Been two weeks…you look lovely, Saoirse." His eyes ranked over her as he breathlessly complimented. He had promised to address her as Miss. Welsh, but it broke as soon as she appeared in front of him. Not that you could blame him. The woman had an unknown power over him.

Shooting an eyebrow up, she was surprised, "You've been counting? Very sweet of you, *mon amour*. But I did ask you another question, which I believe you have ignored. How have you been?"

Straightening his posture, Jiho sat next to her. During their little conversation, Saoirse had moved to a love seat away from the entrance, closer to the walls. Conveniently, it was placed away from the security cameras as well.

Their legs brushed against each other, his dress pants against her exposed legs. Jiho wanted to be closer to her with every fiber in his body, but he had to restrain himself as he tried to stop these feelings from expanding even more than they already were.

"I've been–" the hesitation was there. *How could he say his mind has been in utter chaos since meeting her? How could he just come out and tell her, a woman he'd only encountered twice, that he was starting to like her romantically?* "-fine. How have you been?"

"Still breathing. I just came back from an outing with my godchildren."

"You have godchildren?" Widening his eyes at the news. Saoirse never failed to amaze him with the more information he gathered from her, "But you're so young."

"I am twenty, almost twenty-one, not too young to have godchildren." Her tone was anything but friendly.

Jiho realized too late that her age was a sore topic regarding what she could be responsible for.

Quickly, he muttered out a sorry, a genuine one at that. He was not used to apologizing. Others would apologize to him so often, that the words coming out of his mouth felt weird.

There was an awkward stillness between the two. He was just curious about why someone would place their child in the care of a twenty-year-old. He gave her the respect that she was so willing to take on such a task, knowing he could not when he was her age.

Taking a chance on a subject change. Jiho turned his body, where his left leg was placed on the sofa, touching her thigh, with no indication of pulling back. He would reprimand himself later for not sticking to the promise, but now, he just wants to be as close as possible.

"So, what brings you here? Do your godchildren model for the children's department?"

Staring at the man for a few seconds, Saoirse sighed. She was being a bit mean to the man, letting his curiosity get the better of him, and it was a justified question. "My cousin works here and invited me to meet his girlfriend for the first time."

"You too?"

"What do you mean 'you too'?"

Jiho smiled at her confused expression. Her eyes squinted with her question. He reached over to tuck in a piece of her hair that had flown in her face due to the wind.

"My best friend—more like a sister—has this new boyfriend. It's her first boyfriend, and I wanted to ensure he was the gentleman she claimed him to be."

Saoirse forced a smile that did not meet her eyes, something he noticed. Jiho was happy at her jealousy. It only indicated that she may also like him, though it might be his delusion.

"Your best friend is a girl? Is this one of those 'no, she's just a friend' type of relationship, or is it a really, truly, sibling relationship?" Her snarky undertone was evident no matter how hard she tried to hide it.

"Just a sibling-like relationship. I've never seen Ally as anything but that." He waved his hand, physically showing his discomfort towards the idea as he pulled a face of disgust.

Seeing her chewing her lips in doubt, Jiho gave a soft smile. Feeling a little bold, especially after her little jealous fit, he pulled her closer to him. He had his arm around her as she rested her head on his shoulders.

"I've known her since I was in my fifth year. She was my first friend at school. She did not give up when I refused her friendship, but I'm glad she didn't because now I have someone who will always be a supporter, even if we were to grow distant later in life. Plus, Allyria is just not my type and never will be."

He had laughed at the mere thought of the two friends in a relationship. Again, it was something many people assumed, but they both were completely different from what they daydreamed as their future partners.

"Allyria Turner?"

"Yeah." He quickly answered before stilling, "...How do you know her last name?"

Saoirse's face was reddened with pure embarrassment. She had heard from others about Allyria Turner's sibling bond with a male doctor, but she never thought they all meant Jiho.

"Ah, well, apparently, my cousin is dating your 'sister'..."

At this, Jiho pulled back to face Saoirse's blushed face. Here, she was jealous of her cousin's girlfriend and her relationship with Jiho. It was a weird coincidence that bewildered the man.

"Eric is your cousin...?"

"One of them."

"One of them...Eric's older sister?"

Fidgeting with her hands, Saoirse was still a little embarrassed at this predicament they found themselves in. "She's the mother to my godchildren."

Jiho placed the hand that was not around the siren over his mouth. At first glance, you would think something was wrong, but with a closer look you could see the man shaking.

He was laughing.

A good laugh at that. It was contagious, causing Saoirse to join in as well.

The two continued momentarily, her hand on his thigh, his around her waist. The moment looked rather intimate. Should someone walk in on the two, witnessing this action, they would believe or at least assume the two adults were in a happy relationship.

Coming out of their little fit of laughter, Jiho voiced his thoughts, "What a small world we live in."

"Indeed."

"But I'm glad it's small."

She looked at Jiho with suspicion, noting the space between the two had shrunk, "Why is that *mon amour*?"

"The chance to see you has doubled." The few glasses of wine had given him the confidence he needed.

Thanking his recent past self for all the shitty romance research he had done after the phone conversation with Min-Jung.

"And why do you want to see me? I'm almost positive you do not keep me in your thoughts. You probably have a handful of women flocking to you." Her tone was bitter at the thought.

Ghostly running his finger from the base of her neckline to the point of her jaw, Jiho landed in the middle of her pink bottom lip.

The feeling of her plump, soft, teasing mouth tempted him. A point of no return if Jiho felt them against his own.

He would undoubtedly be forever hers, in this life and the next. Till his soul no longer existed, and even sometime after, Jiho would belong to only Saoirse. If he were allowed to taste her before she could leave.

"You will always be in my thoughts. Since I met you that night, my mind has led to you and only you." He whispered, keeping eye contact.

With a bemused smile, she chuckled, "You have grown confident. Has anyone told you you're quite the charmer, *mon amour?*"

"Many, but none matter more than your own words."

Buzzing with flattery, Saoirse leaned in, "And why does my opinion matter so much to you? We barely know each other."

"You are always there." Jiho had begun leaving soft kisses on her neck in between each word.

It was an out-of-character thing for him to do, but for Saoirse, he was ready to risk it all. And gladly so.

"A person who, no matter how hard I find it in me, or the promises I make to keep you out of my thoughts, out of my dreams, out of my life, you are always there. Always popping out of thin air. I've never lost myself with anyone, ever. Yet, with you, I act like I'm one of those love-sick teens in a shitty rom-com. I have no idea what the fuck I should be doing or how to act around you."

Quickly, he shot his eyes to hers, being lost in them once more. The green had hints of hazel with the light hitting them just right.

Her skin glowing with the sun's setting, and the shimmering of her eyeshadow only helps with the alluring look.

"It's a marvelous thing we both aren't teens in one of those shit shows. So, tell me, what are you going to do as a man? How are you going to act with this newly found confidence?" Saoirse quietly asked.

"I would have you."

"You would have me? Just like that?"

"Just like that. I would have you. You would not need to lift a finger; I would spoil you in ways you've never known. Not in just a flick of lust, but in pure adoration as well."

He was not the same man she met in the dim, dark bar with moving lights giving him a glimpse of her beauty, shying away. Nor was he the man from two weeks ago at the banquet, even with the increase in self-assertion.

This man was serious.

Undeniably.

Saoirse wanted to surrender.

She wanted Jiho's words and actions to be true for her sanity. Longing for a partner to share sweet moments with. But she needed to know if he was playing her a fool.

To know if this is all a trick. So, for now, Saoirse will play the game of cat and mouse. Just to see if Jiho will be faithful to his words.

Tension was in the air. The two were sexually frustrated: longing, wanting each other. Jiho had wondered what she would feel towards him. The pleasures he would cause. He wanted her and her alone.

In his mind, she only wanted physical relations, a play of lust and curiosity, but he did not mind. He did not care if he was not the only one, she had. Jiho was, now, in a sinful state. He did not care if other men or even women were wooing her.

All Jiho could think about was her.

Parting her lips to speak, her words died as the door opened. The two had been behind a wall of plants, tall and thick, hiding them from being seen.

The intruder had been on the phone, talking in what Jiho thought was French, a language Min-Jung usually swore in when they had disagreements.

Because of the disruption, Jiho's cloud of lust had been removed, and coming to his senses, he reevaluated the situation. Seeing the dilation in the siren's eyes gave him joy and relief that she was reciprocating his feelings.

Not wanting a modeling agency's party to be the first place or possibly the only place the two explore these thoughts, Jiho began to pull away once the intruder left.

As quick as he was going to explain and move, Saoirse pulled the doctor back towards her, a handful of his hair in her hand, scratching his scalp slightly. The daring, guarded woman had been the first to act.

The two had shared their first kiss real kiss.

This was not just a little peak like the one from the banquet. But a heated, feverish kiss. An act of lust.

Not reacting at first, Jiho came out of his shock when the woman underneath him pulled his hair again, releasing a soft, small whine. At this sound did he realize what was happening. Grabbing her right thigh, exposing her legs further, he took control of the kiss.

Was this his first kiss?

No.

Was this his second?

Maybe.

Did he watch how the main leads kissed each other for a moment like this?

Yes.

Did he heavily annotate scenes like the one he has in books and poems to know how to explore a person without his own experience?

Abso-*fucking*-lutely.

Tugging her bottom lip harshly, Saoirse gasped, giving him an opening to slide his tongue in, becoming familiar with every corner presented.

The heat from her clothed cunt, mixed with him grinding his hardened cock sent Jiho into overdrive.

The same could be said about the woman as a wave of moans was released.

Sweet, lustful moans.

More was let out as a reaction to him pressing harder against her. Grasping her neck, pressing the sides in, allowing some airway for her to breathe, Jiho devoured her.

Never had she felt like this before. Saoirse wanted to see, at first, what Jiho would do in this situation, but she never expected this from him.

Now, she was drowning. Pulling away from her, Jiho wanted to admire the state she was in.

"Saoirse, if you continue to crumble under me like this, I will not be able to stop. Tell me to stop now, and I will."

She shook her head, giving a no, pulling at his shirt to continue.

"Words. I need words. I need you to verbally consent to this." He sternly spoke.

Saoirse answered between breaths, her chest heaving, "You think I want you to stop, *mon amour*?" She was playing with fire; it was evident in Jiho's eyes. Giving a sly smile, "Please, *mon amour*, continue."

Parting his lips, wanting to know if they would see each other outside of these little run-ins, they were again interrupted when a phone went off.

Looking at each other, accusing one another, before knowing it was hers to answer. Saoirse's facial expression cringed at this. Answering the phone, she spoke in Gaelic.

He pulled himself away, readjusting and smoothing out his clothing; he stood up, giving his hand out after an angry hang-up.

She took it gladly, keeping her hand in his as she fixed her dress. Saoirse gently kissed him, squeezing his hand before setting off.

"Will we meet again? On purpose?" Without turning around, she gave an answer that replied in his head.

"Of course, *mon amour*. Of course."

Chapter Nineteen

The Blended Family

IF YOU WERE TO TELL Jiho at one point in his life, he would see an abusive man be scared shitless while the brother of his mentor was holding a gun to his head; Jiho would not believe you.

Simple.

But here he was, sights on Lisa leaning against a wall, Dmitry with the gun and a girl behind the two.

He had no idea who the third one was, but nevertheless, they had scared the attacker. It would have been a rather funny scene if he had just watched from afar.

Jiho was on his way to the hospital parking garage, finishing his three-day shift, eager to go home and rest, possibly calling his sisters or grandparents. Although he called the other members of his family regularly, Jiho's parents were another story.

His mother ignored his calls as they fought weekly over his dating life. There is constant complaining about having a childless life in his future if she was not allowed to set him up with a couple of her friends' daughters.

His father had messages here and there, but since childhood, Yu-Jun has put some distance between them, not fully being there like he had been in those early years.

As he was approaching his car, a man rammed him into the side of the vehicle. There was some haziness after the impact, but once Jiho could get a steady view of his attacker, it was clear who it was.

He recognized the man as the abuser who had beaten his spouse, a patient of Jiho's, to death before slipping away from the authorities who were called to the hospital.

The hospital's psychologist had talked to the man before his disappearance, informing Jiho that the man was on a psychotic break, believing that Jiho was the one to kill his husband, unable to come to terms with the truth.

The security wanted to walk Jiho to his car just in case, but Jiho did not want to risk the safety of others for his sake, telling them that he was fine on his own and had someone waiting for him already.

Which was a lie. One in which he would proudly say again for the sake of the safety of others.

It was inevitable, to say the least, but he didn't care, as this would not be the first or last time someone was to attack him.

He was able to disarm the man from the knife they were holding after ramming into the doctor. The attacker stumbled as he flung the knife around, indicating his drunken state of mind, too emotional to reason.

Before the man could lunge at Jiho, he felt the cold barrel of a gun, hearing the safety clicking off. The sound made the abuser freeze before them all.

Jiho was shocked and eerily concerned with the appearance of at least two of them: Lisa and Dmitry. The hardened look cast over Lisa's eye left Jiho confused about the change she had undergone since university.

The sound of Dmitry's tongue clicking against the roof of his mouth, taunting the attacker, indicating he has done something wrong.

"I wouldn't do that if I were you. Someone would be rather angry, and believe me, she's not the forgiving type." He chuckled, "The last time I made her mad was because of a little prank I pulled." Dmitry had a playful tone throughout his words, "How was I supposed to know she didn't want all those cats? She did tell me to take in strays-"

Lisa elbowed his stomach, granting a harsh exhale of air from Dmitry, "Shut up, Dima. We are not here to make friends."

"Why are you so mean to me, *Zajchik*? Why can't you just love me?"

The man pouted, still holding the gun in the middle of the fearful man's head, ready to pull the trigger at the slightest movement. Jiho had taken this time to see the trio that had stepped into view.

Lisa was the first person to step out. Instead of the natural tight curls, small micro braids pulled into a half-up-half-down, framing her face elegantly.

She was not in the sweater Jiho had seen on her the last two times. Instead, she was in a rather stunning piece, one that Min-Jung had asked him to get her for her graduation. A black long-sleeved turtleneck underneath her black jumpsuit. The outfit was cinched at her waist, enhancing her small curves and long legs.

Dmitry was the second one in his view. While Jiho had only met the man once, covered in blood, and his clothing had rips and tears, he was surprised to see him in a matching outfit.

Consisting of a full black suit and shoes, his shirt had a few buttons undone, showing a part of his tattoo on his chest rounding to his back. His hair was slicked back, and a few short strands draped over his forehead.

If he had to have guessed, the man was six-foot, give or take. Making him wonder if the rest of the Petrov family was tall.

The final one was unknown to Jiho, but he was intrigued to know it was a girl. She couldn't have been more than fourteen, in Jiho's opinion.

Her height was only around five-three. She stood a bit further from the two adults, eyes shifting around. The unknown girl had on what looked like a school uniform with a familiar logo on the blazer.

"Broduil?" At Jiho's words, the teen looked over at him, eyes narrowing at his recognition of her school. While Lisa and Dmitry were still bickering, holding the man at gunpoint, she approached him. Looking up and down, she offered her hand.

"Daniella Petrov. Top student at Broduil Academy."

Tilting his head to the side, Jiho hesitantly introduced himself, "Jiho Yoo. Former top student of Broduil Academy."

"So, you're Jiho." Her eyes lit with excitement. "You're the one who beat those boys up, right?" Sitting on the ground next to the car's front tire.

Following her movement, he sat next to her before offering some leftover snacks in his coat pocket, scoffing at her words.

"They still talk about that?"

She nodded, swallowing her bite, "Of course. They don't even let anyone in your old dorm. It's been taped off for years now. Even the professors say they get chills walking by the building."

Shaking his head at the utter foolishness that the academy entertained. Jiho turned back to the three standing. The attacker was on the ground, unconscious. His face had tear streaks and snot.

Seeing Lisa and Dmitry still going back and forth, he leaned closer to Daniella, whispering, "So are they dating? Or what? And how did you all just appear, or better yet, why does your brother have a gun?"

"I don't know." Her words were barely audible with the food in her mouth. "Isa is always with Dima, and they act like a couple, but sometimes she's so mean to him."

"Mean?"

Taking a waterfall sip from Jiho's water bottle, Daniella nods.

"She always denies her feelings for him, saying she doesn't like him, but we all know she does. It just…it feels like she's holding onto something that isn't there."

He hummed; returned to his second question, "What about your sudden showing up and the gun?"

She shook her head, "Sorry. Orders are orders. I can't tell you till she tells you."

"She?"

"Their boss and my distant cousin-in-law." Daniella shivered from the cold wind and mentioned the person before continuing. "She's scary when she's mad, and I, for one, am not going to get on her bad side."

Taking his extra jacket from his backpack, Jiho handed it to the girl, which she took with appreciation.

Hearing Daniella say the exact words Lisa did when the two adults came into the ER, he remembered seeing the name on Lisa's phone, "Your cousin-in-law is Saoirse?"

At the name drop, all three snapped their attention to the doctor, "How do you know her name?" Dmitry snared.

Jiho raised his hands in surrender and let a nervous chuckle out towards the Petrov man, still holding the gun.

"Well...you...see...umm...I've met her, and my friend is dating Eric too..."

"Ally is dating Eric?"

Jiho confirms Lisa's question.

"For how long?"

"I don't really know the timeline, but I did meet him not too long ago."

But he paused.

If Saoirse is Eric's cousin by blood, he thought, *as well as an in-law to the Petrov family, and Viktor is the brother to these two, then-.*

"Emilia is Saoirse's cousin, and she's married to Viktor...Emilia is Eric's older sister, right?"

"You know my brother?" Daniella's voice held hope, for which Jiho could not know why, but he nodded, "Have you seen his kids?"

"Yes." He smiled softly, "They are adorable. They call me Dyadya most of the time."

Shocking the two Russians at the closeness their brother must have with Jiho. Frowning his eyebrows, Jiho finally put the last piece together.

"Saoirse is the godmother to them…"

Daniella suddenly held his hand, spooking Jiho a bit before relaxing, "You have a lot of information about the blended family." Turning her attention to Dmitry, she asked, "Can't we just tell him now? I don't think Irse would mind it if she knew about this."

Her request was denied. As Lisa looked down, her thoughts were mushing together. Wondering how close her boss and crush were for him to know all this. Seeing Lisa's sad state, Dmitry interrupted with a loud clearing of his throat, gaining the attention back on to him.

"We need to go, *Pcholka*."

Lifting the unconscious man over his shoulder with no signs of struggle, Daniella let out an aggravated sigh.

"Fine." She mutters, standing up before dusting herself. She gives Jiho a soft cheek kiss before giving him a smile. "See you soon, yeah?"

Nodding his head, utterly stunned at the girl's personality switch, he watched as Daniella pulled Lisa away, following her brother.

Once alone on the cold ground, Jiho buried his face into his arms as his legs were pulled into his chest, "What the fuck just happened…"

Chapter Twenty

Damaged Images

THE NEXT DAY, Jiho woke up to a minor heart attack.

What does that mean?

When he opened his eyes, he saw Dmitry standing over him with a wide smile, not a care in the world. It was one of the most horrifying things to wake up to.

"Wakey, wakey, sleeping beauty. It's time for us to go on a little errand run." He laughed at the confused look on Jiho's face.

"Errand run?"

"Yep." Dmitry walked towards the closet, rummaging for some clothes, "I'm taking you on a little field trip with me. We must hurry if we want to be on time. You slept in a little too late, boss."

"Boss?" Jiho was confused about everything happening. "I'm not your boss. How did you get in my house? How do you know where I live?"

"Not important right now." Waving him off, Dmitry throws an outfit at the foot of Jiho's bed before leaving the room. "Get dressed. You got five minutes."

He had no clue what was going on. All he knew was not to keep the man waiting, unsure if he still had the gun from the previous night.

Quickly getting ready, he jogged downstairs to see Dmitry drinking coffee with Daniella, both waiting for him. Once in her vision, Daniella ran over to Jiho, hugging him. The action caused him to stiffen before awkwardly patting her head.

"How did you sleep?" She looked up at him, not removing herself.

"...Good. What about you?"

"Terrible! Dima didn't take us home till two this morning, and I only slept four hours till he barged in, waking me up."

Frowning, she stuck her tongue out at Dmitry before smiling back at the doctor, "But seeing as it's you we had to pick up before our little run, I'm not too mad."

"And why is that *Pcholka*?" Dmitry held a playful smirk on his face.

"Shut up, Dima," the young Petrov hissed, letting Jiho go, "or I'll just go and tell Isa more embarrassing stories about you."

The smirk had dropped at the mention of Lisa's name. Dmitry's demeanor rigged as his eyes waved over to Jiho. Shaking her head, Daniella quickly refused, "No, don't do that."

"Do what, *Pcholka*?" He gritted his teeth, still holding some playfulness in his gaze.

"You know what, Dima." She said, hands resting on her hips. "It has nothing to do with him, so stop."

Standing up, Dmitry smiled, "Fine. I'll wipe my hand from it." Motioning his hand in a way, he walked over to the front door, "We ready?"

Nodding, she grabbed Jiho's hand before walking out of the house and into the car. Before he could open the backseat door, Dmitry placed his hand on his shoulders, "You sit up front with me."

Jiho let out a staggered breath, "So where are we going?" Looking out the window as the trees they passed turned into blurs.

Subconsciously, Jiho ran his hand over the scars on his left arm that were now displayed as Dmitry laid out a short-sleeved shirt. There was no need for a jacket as the day's weather was on the warmer side.

He was not ashamed of his scars as they reminded him of the struggles he had and the progress he'd made. Jiho was just nervous for the two Petrov siblings to ask about it, which so far, they haven't.

"That's for us to know and for you to find out." Dmitry taunted; it wasn't until Daniella slapped his arm from the back seat that he answered, "Shit. Okay. God, always so violent, aren't you, *Pcholka.*"

"Answer the man, Dima." She narrowed her eyes.

"Fine." He rolled his eyes. "Just relax, boss, you'll be fine with us."

Taking in the worried state of the passenger, he couldn't help but sigh before reaching behind Jiho's seat and holding out a neck pillow.

"Just sleep or something. It's about a two-hour drive."

"You sure? I can stay up just to keep you company..." Jiho hesitantly offered, seeing as Daniella had already passed out from exhaustion in the back.

Chuckling at the waves of nerves Jiho had, he shook his head, "No. It's okay; I'm used to it already."

Reluctantly he caved, nodding towards Dmitry, "Okay. Well, wake me when we are about twenty minutes away, yeah?"

"You got it, boss."

UPON THE REQUEST TO be woken up before they reached the destination, Jiho was left confused once he opened his eyes.

They were closer to the ocean and more lavish houses. The scenery of the blue skies and reflective waters reminded him of the trip he took with his sister.

Of his family.

Of Eun-Ya.

He remembered the two families coming together for a weekend trip one time. How the two small children learned how to swim from Taeyoung. The sand building contest both their fathers held. Jiho and Eun-Ya covered her grandfather with sand while he fell asleep.

He was grateful to have that memory. He was thankful for the progress in living a happier life and not letting guilt, which is still alive in him, weigh him down. Making Eun-Ya happy with being a doctor and his promise to Taeyoung and Kyong to live as he wants to. To find his own happiness.

The car did not stop until they reached a dead end, the last house on the street.

It was more prominent and secluded than the others, as the gates covered the architecture's bottom half.

"What are we doing here?" Daniella's sudden question startled Jiho, who jumped from his seat. Her giggles were loud, sending Jiho's cheeks and the tips of his ears turning pink.

"Don't start, *Pcholka*. We must do this." Dmitry waved to one of the security guards at the entrance.

"But his son is always trying to hit on me." She whines.

Confused about who they were talking about, Jiho only raised an eyebrow to Dmitry.

"One of the sons here has been trying to get with her for the past year."

"And it's terrible. I could tolerate it if it were only at the check-ins, but the boy goes to the academy, too!" Letting out a tired sigh before looking at Jiho once they all exited the car. "Can you scare him for me?"

"Scare him?"

"Yeah, your name has its own legacy at school, and he is always saying he could take you on, but I know that's just bullshit-" Daniella's anger rose as they reached the door.

"Language *Pcholka*."

"Untrue. Happy?" Stepping between the two men and the doorbell, Daniella asks, "Can you, Jiji?"

"Jiji?" He raised his eyebrows, and a small smile was placed on his lips.

"Can you?" She pleads, holding his hands in hers, pouting in anticipation.

Looking over at Dmitry only to get a shrug in response, Jiho sighed before nodding. Clapping her hands, Daniella hugged him once more before ringing the bell herself.

Not waiting long, the three were escorted to the living room where a man in his sixties stood, arms open with a smile.

Another man around Jiho's age was sitting with his back to them, and one who he assumed was the boy Daniella hated as he grinned at the girl.

"Dmitry! My boy, how are you doing?"

"I'm well, Mr. Harriet." The name Dmitry barked in equal amusement, sparking recognition in Jiho's mind.

Taking another look at the boy sitting with his back towards them, he couldn't tell if it was who he thought it was.

Deciding to keep his mouth shut, he did not move forward to greet anyone. Instead, he placed an arm around Daniella as she hugged him, as a way to protect her.

"How are you? The family?"

"Good, we've been trying to set up a good time for dinner with Miss. Welsh and her parents, but we haven't been able to get in touch."

Chuckling at the poor man, Dmitry smiled, "Yes. Well, they have all been busy as of now. So, they do apologize for the inconvenience; please understand."

Mr. Harriet smiled tightly, not believing a single word, "Of course. But please do tell me who you've invited. I don't know who this person is to have in my home."

At that, the attention was solely on Jiho, including the one sitting with his back towards him, who only paled in fear.

Jiho had been right in his assumption.

It was Jassin *fucking* Harriet.

The bastard who assaulted Ally.

Once Jassin saw Jiho, he could not help but shake in fear; standing up, he began to stutter out a question as his family looked in confusion. "What are you doing here?"

"Jass, you know him?" His father asked.

"Ah, sorry." Dmitry chuckled, "Where are my manners? Let me introduce Miss. Welsh's most important guest, who she ordered to be treated with the respect we all give her-" watching Jassin pale in complexion at the statement the Russian gave, "-this is Jiho Yoo."

Seeing both sons look sickly at the name, Mr. Harriet remembered what happened a few years ago when Mr. Turner had phoned him angrily about what his son and nephew had done to his daughter.

"Based on your faces, you know him?" Daniella gloated.

Staring at Jassin, Jiho did not smirk or frown; his face was void of all emotion, chilling the assaulter to the bone.

"Jassin." His tone was deadly; even Daniella and Dmitry were impressed.

"Y-Yes?" The man straightened his posture, looking down at the ground.

"You've been out of trouble? Or have you been doing things you shouldn't have?" Jiho's gaze did not flatten, still loosely holding onto the smirking girl. Nodding his head, Jassin was too afraid his voice would crack, "Words, Jassin."

"I've been out of trouble." He meekly answered, stuttering here and there.

Nodding, Jiho pulled Daniella over to the other side of the Harriet man, sitting down before gesturing for them to do the same.

Watching this with amusement, Dmitry was laughing. Jiho did not mind this as his gaze was on the sons.

If Jassin could do that to Ally, he thought, *then what makes his little brother any different*? Not trusting either of them, the two Harriet boys could feel the heat of his glare.

"I have no idea what your sons did to get on Jiho's bad side, but I have to say I'm glad it's not me." Wiping his tears away, he looked at Mr. Harriet, "Why don't we talk, just the two of us. I'm sure Jiho and my *Pcholka* can watch your sons. Right?"

Dmitry looked over to the other two regarding his question. Jiho did not answer, as his attention was not on him. Shifting his eyes to his sister, Dmitry waited.

"Just go, Dima." Daniella huffed, "I need to make it back in time to have dinner with the others."

"Well, you heard the lady, let's go." The two disappeared from their sight, leaving the four alone.

Jiho could see the youngest looking at Daniella in a way he did not like. It made him think back to how Jassin had looked at Ally before that night. In places like classes, in passing, at the canteen, whenever the two saw him, Jassin was looking at Ally.

"What's your name, kid?" Jiho broke the silence after ten minutes.

"What?"

"What's your name?"

Gulping, the boy looked directly at Jiho. He had heard about the rumors of this man.

"Benjamin."

"Well, Benjamin, has Jassin told you how he knows me?" Still, his face did not lift from the void he was in.

Benjamin looked over to his older brother to see his eyes downcast at the floor. This was a side to Jassin the young boy had never seen. Usually, Benjamin would see confidence, even arrogance, but now, all he could see was shame and fear.

"No."

"Why don't you tell him, Jassin." Receiving a small no. Jiho gritted forward, "Either tell him willingly, or I'll make you."

Silence.

Shakely, Jassin nodded.

"Good."

Slowly, he turned his body to his little brother before looking at Jiho, pleading for any sign of mercy only to be handed none.

Uninterrupted, Jassin told his little brother.

Told him how he had to drug a girl, having their cousin and some of his friends hold her down so that Jassin could finally get with the girl who constantly turned him down.

He told Benjamin about the beating he endured from Jiho and how all the rumors about himself and Jiho were true. The rumors of Jassin being an assaulter and almost raped a girl were true.

The rumors of Jiho placing those in the hospital and the violent nature were true.

"Now, do you know why I made him tell you this?"

"No." Tears formed in Benjamin's eyes as the image of his brother was destroyed.

"Dani here," bringing the smiling girl closer, "told me no matter how many times she says no, you don't give up. Is that true?"

"...Yes."

"She is very important to me and the people I care for."

Jiho stood, hearing the office door where the other two were open.

"So, if I hear any more of you harassing her, then we will have problems. I don't hit kids, but I can put my anger on your brother again."

Seeing Jassin flinch at Jiho's words, Benjamin nods in agreement. Clapping his hands together, Dmitry smiled towards the four.

"All done. Are you two ready to go?"

"Yep!" Daniella ran over to her brother while Jiho walked calmly, bowing his head towards Mr. Harriet, the three-bidding goodbye.

"YOU WANT TO EXPLAIN WHY Mr. Harriet's son shit himself looking at you?"

Dmitry broke an hour or so of silence as Daniella fell back asleep, snoring softly. Jiho had made it a point to look out the window instead of the two Petrov children. A way to avoid the explanation of his behavior change.

It was a cowardly thing to do, but Jiho did not want to go through it all again, as he had already done while in front of *Jassin*.

The name sickened him to the core.

"Not really." Jiho muttered against his palm. Opening his eyes and turning his head, "But I know you're dying to know."

"You're damn right, I'm dying to know." He laughed, "I've been trying to knock that arrogant son of a bitch down for a while now. Jassin thinks he's hot shit just because we do business with his father."

Side-eyeing the driver, Jiho thought of a good deal for getting more information about Saoirse.

"If I tell you why the bastard basically shit himself, you have to tell me more about Saoirse. Deal?"

Scoffing at the offering, Dmitry jokingly let his inner thoughts come out, "You like my cousin-in-law, don't you." Only he was laughing as Jiho burned red from embarrassment.

How did he, of all people, figure it out, Jiho thought.

Once Dmitry realized that he was the only one laughing, he turned to see the red mess Jiho was in.

"Wait, you like Saoirse?" Dmitry gasped at the deeper shade, saying, "Oh, you *really* like her."

"Do we have a deal or not?" Jiho quickly asked, turning his face away from the teasing man.

"Yes." He responded after a few seconds of debating, "We have a deal.

Running his hands over his face, Jiho began the story once more. Tell the driver of all the events that happened on a specific day.

From the start, when Ally asked him to go with her to the party, to losing sight of her, finding her in such a way, to beating the shit out of the boys, which included Jassin, and finally taking care of Ally and informing her father.

"Well, shit…" Dmitry breathed out.

He knew the Harriet family got things done by any means but hearing that one of their own could take it that far made him sick, especially since their other son had his eyes on Daniella.

"You don't need to worry about Dani." Jiho could read the expression clear as day, "I already made it known what would happen."

"...Thank you."

He appreciated that his sister had someone to look after even when the two did not know each other well. Dmitry held some bias against the man as Lisa obviously still liked him.

But hearing Jiho take care of the situation before it came to life made him understand why she felt that way. Knowing Jiho did not like Lisa the way she did brought joy to him.

"So, what do you want to know about the head of the Welsh family?"

Jiho thought about it; he had to ask something he was dying to know, as it was one explanation for another. The endless list in his mind made it difficult, but one kept popping into his head every time.

"What is it that Saoirse does?"

"A loaded question, huh." Smirking at the man, "Well, she's a jack of all trades. Saoirse doesn't just do one thing; she does it all. That's why her father placed her above all her other siblings."

"She has siblings?" Jiho question. They had finally reached his house, putting the car in park.

"You only get the one." Dmitry smiled, "Have a good night, boss."

Chapter Twenty-One

Together Again

JIHO WAS FEELING ON top of the world.

His three sisters had planned to stay with him for two weeks after Nari and Iseul met with Min-Jung in Italy.

He was incredibly excited to see them all in the flesh. Face-to-face after a little over nine months away from each other.

He had not known the three girls had planned this little trip behind his back for five months, but he was not disappointed.

The twin told him less than a week ago, and due to the amount of vacation time he had collected from the overtime he put in, Jiho was approved to have the two weeks off to just spend with his family.

Due to his excitement, he finished his charting quickly, said his little goodbyes, and packed his things. Setting off towards a floral shop to give the girls a 'welcome' present once they landed.

He settled on the same types of mixed flowers: carnations, roses, cornflowers, forget-me-nots, and alstroemerias–for the girls but in their favorite colors.

Nari loved the vibrant jewel tones of blues and purples, Iseul preferred the opposite of soft, welcoming pinks and greens, and the baby, Min-Jung, loved any warm colors, gentle and harsh tones.

Each bouquet was relatively small for him, holding all three in one hand. He had hoped that compared to his sisters, they were the right size, which would require them to use both hands.

Throughout the month of their sibling vacation, they traveled to all the must-see locations in their home country. Staying with the favored sightseeing places: Busan, Gyeongju, Incheon, Changdeokgung Palace, Jeju Island, Haeundae Beach, Myeongdong, and Seoul.

Seoul was the last on the trip as Jiho and Min-Jung would help the twins settle in their housing for their second year in university.

The drive took an hour before he was able to pay for parking. Leaving behind his backpack in the trunk, taking only his wallet, keys, and flowers.

Once entering the airport, Jiho searched to find which gates his sister would be coming from after customs and receiving their baggage. The possibilities were endless for him. Thinking of how they would all react toward each other after their time apart.

During these months, Jiho witnessed his trend following, sheltered sisters all finding their own style to his happiness.

"Oppa!"

The three girls had all raced to their brother. The first to reach him was Iseul; being the tallest of the other two gave her the advantage.

She embraced the whole tortured artist style. Her low bun was set in place with a pen, and the turtleneck kept her neck warm, with the wide-leg pants. Her heeled boots gave her tall stature a bit more height; instead of reaching Jiho's shoulder, she was at his chin.

The next was Nari. Now, she was only a few centimeters shorter than her twin, something Iseul held over her. Having grown up wearing the same outfit as Iseul, Nari wanted to expand her identity as the fashion designer she became today.

The woman was often seen in her work or a mix of them and second-hand pieces. Her off-the-shoulder silk top-which was being held with thin straps on each shoulder-was tucked into a long denim skirt. Her kitten heels helped her reach the shoulder height her sister came with flats.

Lastly, to her demise, Min-Jung joined in the group hug, careful not to damage the bouquets in Jiho's hand.

Compared to her two older sisters, Min-Jung's style changed drastically.

The once shy girl transformed into a confident young lady. Her long sleeves were replaced with tight-fitting corset-like tops, and her bottoms still occasionally had jeans in them, but more linen bottoms had made a prominent appearance in her wardrobe. Loafers and, like Nari, kitten heels stuck to her after years of Converse.

All three had held on to Jiho as if their life depended on it. For the first time, Jiho let out a soft sob; tears of joy were let out.

He never realized the longing he had for his sisters and his family. Ally would always be considered a sister to him, but she had her own life and family there for her. He loved her like a sister and best friend. She was, in a sense, his twin.

But he missed the three in front of him. He was there for all their births, birthdays, and little celebrations.

"I've missed you three so much…" Jiho spoke in Korean, glad he did not talk in it only ever over the phone after all this time.

Pulling away, he gave them each their personal flowers. Something each enjoyed very much.

"Please don't cry." Iseul stated.

Nari was the one to wipe his tears, as she was on the verge of crying.

He nodded in agreement, giving them a content smile, "Are you all hungry?"

They began to walk back to his car. Jiho grabbed the heavier bags and suitcases while the girls had their carry-ons and small bags.

"There's a nice little takeout spot on the way home we can get."

"I'm dying for food. They don't have big enough meals for me on the plane." Min-Jung pouts, rubbing her stomach. She ate as much as their father for the smallest of the four, putting the others to shame at buffas. The twins agreed with their baby sister, complaining that the sizing was only enough to feed a child.

"Okay, I'll get you all the food and wake you up when we get home." Once in the car, Jiho let them all rest for the car ride back. The soft tunes played in the background.

PUTTING THE CAR IN PARK, Jiho woke them. As they were gathering their belongings, he ran into the house, placing the food down before grabbing the rest of their luggage.

Once set in the living room, all four Yoo children settled at the dining table, opening the lids, and handing out utensils.

Each person had a shot of liquor, except Min-Jung, who only had soda, they fell into a game of 'twenty questions.'

"How's university life? Italy?"

"Nari-yah hasn't slept in our apartment for the last three weeks-"

"Iseul-ah when on two dates with an older man before we left-"

"I kissed a girl-"

Jiho stopped mid-bite as he processed all the information that had been thrown at him. His sisters had more action than him; he was unsure how he felt.

On the one hand, Jiho was happy they were coming out of their shell and being experimental with their lives. But on the other hand, they were still too young for romance in their lives. Amid these thoughts, the three girls started to bicker with one another for not telling each other about these things.

"...What?" The silence was thick. Jiho's eye contact with all of them was uncanny, "What do you mean Nari-yah hasn't been home for three weeks? When was Iseul-ah interested in dating? When did you kiss a girl-actually when did you have your first kiss?"

Still, no one answered.

Instead, all three of them continued to eat, passing some food to each other, and refilling their cups. Jiho was annoyed now. He was only curious, not angry.

"I'm not going to scold you. I just want to know what's going on with you three."

Min-Jung was the first to say, "You promise?"

"Promise."

One word broke them all into smiles. Quickly they set their utensils down before speaking, "Okay, so my first kiss was at the twin's eighteenth birthday party, with Hyuk-seonbae-"

"Seo Hyuk-ah?! The one with that scar on his arm?" Min-Jung nodded at Nari's question.

Nari had always disliked Hyuk due to his little fast track of dating those around the neighborhood. His flirtatious ways made it hard for her to even agree to invite him to that celebration, but Iseul shared a desk with him and had to ask him out of respect.

"Gross."

"Shut up; it was a small peck." Min-Jung scrunched her face inwards as she recalled the memory, "His mouth smelled bad. We agreed never to tell anyone. But anyway, this girl is in my Italian class, Mia, and we were studying late. There was this movie on, and the two main female leads kissed. We got curious and just did it. That's all."

Min-Jung saw Jiho ready to ask more but shut it all down with one look.

"What about you two?"

Nari and Iseul had a silent conversation, all through their eyes, seeing which twin would speak first. Deciding to go from youngest to oldest, Iseul started.

"Well...mom set me up with one of her friend's sister's sons. He's only, I can't stress this enough, twenty-four years old-"

His eyes nearly fell out of his head.

To hear his nineteen-year-old sister date someone only three years younger than him was shocking. Subconsciously, Jiho knew he couldn't judge the relationship as he was in a...well, he didn't know what to call his relationship with Saoirse.

"Stop. Don't say anything. He's nice and works for a terrific company. Very sweet. So considerate, which is rather hard to find nowadays."

Her smile melted their hearts. They could tell Iseul was smitten with this man.

"I really like him. And I want to see where it goes. If this continues, you three will be the first to meet him."

A satisfied nod from Jiho was all it took to have everyone look at the last one, Nari. She was nervous.

Trying to explain to one overprotected brother and two nosy sisters was a handful just thinking about it.

"It's nothing bad, first. I just stayed closer to my classes at a friend's place."

"Just a friend?" Min-Jung smudged.

Scoffing, Nari was already over her little sister, "Yes, just a friend."

"Does he believe that?"

"Of course he does-"

"It's a man?" Jiho pipes in. Now, he had to worry about all of them dating other people simultaneously.

Blushing with embarrassment, she nodded, "He's nothing to worry about. Honestly, I don't believe he likes me like that."

"Believing and knowing are two different things, Nari-yah. You are just like Ally, overthinking and doubting everything."

With questionable looks, Jiho explained how his friend self-doubts herself before getting together with Eric. They were not surprised Ally was dating a fellow model.

Once Jiho told them Eric's name, the three sisters went on their own little rant about him. Since Nari and Iseul attended a top art school, they had the chance to see his work life during Seoul Fashion Week.

Their class got to speak to him about his expectations within the fashion and art industry. Their interaction was pleasant, with kindness and well-thought-out sentences. Eric was respectful towards them, other students, and staff, a rather refreshing take from some unnamed professionals. Min-Jung never met him but was always up to date with European and Italian fashion.

Seeing him work a lot in Paris and Italy, you could say she found him attractive, and as every seventeen-year-old, she watched his clips of interviews and personal videos, finding him funny.

"Back to the topic, I will give you the advice I gave Al. If you like him, just tell him. The worst that can happen is him not reciprocating the feelings, which means it wasn't a relationship that was meant to be."

"What if I've turned him down once before...more like four times?"

Blinking several times, Jiho cleared his throat. No one could deny the Yoo family was good-looking in their own ways, but Jiho never thought his sister could be such a heartbreaker.

"Umm, I won't lie...he might not believe you, but that doesn't mean you shouldn't try." Grabbing the trash off the table, they began to clean their meal.

They wanted to take the conversation to the living room, where they all agreed to sleep for the night as there was a pull-out sofa, couch, and mats to sleep on in the downstairs closet.

"It might be a good idea to list why you like him and tell him personal things you always think about when your thoughts wander. How he makes you feel when he's near but also when he's gone."

Deciding to shut this conversation up, Nari nodded in agreement, "So what about you?"

He flopped on the floor, placing his arms behind his head.

The girls separated; Nari was in the single armchair, Iseul was lying on the pull-out couch on her side to still see everyone, and Min-Jung was on the floor with her knees pulled to her chest, sipping on her drink.

Around them were snacks Jiho had placed before leaving for work that day, as it was only a meeting and a few rounds. The man was well prepared for his family and their appetite.

"What about me?"

"Don't play dumb-."

"You're not stupid-"

"Stop being an idiot-"

"Wow…you three are really the same…"

Iseul was tired of being in the dark; Nari and she knew the oldest and youngest talked about something private. She saw the side eyes they threw at each other, silently shaking their heads, denying anything.

"We want to know what happened? One day, you were fine, and then you weren't. It was like you were somewhere else for two weeks. Then, out of nowhere, you bounced back to being happy. So, what happened?"

Although it has been a while since he's seen Saoirse in person, Jiho still thinks about her. He promised himself to forget her, but after that kiss, Jiho was trapped.

He would forever be in her clutches. Coming to terms with the fact, Jiho understood it was only a matter of time till he had to tell his family about her. Unfortunately, he could not keep the siren to himself.

After talking to Min-Jung a few times before his little shutdown, he was relieved that it was something some woman wanted in a relationship.

The feeling of always being wanted so openly was a good thing. Jiho just had to remember, in his sister's words, 'to feel wanted and not controlled is the way to go.'

He took a deep breath after the inner debt happening; each sister waited patiently, "There's this woman-"

Not even after the sentence did the twins erupt in questions left and right. *This is going to be a long night.*

Chapter Twenty-Two

Respect My Decision

"YOU'RE NOT A NUN ANYMORE? -"

"You lost your virginity? -"

"Oh god." Hiding his face, Jiho was burning red.

It was no secret the man was a virgin.

He never hid it from his family or Ally. Even Viktor knew, but only because he was talking about all the fun places, he and Emilia had sex at when they were younger, asking Jiho if he had some 'adventures' as well.

It wasn't something he held for religious morals; it was just something Jiho wasn't worried about losing immediately.

"You want me to tell you or not?"

The twins zipped their mouths before handing the imaginary keys to Min-Jung.

"Okay. So, there's this woman, her name is Saoirse. She's cousins to Eric and Emilia, and I...*really* like her."

"Is she the reason you were so weird lately?"

"Minnie, you knew this?"

Min-Jung was indifferent to being called out; she shrugged, "It's been all over the blogs for 'Current Media News

International' class. He wasn't hiding it; you just had to tease him, and *poof* you got all the information."

Quickly cutting in as he saw the twin open their mouths again, Jiho pleaded with them, "Don't get mad at her. I told her when she called me with a photo of us and asked her not to tell anyone."

"So…Are you in a relationship or a fling?" Nari was a little angry with the lack of trust her brother had in them.

Nari's a somewhat hypocritical person when it comes to things. She wanted to be the first to know what was happening but never wanted to air her life for people to understand.

Every member of the Yoo family had something that pissed everyone to no end; Nari's hypocritical behavior, Iseul's bold and hurtful passing comments, Min-Jung's unapologetic attitude towards privacy in other's lives, and Jiho's lack of openness towards new people.

It was a headache for people around them once the siblings were together in one room.

"Bet you she's just wanting to get a free ride for money." Iseul mutters into her glass.

"She has her own money. Saoirse's the head to her father's company as he's retired already." The glare Min-Jung gave had Iseul rolling her eyes.

The youngest defended a woman she had never met, an uncommon action, but Iseul was getting on her nerves. She was going to stop with Saoirse. Though they had not personally met, Min-Jung could see how she'd just lit Jiho's world. She was willing to defend Saoirse against the family if she had to.

"How do you know that? You've talked to her? What does her family do?" Nari cut in.

"Her family owns the majority of companies in Ireland and France." Min-Jung turned her body, facing the firstborn daughter head-on. Narrowing her eyes, she continued. "All you must do is look her up, and you have all the information you need about their family success. I've never talked to her, but I've seen the photos taken by the press; Oppa and her looked so happy."

He had just watched this small piss contest with sadness. He knew the reactions would differ for each sister but never thought it would become an argument.

It hurt him.

Jiho thought they would show happiness for him in his endeavors, but they couldn't even pretend–except for the youngest. Having had enough of this bickering back and forth, Jiho sat up.

"Can you three not start a war over my love life? I won't sit here any longer and have you trash a woman you've never met when she's only brought me feelings of joy and safety."

"We're just worried for you."

"No, if you were worried, you would be asking questions regarding where we met, how safe it feels around her after everything I've been through, and we all know I don't just let anyone in my little space. You wouldn't question if she's a gold digger or if it's true about her family being well off. You wouldn't have this snobby attitude and tone."

Jiho understood this side of them was who they were. No one will be a cookie-cutter, sweet, overly kind, always understanding person. That's unrealistic. With Saoirse ingrained in his mind, he couldn't stand to hear anything negative about the woman.

In his opinion, Min-Jung was the only one in the family with an open mind. When he told her about his first kiss, she didn't judge him or make him feel awkward for having it during his last year of university. She was supportive, keeping things light and warm with her comments.

That said, she investigated to see who would take one of her older brothers first, as Jiho did not give any details regarding the actual person. The sneaky little seventeen-year-old found who the person was, and *he* is now one of her hidden cards to tease Jiho with.

With a deep sigh, Nari broke the silence, "We're sorry for reacting in such a way, but you have to understand; we are just worried." Placing a hand up to stop Jiho from speaking, she continued, "We don't want the first person you are serious about to leave you heartbroken. We just want to be sure she's up to the standard we believe is the same level as you."

"She's right. You're our only brother. You are the only son in our family and the only grandson to our grandparents on both sides. We must make sure they are equal to you or at least within reach. You are the future head of household back home."

Iseul was one for tradition and customs. She desperately wants to see Jiho settle down and have children but wants only the best for her older brother.

"This is the twenty-first century. If I believe she is worth this argument, then she is. I don't need you to baby me. I'm the oldest. I know what I want, and I want Saoirse."

"How long have you known her? How can you tell this is what you want?" Iseul's doubtful comments hurt Jiho.

He just wanted to have support; never did it cross his mind that the ones he holds dear would be so quick to stomp on his happiness.

"Al brought me to a bar-"

"Was she drinking? Got so drunk she started to flirt with you?"

"She wasn't drinking. All she did was paperwork till we started to talk, then we met each other at a banquet and recently at an evening company party for Al's work, where I met Eric, her older cousin."

"So, you've met her three times and suddenly want to be in a relationship?" Iseul scoffed.

Min-Jung had been silent the whole time. Her remarks would not be said as Jiho was willing and needed to argue for his own sake.

It baffled him to know they all got along not even two hours ago, but now it felt like he wanted them to leave and never return.

"I know we only saw each other three times, but I've never felt like this. I have you three and Ally, but you all are my sisters. With Saoirse, I feel the same safety as I do with you, but I also have longing and romantic feelings for her. It's too early to tell if she wants me the same way, but she's the one for me. Even if I don't get her, I will only want her. I've accepted this. So just be happy for me..."

The women were at a standstill with emotions. On the one hand, they wanted what was best for Jiho and continued with this nitpicking debate; on the other, the three young women had never seen him beg in desperation for this random person.

It was eerie.

After his small speech, Min-Jung silently decided to support Jiho fully with no hesitation. She knew he needed to deal with these feelings and have this experience to be more confident in himself, breaking this fear of being a failure.

She wanted her brother to live life with full intent. If things work out with Saoirse, Min-Jung would be extremely happy for the two, but if it ends in tragedy, she'll be there to support and help him through his first romantic heartbreak. Smiling confidently, she crawled towards Jiho, giving him a side hug, and watching the other two's responses.

Nari didn't believe her brother was too serious about *Saoirse*. She thought it was a case of his puppy-love portion in life that he never had. Feeling fed up with the drama, the back-and-forth, she gave up.

Nodding in agreement, half-heartedly. If this were true, something Jiho was dead set on, Nari would bring this conversation up later.

Iseul could not let this go in the back of her mind. She wanted to continue, to knock some sense into her stupid older brother. He had brain smarts, but that was it. Jiho never experienced anything outside academic reasons or if Ally dragged him to social events. But seeing she was the odd one out, she huffed, looking away and muttering.

"Fine."

Looking down, still hugging Min-Jung, he had to set some things straight with them, "I know you're skeptical about this, with me proclaiming my intentions for Saoirse, but it's my life. I'm not asking you to be the best of friends if you met her at some point. I am asking you to respect me, my decisions, my efforts, and most importantly, Saoirse."

The tension was high, but the sisters let his words sink into them. Realizing the truth behind them, the twins looked at one another, conversing about whether they should allow this or be the unreasonable younger siblings they could be.

Sighing at the results, Nari and Iseul felt left out of the hug. They give off a shy smile before making their way to join the other two.

"You're lucky we love you enough to be doing this," Nari states. She was on the fence a little, but if Jiho really believed in himself to handle all the mess that might come with pursuing a relationship, then she could only watch.

"We'll trust your judgment, but if we don't like her or if she does anything to make you cry, we get to hurt her…and tell you 'We told you so' as punishment. Okay?" Iseul finished Nari's thoughts.

She was unconvinced about the whole thing, but losing her brother was not worth it…for now.

Chuckling at his sister's antics, Jiho nodded, tightening his hold on them. Happy they could at least enjoy each other's company without any arguments for the night, Jiho started to stand up, still holding on to them.

The overlapping pleas and commands to stop made things more interesting as he began flinging one after the other onto the couches, tackling them left and right. It was something they had grown up doing. When they were younger, Jiho allowed them to overtake him, pinning him down as they attempted to tickle him or make him tap out.

But as they all grew up and could hold their own with each other, he was difficult to beat, just like now. It helps that their father was adamant about them taking martial arts.

They all took the same classes, jiu-jitsu, judo, taekwondo, and tai chi. Their father had wanted them to defend themself when faced with danger after the murders during Jiho's childhood, placing a little bit of peace in the father's heavy hearts.

During their time apart from Jiho in boarding school, the twins in their middle school and Min-Jung in her primary school ventured into different areas while maintaining their four main interests.

Jiho went into kickboxing to deal with stress without a partner to spare with. The twins each took on aikido, perfect for the two. The youngest went a completely different route in acrobatics when she saw the high schoolers practice on the way home, wanting to be just like them.

These different and similar fighting styles made things interesting when they playfully attacked each other. Surprisingly, Nari won most of the time as she could concentrate more on aikido, unlike Iseul, allowing her to redirect the other's hits without breaking her own.

Iseul and Min-Jung tied in wins as they held taekwondo in higher regard, teaming up sometimes until they were the last ones standing. Jiho will never admit it out loud, but he never puts too much effort into these fights simply because he hates hurting them. That doesn't mean he put zero strength into his attacks; he simply tapped out before the others could realize.

Jiho had nothing to do besides studying, hence his higher level in fighting, but the girls had their own hobbies that they were now pursuing outside of physical activities.

Nari for fashion, Iseul for painting, and Min-Jung for languages. Jiho never underestimates his sisters for a second. If he did, he would lie just to help his ego, nothing more.

In the end, today's winner was Min-Jung, something she was excited about as she did her winner's dance. If they were in public, the other three would just walk away.

Flailing arms moving in every direction, and her legs cemented to the ground as her upper body bobs up and down; she looked like one of those car dealership inflatable tube men.

"Can I ask you something about Saoirse?" Iseul broke the laughter.

He hesitated a moment, not wanting his effort to make them forget their disagreement to go to waste. But seeing the pure curiosity in her expression, Jiho nodded.

"How does she make you feel when you're with and away from her?"

He sat between them, breathing heavily on the couch, "When I first met her, she reminded me of home, when we all hiked that big mountain, just to see the sunrise hit the green fields. A sense of calm came over me. Talking to her makes me want to run and hide, scared I'll say the wrong thing or something embarrassing, but I also want to stay and be around her more. She is direct with her opinions most of the time. But I feel she holds herself back sometimes."

Jiho allowed the cushions to swallow him as he relaxed his body, "I lose my current self when I'm with her, not in a bad way, but I become my past self. Me before Eun-Ya was taken…"

Tension placed in the girl's body at the name. It's been a while since their brother could say the name; usually, tears came with it, but seeing him remember his short time and fond memories with the dead girl, they knew he was healing. The girls place their hands on his shoulder, back, and arm, giving them comforting squeezes or rubs.

"When I'm away from Saoirse, I can only think about her. How she does this little nose scrunch when she finds something amusing. Or when she gives me a soft smile when sneaks up behind me. The way her eyes always catch my attention, the little fidgeting she does with her hands when embarrassed."

"You really noticed her, huh?"

Turning to Nari, Jiho looks down at eye contact, blushing, "How could I not? She holds the whole room's attention with her mere presence. No wonder why I call her a siren in my head."

The girls giggled, "No matter if I'm around her, or not Saoirse stays on my mind. She's all I can think about."

"I remember Eomma was the first to fall, but Appa fell harder. I think you fell first and harder." Min-Jung teased. Rolling his eyes, the man pulled her hair, earning a light slap on the arm.

"So," Iseul grabbed his phone off the table, waving it around, "do you text or call her more than us?" Jiho's eyes widened. He blinked a few times.

"I would also like to know this. I want to see pictures, too." Nari reached over, grabbed the phone, and held it to Jiho.

Taking the phone slowly, he tried to think of excuses for not having her number. How each time they met by accident, he forgot to get any form of contact with her.

Panicking, Jiho's eyes shifted left and right. Seeing the gear going in his head, Min-Jung gasped. The three older siblings looked at her.

"You have her number, right…?"

The words came out slowly. Wincing, he knew they caught him. He would never be allowed to live this down from any of them soon.

Iseul was the first to break into a fit of giggles, then Min-Jung, Nari, and finally Jiho. It was a simple thing to have, yet he did not.

The girls looked at one another before screaming a common phrase they nailed down when Jiho lacked common sense in everyday situations.

"You're an idiot!"

Chapter Twenty-Three

Ilya Repin

"WHY DON'T YOU THREE goes find us a seat while I order your usuals?"

The siblings had gotten out of the house for an outing. True to the nature of their manners, the three sisters drew straws to see who was going to dictate the day.

Iseul was the winner and had mapped out the entire day down to their food. She had been excited, much to the annoyance of Min-Jung who awakened to harsh, loud screams early this morning.

Agreeing with him, Iseul took the lead and picked a corner not too far, giving them privacy from others but still in view from the counter.

"Welcome, what can I get you?"

"Can I get two iced americanos, one ice mocha, and one cappuccino? And three breakfast bagels and…two of your avocado toast?" Jiho took out his wallet as he placed the order.

Getting a repeat of his order confirming the staff had heard correctly, Jiho paid before getting a small device indicating when the drinks were done.

Once he was within earshot of the table picked, he could tell the conversation was just for the three of them, as Min-Jung silenced them. Paused midair before carefully sitting beside Nari, he looked calculated at the three, "What are you guys doing…?"

"Nothing." The answer was simultaneously said, not easing Jiho's concern.

"Right."

Taking a moment to look at him, Iseul eyed the other two, trying to signal something in Jiho's direction. He wasn't stupid to just take their words without warning. Jiho grew up with the troublemakers.

They only got this quiet when they had something up their sleeves. Before he could ask or see what the girls were trying to do, the device went off-causing the man to hurriedly get their order.

Grabbing the tray, he thanked the staff before returning to his seat. With the caffeine in reach, each held their respectable regular orders.

Min-Jung was surprisingly into the cappuccino, something she had liked while abroad in different places. Iseul loved her mocha; whether it was iced or hot, she would consume it daily.

Nira and Jiho loved the simplicity of the americano–it could be sun or rain; they always have the cold drink in hand, sometimes with an extra shot.

Jiho was the one to hand food out to everyone. The twins had the avocado, although Iseul also had half of the extra bagel. Min-Jung usually ate one bagel and whatever the others couldn't finish. The additional order was for later when he eventually got hungry as he wasn't a morning eater as of late.

"They did not stir the chocolate all the way…" Iseul sighed in disappointment.

"You want mine?"

"No, it's okay. I know you don't like chocolate too much, and I can stir it myself. It's just a little annoying, is all." Iseul held her hand in protest as her brother reached over diagonally for the mocha.

Shrugging his shoulders, Jiho's eyes land on the lip of his cup. Written in marker is a number with a drawn-on smiley face. He was confused for a minute, unsure if the barista had mistaken his order with others, as there was no indication of any extra friendly behavior.

Looking up, he was met with a shy wave and smile from the barista who handed him the tray. Not that the person wasn't attractive to some, but she wasn't his type. Not sure how to reject the person without embarrassing them, Jiho looks away, tuning into the girls' conversation.

"-I was thinking we can have a little walk around this park not too far," Iseul shows them the map on her phone, "it's also a three-minute walk away from the restaurant."

"But won't we be tired of walking?" Nari questions, taking a big sip of her coffee.

Huffing a little, Iseul pouts, "We'll take little breaks here and there. Please? We will do your stuff tomorrow and Minnie's things the next day before we do things as a group."

One thing about Iseul that many people would not know when they first met her was her professional skill as a guilt-tripper. It is not necessarily a bad thing but not a good thing either.

Jiho, Nari, and Min-Jung all looked at each other before nodding or voicing their agreement with her wishes. Clapping her hands in excitement, Iseul did a tiny dance in her seat.

With shame, Nari placed her face in her hands, Min-Jung laughed and Jiho just smiled. He was about to comment when a throat cleared beside him. Seeing what caused the sound, he found the shy barista.

The happy mood died as soon as the worker came up to him. A coat of blush scattered her cheeks and the tip of her ears. It was clear to everyone that this person was nervous.

Nari was the first to speak, switching out of their native language. Having siblings fluent in English helped her with conversation.

The twins could hold their own while speaking the foreign language only briefly. Just enough to get their point across, her words coming out a bit awkward, "Can we help you?"

"Um, I was wondering if…um…you happened to see the number on your cup…?" Her voice was timid, causing him to have a hard time hearing.

He nodded.

The pink hues darken with every word, "Cool. I didn't know if you did, so I had to make sure…Did you want to maybe go out sometime…?" Jiho gave her some respect. This was clearly something out of her comfort zone: coming to someone and asking them out.

But he couldn't.

Not when he's planning on doing the same to Saoirse, whenever he sees her again.

"No." Iseul answered. She may not entirely like the idea of Saoirse, but this *foreigner* was not the one for her brother. Iseul was sure of it.

"I'm sorry, are you his girlfriend…?" A level of defeat was placed in her question.

"No, sister; we all are. You are just not his type." Iseul spat, her English better than Nari's. When Min-Jung sends her a pleading look, she only continues, "He likes confidence. A woman of class. One who doesn't act like a child. So, the answer is no."

Jiho called her name quietly, indicating she had gone too far with speaking for him. He could see that his sister had become a *little* harsher over time.

There were times on their sibling trip when people would flirt with him, and the girls would reject whoever came his way before he could himself.

Nari was a simple 'no,' while Min-Jung lied that he had a girlfriend already or that his wife was waiting for him. But Iseul was mean with her answers, ensuring they would never be tempted to ask again.

"Oh…umm…okay." The poor girl looked like she was going to cry. It seemed to take a lot for her to approach Jiho, and Iseul destroyed her small courage in seconds.

"Iseul Eonni." Min-Jung spat her name, switching back to their preferred language. Hitting her arm hard, "Why must you be so rude?"

"What? She asked a question, and we know Oppa can't turn someone down properly, so I ensured she would never ask again if he ever came back here." Shrugging her shoulders.

Sighing, Jiho knew she was right about the rejection part. He would always feel bad or say worse things to keep people away. He remembered rejecting an old classmate when she finally asked him out. The girl ran away crying after Jiho listed reasons why he would never be with her in the way she wanted.

In simple terms, Jiho was a fucking dick to people back during his schooling days, something he has worked on with the help of Ally, and just like his physical damage, his verbal ones hurt the same.

"She was scared, Iseul-ah. A simple, 'he has a girlfriend' would have done the trick."

"I thought you were serious about this, *Saoirse*?" Her voice held some disgust and resentment that Jiho had ignored, "Do you not want her anymore, Oppa?"

"I do want her."

"Then there's no need to give that girl hope you might be on the market."

Taking the last sip of her drink and popping the last piece of her bagel, Iseul stood up, indicating that she was over the debate on her behavior and wanted to leave. Since it was her day, the three stood, walking behind her.

Their first stop would be across the street at the art museum, where they were having a showing of realism art by three of her favorite artists: Ilya Repin, Gustave Vourtbet, and Edouard Manet.

Not knowing when she'd have access to this opportunity again, Iseul brought her non-flash camera and two sketchbooks to fill as much as she could before they had to leave, as the family agreed to after an hour and a half there.

If it were up to Iseul, she would stay at the museum till the staff kicked her out, but Min-Jung could not stand in one place long enough and look at the artwork as she was more interested in reading about the detail, being engrossed with the swoon-worthy words. It was something she was grateful Jiho had taught her.

Before entering primary school, Min-Jung hated to read; she would rather play outside and watch the dramas their mother had on. But she got curious when she found Jiho sitting on their back deck one summer, a book in hand.

That day, till he had to leave, he would read to her and sometimes the twins–when they had time to join after their own hobbies. It was peacefully captivating how Jiho would read, translating the words to fit how the author, in her opinion, would have wanted.

Seeing how excited her older sister was about this, she would cave into staying another hour if questioned.

Nari loved visiting museums with her sister as it gave her inspiration for new stencils and design styles. This is why she also had her own sketchbook and camera with her.

Jiho didn't mind attending these things with the twins; he could enjoy these creative individuals' work. Crediting them for doing what they loved–having the ability to push through some people's judgment and ridicule. It allowed him to daydream of a different life where he could have been whatever he wanted.

Jiho had paid in advance for the tickets, wanting to give his middle sister a fast pass into her domain of expertise.

He was lucky that there were few visitors today, giving them a more intimate atmosphere as they slowly walked by each piece, admiring the time it took to complete and the work it took for such detail. Min-Jung was off in her own little world as she sat not too far from his line of vision, finding one painting interesting.

Nari was two paintings away, frantically looking up and down from her sketchbook and the painting in front of her.

There were many intricate gowns in the one she was seeing, not knowing how some ruffles, puffs, and hemming enhanced certain features, fitting the body without misconfiguration of natural bodies during those times.

Iseul was on the other side of the room. Standing face-to-face with Gustave Corbet's work, a self-portrait of himself. His hair was a mess, his hands were tangled in them, and a wild look was placed on his face.

Jiho saw the tears well in her eyes.

Knowing it was a piece that spoke to her more personally, Jiho left her to her own devices in admiration. She had always had this soft spot for the raw emotions past artists were able to capture just by memory alone.

Jiho took his time watching as each family member had their own experience. His eyes stopped on one painting.

Walking closer to the painting, he read the little information card placed next to the work on the bottom right corner—*Ivan the Terrible and His Son Ivan by Ilya Repin, painted on 16 November 1581*—a cord of ache struck Jiho's heart.

It was painful to relive that feeling.

Kyong's words still echoed in his head every day. Taeyoung's reassurance was something he also reminded himself of out loud every day.

These old conversations were the things to help Jiho when days seemed too challenging to continue, having the guilt crawl back into his soul. His connection to the devastating man, whose eyes burned red with sadness, brought many hidden and forgotten emotions to Jiho.

Feeling the cold around him be replaced with warmth, he blinked away, tears forming. The girls saw him walk towards one of the paintings as if he were in a trance, worried about its effects on him.

They were all on edge.

Iseul was the first to understand what was happening. She did not think *that* painting would be here, unable to give her brother a proper heads up.

Min-Jung saw her sister's fallen face, rushing to Jiho, wanting to be there to comfort him as much as possible. Nari was the furthest away, but her slight jog made her reach Jiho simultaneously as the other two.

"You okay, Oppa…?" Nari's worry was noticed.

"I'm sorry…I wouldn't have suggested coming if I knew this one would be shown. I thought it was already bought for a private collection." Iseul's frantic statement eased his tense posture.

"I'm okay." His voice was shockingly even, causing all three to look at him suspiciously. "I just remembered some things. But I'm okay, I promise."

Tugging at his sleeve, Min-Jung became the center of attention, "You sure? I know it's hard to see some things, and we," pointing to herself, Nari, and Iseul, "all worry for you. We care for you and your mental health. So, are you sure you're, okay?"

Jiho let out a sound of conformation, almost like a hum. Bringing his attention back to the painting, admiring it again.

"It's crazy to think something from the 1500s would have a strong connection in the present. It makes you think about what–from this point in time–will make an impact in the future."

The girls all looked at the painting. They didn't fully understand the extent of relatability this had on their brother. It was a stunning, extraordinary painting, but they couldn't and probably will never understand how much this art meant to Jiho.

The seconds turned to minutes as the four siblings stood there, trying to wrap their heads around the importance.

The pain in the man's eyes as he cradles his boy, the blood seeping from his head onto the father's hand.

The objects in the painting, around the father and son, had been knocked over, the rugs overlapping, some bunched up, messing up the perfection the floor once had before the loss. The light shined on the two while darkness was behind them.

An emotional piece that Jiho wished to have but knew it would never serve him in the way he needed. The way Jiho knew he needed to heal. This painting would only serve as a negative reminder, but a reminder, nonetheless.

Iseul wanted to improve the atmosphere by telling them she was done with the museum. The other two saw what she was doing. Agreeing to this, they pulled Jiho away from his trance, babbling about the cool things they would do and see while looking around for little shops.

Jiho had a gut feeling that this day would have something unexpected happen. All Jiho could do was wait for whatever his sisters were planning, praying that it wasn't bad.

Chapter Twenty-Four

Run In

THE SIBLINGS WALKED side-by-side in twos: Iseul with Min-Jung and Nari with Jiho.

Although the two youngest tend to get on each other's nerves, they were getting along well at the moment-it was a weird predicament.

They entered pop-up shops; ones where handmade items were being sold, they stopped in each one, where Jiho paid for most things.

Most of the time spent in the shops was him complementing his sisters in all the outfits they had come out in. Although the three Yoo daughters had different styles and ways of dressing, they could use the same clothing item and put their personal taste into it.

"It's almost time for our reservations. Should we head over?" Nari states, checking her watch, a gift their father had given her for winning a design contest in her first year at university.

It had just dawned on Iseul that all their time was spent looking around this shopping center, and they didn't even walk around the park like she wanted.

The day wasn't going according to plan, irritating the girl, but nonetheless, she enjoyed her time, so there was no need to sulk too much over it.

"How far of a walk is the place from here, Oppa?"

Checking the time on his phone, ensuring they did not go too far from their end destination: "It is about a twenty-minute walk if we take these shortcuts."

Min-Jung was chanting out the restaurant's name, bouncing from one foot to another, excited for a change of environment.

Instead of Iseul taking the lead, Min-Jung snatched her brother's phone before dragging her sister towards the food.

His disapproval could be heard, as well as Nari's snickers. The first daughter knew why her sisters had taken his phone and were trying to get there as fast as possible, wanting the surprise to be a surprise.

Snaking her arm around her brothers, interlocking them, the two followed at a slower pace but were still able to keep up.

During their short walk, Jiho took the opportunity to check on her. He felt their relationship was a little less than the other two as she was so secretive with her emotions, "So, how are you doing these days?"

"That's how you're going to start this conversation?" She laughs at his awkward nature.

Shrugging, he looked away from her gaze.

"I'm okay. Nothing new, really."

"But something is going on, isn't there?" Jiho counters.

He knew she hated being open to others and sharing her feelings, but he wanted to be a support system for her. Expectantly, now that he's making progress in healing.

"Tell me what's going on? How is school? Friends?"

Nari pondered. For so long, she had kept things from Jiho, not wanting to add more problems to his life, "Well, school is going fine. I've made top marks in my classes, and my teacher has brought up internships for designer companies near home and in Japan."

"That's great!" Jiho's face lit up at the news, ruffling her hair a little, "How come I've never heard about this till now?"

Her face contorted into insecurity; it wasn't kept from him specifically. In fact, the whole family didn't know. Not even Iseul knew of this, and they did live together, "It just never came up in our calls. It's not a big deal-"

"It is Nari-yah. Don't act like it's a passing grade." A habit she never truly broke. Thinking that her accomplishments never meant a lot to others, "This is what you worked so hard for."

"I guess."

"You guess?" Jiho's eyebrow shot up.

Nari was silent.

Scoffing at his sister's nonchalant attitude, he scolded her, "This is something to celebrate and announce to everyone. What's making you hesitant? Do you think your dreams aren't important?" Nari was caught, her sharp inhale told him, "Why do you think that?"

"Why wouldn't I?" She answered after a few minutes of nothing, "It's always been you…and Eun-Ya's dream…"

"…What?"

"Christ, Oppa."

The woman muttered under her breath. Jiho waited for her to continue the much-needed rant.

"All our lives, we've been told to be careful of you. To make sure you reach your goal. My earliest memories with Appa and Eomma were being told not to mention Eun-Ya unless you did. I didn't know who that was till I was in my teens."

Jiho never knew this. He found it odd that the girls always tensed at the name, thinking it was because they knew what had happened and felt pained hearing it. He never thought their parents would put a ban on the topic.

"We could never mention our wants and needs without people bringing you up. How you needed to be the priority. So, I just stopped talking. Appa would find some past awards we won, buying us these gifts to compensate for not being there, but it's meaningless."

"Yoo Nari!" Jiho semi-shouted, "You matter, okay?"

"Wha-"

"You matter. Your dreams matter. Your work matters. Your accomplishments matter. Even your failures matter."

They had stopped altogether. The younger two's attention was caught by Jiho's shout. Seeing their older siblings were in a serious conversation, they stood out of earshot but within line of sight.

"You. Matter. I don't care what the fuck our parents told you. If I didn't say it, then it's not true. Did I tell you not to mention her?"

"No…" Nari said meekly.

"Did I ever tell you my goals in life outweigh yours? Iseul-ah or Minnie's?"

"…No."

"So why did someone else's words overrule mine?" He asked.

It was a valid question; *why did she not just ask him*? Growing up, Nari wanted to, but the warnings her parents, grandparents, and neighbors all gave made it hard too. So, she opted to ask those around to get the information she wanted.

"I wanted to. I just couldn't."

Squeezing her arm, Jiho was able to get her attention solely on him instead of the trees around them, "Ask me next time, and I will fly out just for you. No matter how small or big it is. I can always take my meeting through a call." The last sentence made her smile, "Your dreams matter. And I want to celebrate with you, Iseul-yah, and Minnie. Always."

Nari nods, "I hope you know I'm not going to be all teary-eyed because of this…"

Jiho lets a booming laugh out, his head thrown back. The younger two see the happy mood, letting out a sigh of relief. His cheeks hurt from his grin, "I would never dream of it."

"Good. Now, let's go. I'm starving, and that talk made me even more hungry."

Within three minutes, the four were in front of oak doors. Stained glass in the middle, shaped like an oval and handles were vertical, reaching from the top to the bottom.

Holding the door, the girls entered from oldest to youngest before Jiho entered, making his way to the front.

"Welcome. Do you have a reservation?" The host asked. He was simply breathtaking, in Jiho's opinion. Although he was very much attracted to the opposite sex, he had no problem admitting when someone was beautiful.

The host seemed to be around Min-Jung's age but held such professionalism that was making Jiho doubt his ability to guess correctly.

"Yes, should be under Y-" he was interrupted by a voice that had relentlessly tortured his mind, body, and soul since they met.

The same voice that not even a few weeks ago whimpered under him from just a kiss. He wanted to see her again, just not with his judgmental sisters-some more harsh than others.

Saoirse was in front of him, in all her glory.

"*Mon amour?*"

She was again in lighter clothing, but there was a difference. When they shared a rather intimate moment, Saoirse wore a dress that flowed around her body without revealing her shape.

The clothing was loose fitting except in the chest, the only tight silhouette to be seen. Now, the woman was in a white-on-white pantsuit with a lace top. Her figure showed throughout, not hiding anything.

This was still a more pleasing color pallet to Jiho. The tones not only suited her complexion more than the darker ones, but like his reasoning last time, she looked relaxed, free from any responsibilities.

Although today, it would seem she was attending meetings or some higher clients with the powerful sight and she was capable of handling everyone in the room without a second thought.

He had missed her.

His mind, once again, had not done her justice.

"Saoirse." Jiho whispers, afraid his mind is playing tricks. The woman gave a soft smile, her eyes gleamed.

Before she could get close to him, Saoirse was startled by the sudden repeat of her name by the three girls beside him.

"Saoirse!" Each having a different reaction.

One was heckling, the other snaring, and the last joyful.

It was very unsettling for Jiho to see. He knew at that moment they had something to do with the run in. He just hoped they wouldn't embarrass him or scare her away.

Chapter Twenty-Five

Awkward

AFTER KNOWING LOOKS Nari, Iseul, and Min-Jung gave him, they all stood there, unsure of what to do.

Min-Jung knew she would be the main speaker for the three sisters as she could fluently translate the questions they had in their minds. It was better for her to speak as Jiho would want to keep the peace.

Jiho and Saoirse felt uneasy with their stares. He could not entirely stop his sister's plan, but that did not mean he couldn't do some damage control along the way.

Trying to figure out who these people were, Saoirse was irritated. The judgmental looks for two of them, and the curious one made the following words out of her mouth come off as standoffish.

"I'm sorry, who are you three?" She crossed her arms, popping her hip to the side, challenging them.

Iseul shot both eyebrows up, shocked at the woman's tone towards them. It was one thing to be suspicious of people, but to be so bold to outwardly question them in that manner sent her over the edge.

Sticking to their native language, Iseul asked who she was talking to in that way, her eyes burning with disgust. Confused by what she was saying, Saoirse looked at Jiho for an explanation.

Manners were a big thing that was instilled in Iseul at a young age as well as the other three. Seeing this woman who looked around their own age be high and mighty sent her into a frenzy.

Nari nudged her sister, calling her name out quietly, telling her to stop. She opposed Iseul for going off the plan, knowing things would be in chaos once the opportunity showed itself, but they were twins; they shared a womb for nine months, she would stand with her.

Min-Jung hissed quickly at both, telling the twins to be quiet and to stop with their looks and hasty attitude. She tried to be discreet, though Saoirse still heard them speaking in Korean. Turning back to the woman, Min-Jung smiled pleasantly before introducing themselves as Jiho held his head in his hands.

"Ignore her. That's what I usually do. Anyways, I'm Min-Jung, but I do go by Minnie. These are the twins Nari and Iseul." Pointing to each, "We are Jiho's younger sisters."

She giggled at the shocked face Saoirse had. It was pleasing to her to see such a reaction come from someone older than her.

Hearing the introduction, Jiho peeked through his hands to see the realization hit Saoirse like a truck. He never brought up the sibling topic while they bumped into each other; now it's come to bite him in the ass.

It's not that he would have never told her about his family–he would have–but Jiho never got the chance to ask for contact information from her or anyone else he knew, making it hard to see the siren.

As he was looking at her, he caught a glimpse of the host getting closer to her. Jiho reaches over, grabs Saoirse by the wrist, and gently pulls her into his arms in a blinding blaze of possessiveness. Their bodies were pressed together.

He had missed how her soft skin felt against his hands, the golden speckles in her eyes that shone under the sun through the skylights.

There was nothing in the world that Jiho wouldn't do to stop time as it was and just be in Saoirse's embrace. Her nose scrunched up as Jiho realized he had been staring at her for a while now.

The boy was confused, and so was everyone else. He had no idea what was happening, and the sisters blinked at Jiho's sudden surge of confidence in making the bold move that would typically not be seen in their hometown.

"Umm…can you let go of my sister?"

THE SIX SAT AROUND a circular table in a private room. Not wanting to cause any more of a commotion in the front of the house, the host–Brandon Welsh–had gotten another staff member to cover for him.

The two families were eyeing each other; Jiho sat in the middle, his eyes to his lap, between Saoirse (holding her hand) and Nari. Next to Nari was Iseul, who had to sit next to Min-Jung, pouting at her brother's choice in woman.

Being the friendly one of the three, Min-Jung understood Saoirse wanting to sit between Jiho and Brandon, having that sense of comfort with three strangers nearby.

"Thank you for not kicking us out after someone," Jiho sent a disapproving glare at Iseul, who only looked around the room to avoid his gaze, "decided to show her rude side."

"Don't thank me." Brandon said sharply, "If I had it my way, you would never be allowed to step back here." Huffing, the young Welsh boy crossed his arms, "So why don't you tell me why your sister decided to be rude to mine, and how do you know her?"

Shooting a question within a question, Brandon tapped his finger on the table, waiting.

He felt something was going on in Saoirse's life lately as she came home smiling after meeting their cousin's new girlfriend, the problem at the banquet, and the bar, three things she had never found joy in doing before.

"Donny." His attention was pulled to Saoirse, giving him a warning look, "Be civil, please. I didn't exactly have my arms open to them. Iseul-" saying her name as a question towards Jiho, who confirmed she pronounced it correctly, "was just responding in the same tone as I did." Jiho squeezed her hand as a gesture of appreciation for her understanding, "I am sorry for sounding like a-"

Cutting off the woman's sentence, Iseul spat out a few words, still in Korean, as she cut into her food. Smirking at the two confused people.

"Iseul-yah!" Jiho slammed his hand on the table, startling everyone. He could feel Saoirse tense at the action, trying to pull away.

Fuck.

His thoughts were running all over the place.

Iseul had promised to behave when she finally got to meet Saoirse, but calling her such a nasty name was too far for Jiho to handle any more disrespect.

"Apologize or wait outside."

Bewildered by the two options, Nari tried to calm him down, placing her hand on his shoulder. Calling his name sweetly, trying to find any sympathy in him.

"No." Jiho shrugged her hand off, "She's being nasty without reason. I won't let you both make a fool of our family with this behavior. Apologize."

Nari and Iseul both looked at one another. This was not their first time being scolded by their brother, but it was the first time he'd done it in front of someone besides family.

Min-Jung predicted this meeting between Iseul and Saoirse would be a shit show as soon as her sister opened her mouth in front of the other customers.

Deciding to find more interest in the spread before her, she kept her words in, with no intention of being Jiho's next target on his shit list, something she's lucky never been on.

She felt terrible for the woman as her sister's words were quite colorful. Not that Saoirse understood what they were saying, if she did, there would have been a fair fight.

Feeling a tap on her shoulder, Min-Jung turned to see Brandon motioning her to come closer to him,

"Why does your sister hate mine?" Shifting his eyes between her and the other four before them, he spoke softly, "What did she say about my sister?"

There was hesitation on her part, she could tell him and see where that led, but she could also keep quiet and avoid being thrown into an argument between the older ones.

Taking the first option, Min-Jung leaned over her right side.

"Iseul Eonni doesn't like the idea of Oppa dating, especially a foreigner. She promised to be nice but changed her mind when your sister didn't greet us nicely." The two spoke in hushed whispers, not trying to have the arguing group see what was going on, "And she basically called her every name in the book."

Hearing some shrieks here and there, the two looked up, seeing Iseul red in the face and Jiho with sadness and anger. Nari had tried to get her sister's attention to calm her down, and Saoirse just sat there confused as ever, squeezing Jiho's hand whenever Iseul would glare at her.

"Now she's going on a tangent on why she shouldn't apologize when she's not getting one back."

"...That seems kind of stupid...no offense."

"None-taken." Min-Jung smiled, "She needs to know Oppa is in control of his own life, not her. Even if that means getting yelled at for the first time."

"Your brothers never yelled at you?" Brandon was astounded.

Shaking her head, she pouted, "No, he just stops talking to us, but he needs to step up. Tell the twins they are overstepping. Take charge of his life for himself."

Brandon looked at the youngest with more respect than started. She was more mature in his eyes than her sisters.

Seeing the recognition on his face, Min-Jung continues, "My brother may be book smart, but he's new to the real world of people. I, however, am not." She chuckled shyly, "I help by listening; my sisters talk over him. Something I can't help with unless he wants to help himself."

At the end of her sentence, they both realize the arguing has stopped, greeted by the sight of an angry man, Nari holding on to Iseul and Saoirse in between the siblings-separating the three of them.

During their little conversation, Jiho and Iseul went back and forth on why she should apologize to Saoirse. He also wanted her to either be respectful or leave dinner.

There had been mentions of how Saoirse would end up like Eun-Ya, leaving him all alone and broken for the family to pick up again, sending Jiho on a warpath once those words left his sister's mouth.

Not knowing why she would say such things, especially after knowing about his past and having that heartwarming moment earlier, Nari had pulled Iseul up from out of her seat, getting as far as she could from Jiho, afraid of what would happen. He could not think straight; it was like he returned to his past self; a light switched inside him.

Saoirse only knew bits and pieces of what was happening as Jiho mixed his response in Korean and English, feeling the fight was getting worse by the minute. Once he had gone quiet, she knew something was said that could never be taken back.

Getting out of her own seat, she stood in front of the twins, making Jiho halt.

"*Mon amour*? What are you doing?" She slowly questioned, unconfident of what could occur.

She was troubled by the man in front of her. This was different from the person Saoirse had come to know within the last nine months.

She had heard things from Lisa about his university days, how he handled the Harriet boys for Daniella, and how cold Jiho was to people from Dmitry.

Jiho watched how apprehensive Saoirse was with him, and the judging eyes snapped him out of his angry daze. The overwhelming feelings crashed over him. His breathing became heavy and quickened by the second.

"*Mon amour*? Are you okay?" Seeing the conflicting emotions in his eyes, frantically looking around as his body shrunk into a ball, Saoirse motioned for everyone to leave.

Min-Jung knew about his panic attacks as he only really confided in her a few years ago. Quickly letting them know what was happening, Brandon showed the girls out, reluctantly leaving his sister behind at Min-Jung's advice.

Once out of the room, Saoirse stepped towards Jiho, wanting him to control how close she could get to him without being pushed deeper into a panic state. When he was within arm's reach, she opened her arms, and within seconds, he latched on to her, clinging to dear life just as he did when Emilia first helped him.

The comforting words helped his foggy mind become clear. The different texters he felt made him think of the tricks Ally had him do. Jiho began to list the three things in his head, finding them quickly, most of which were linked to his siren.

Saoirse had not tried to ask what happened when he pulled away. She only questioned his health, his awareness of the area around him, and what he needed from her.

"Water, please." His voice croaked, raw from the cries he had just screamed a few minutes ago.

Reaching over the table, balancing on the balls of her feet, she found a glass and some food left over on a small plate. Taking both in her hands, she sat in front of him, crisscrossed before handing him both.

A questionable look was there when Jiho saw the food. Giggling at his expression, Saoirse explained her reasoning.

"It helps fuel the body if you have food and water. If you can handle eating, I would greatly appreciate it."

He nodded and chugged down the drink before having a napkin held by his face. Wanting his siren to help, he leaned closer, allowing Saoirse to wipe the dribbles of water that missed his mouth.

There was no conversation as he ate the food on the plate; Saoirse wanted him to talk when he was ready, not when she wanted, knowing it was hard for some to show that side of themselves to people they hardly know.

Once finished, Jiho leaned back against the wall, shutting his eyes before exhaling deeply. He stared at the ceiling once they were open, which had a moral painting, showing the elegant brushstrokes bringing him peace of mind. It was the calming atmosphere that he wished to have had to begin with.

But that was too much of a thing to ask for.

To pray for.

He let out an amused sigh. Saoirse looked over at him, finding his gaze was already on her; giving him a half smile, "I'm all ears if you want to talk."

Taking a moment, he took all her in. The pinned hair, light blush, and bare fingers cupping her own face-patiently waiting.

"I really wanted to see you." He confessed. Seeing the corner of Saoirse's lips lift higher, he quickly continued, "I just didn't think it would be with my sisters."

"Yeah," she scoffed, "I don't think they like me...at least the twins don't."

He ran his scarred hands over her soft ones, "I'm sorry for them. I don't know what was happening in their head, but they should not have been so rude."

Resting her head on his shoulder, Saoirse shrugged, "I understand."

Looking down at her, he made a sound of confusion.

"I would be a little mean towards potential partners with my family members." Chuckling at her memories, she said, "I was a little mean with Ally, but after she told me about her intentions with Eric and said I reminded her of a friend she had, I kind of let my guard down."

"Ally's a good girl." Pausing he cleared his throat, flushed, "And I'm glad she's with Eric."

"Can I ask you something now?"

He nodded, facing her straight on, "Of course."

"What did your sister say that made you snap like that?"

He looked down, tracing shapes on her skin, sighing at her question.

"Does it have anything to do with these markings over your body?" She raised his hand, "I also remember seeing some scars on your arms and chest."

Straightening his posture, he confessed licking his dried lips, "I am not perfect. I have seen some things that shouldn't have happened to a child, and I've done some questionable things as a person. I don't have a strong mind."

Taking a breath, bringing his eyes to hers, "I am healing from something difficult to talk about right now…It's fucked with me for a long time, and I have no idea what I'm doing. I'm a complete mess underneath my appearance."

"We are all a mess, *mon amour*." Scooting closer to him, Saoirse looked deeply into his eyes, cupping his face tenderly. "That's what makes us human. It's okay; you don't need to have everything figured out, and you can tell me when you feel ready."

Saoirse's smile was infatuating. Grabbing the back of her neck, Jiho rested his forehead against hers.

He was content.

He was at peace with her around.

Jiho wanted to stay this way for as long as he could with no interruptions, without his family's comments and their views.

He wanted to be there for her as she was there for him.

He wanted his siren to be his officially.

Pulling back, he looked around her face, memorizing every detail. He engraved them in his mind in case his question would be rejected.

Letting an airy chuckle, Saoirse asked, "Why are you looking at me?"

"This might not be the right timing, but" taking his phone out, "can I finally have your number and take you on a date?"

Chapter Twenty-Six

Solutions

THE DAY ENDS AS Jiho bids goodbye to Saoirse and her brother, apologizing for the mess his sister has caused.

Saoirse paid no mind to the actions of his family as she was not concerned with their view of her, seeing as they didn't know her.

Brandon had regarded the family in a bad light, and the only redeeming members were Jiho and Min-Jung, especially the girl. So much so that the two exchanged contact information. It is difficult for Brandon to find and make friendships due to his family name.

Once they left, the walk was silent. Even the car ride had no music playing in the background.

Min-Jung sat in the passenger seat as the twins were in the back. Jiho had no strength in him to argue anymore.

Conflicted with his sisters, he was unable to wrap his head about their actions. They were the ones to help when times had gotten rough between their parents and him; now, he wanted them to leave after only day three.

Opening the front door, he went to the kitchen. Nari and Iseul followed him, but still, no words were exchanged between the three of them. Min-Jung had stayed away but was close enough to them in case it resulted in another panic attack.

Jiho was still unaware the two had chased after him, as his back was facing them. Once he had taken the last drop of water from his glass and placed it in the sink, he turned around, jumping. The two had scared him in the process of not speaking.

"Yes?" His demeanor held defeat–he was already over the conversation. Nari bumped her shoulder into Iseul, clearly telling the woman to speak.

"I'm sorry…" Iseul mumbled out.

"Iseul-ah…!" Nari whispered-yelled, annoyed at her sister for forgetting.

Jiho had a problem with those who mumble when apologizing; if you could not speak in a clear, loud voice so that the other person could hear how sorry you were, then you weren't apologetic in the first place.

"Okay, okay." Straightening up, Iseul finally got the courage to look their brother in the eye, "I'm sorry I acted like a complete bitch to Saoirse and her brother. I'm sorry I said those things about Eun-Ya and compared her to Saoirse. I'm sorry I caused you to have a panic attack. I'm sorry I hurt you, Oppa."

Min-Jung poked her head at the second 'I'm sorry' to see Jiho's face remain still. She was somewhat surprised.

Usually, all they had to do was apologize, and they were forgiven. Returning to Jiho's good graces was easy, but this time was different. Instead of a smiling face, all there was a stoic expression that was out of character.

"I don't believe you Iseul-ah…" Jiho crossed his arms with dismay; her face fell, "I just can't. Not after I asked you to respect my decision and Saoirse. At the first chance, you disregarded my wishes and became this person I don't know or wish to know." Each sentence hurt more than the last as Jiho spoke the truth, "I cannot believe the amount of hate you have for a person you don't even know."

He scoffed in disbelief, "I never thought of you, Yoo Iseul, to come out the gate with this crown on your head, thinking you are better than everyone. Thinking you have every right to pretend not to speak English. Not only making rude comments in front of Saoirse but also leaving her confused about what you were saying."

"Oppa I ju-"

"Just? Just what? Just sorry for making someone feel less than for not knowing a language we four speak?" Jiho kept his face neutral. He had been so close to booking her and Nari an early flight home for the stunt they had pulled.

"Oppa," Nari steps in the spotlight, shielding a teary-eyed Iseul, "she just wanted to ensure this random woman was good enough for you."

"Good enough for me?" The question felt weird between his lips. His face scrunched, displeased, "How would someone be good enough for me? What are the standards?"

"She has to be caring-" Nari blurts.

"You all saw how she was with me during and after my panic attack caused by you." His eyes darted back over to Iseul, still hiding behind Nari.

Taking a moment to think, Nari counters, "She has to be willing to have children."

Shaking his head, he said, "That's up to her and her alone. It is her body; I will not make her go through anything she doesn't want to. And we can always adopt a child if it comes to it."

"They have to have their career in order."

"Saoirse has a full-time job that I don't think she can leave anytime soon." Rolling his eyes, he grew tired of these silly little things that were the reasoning behind their actions.

"The person has to speak our language." Iseul fires.

"She doesn't have to be fluent. Only enough to talk about basic things with Eomma and Appa, who both speak decent English-" Jiho counters.

"She has to be Korean!" Iseul spat.

Scowling his eyebrows, the corner of Jiho's lips turned into a frown, "What?"

Taking a step forward, Iseul spoke slowly, "She has to be Korean, same as us."

Jiho was astonished and frankly repulsed by his sister's blatant prejudice against foreigners. It wasn't something he had thought was such an issue for the others.

He could understand the reasoning from his grandparents and maybe his parents, but his sister, who has never brought up foreigners as an issue, wholly blinded him.

Min-Jung felt the same; she could not believe what was happening.

After Jiho had stated he did not believe in Iseul's apology, Min-Jung video-called Brandon in case something was to happen and needed some help. Brandon had heard all that was unfolding, thanks to Min-Jung. The two were confused, just as Jiho was.

"Why does she have to be Korean?" He placed his palms on the flat countertops, leaning on them for support, "Why is it such a bad thing to be a foreigner now? What about Ally? You didn't have a problem with her being close to me? Why now? Why Saoirse?"

Nothing was making sense anymore.

"You can have foreigners as friends but as a wife?" Iseul shook her head, unable to imagine it, "That's ridiculous even for you, Oppa."

He was desperate to understand his sisters' logic, gripping at the roots and running his hands through his hair.

He was stunned at her stupidity.

Her views were too much for him now; Jiho did not want to fight about this anymore.

"I'm going to bed to sleep on what you just told me, hoping it was all part of a dream." He slowly backed away. This was not his little sister; this was not someone he knew. This was a different person who he wanted no part of as her views were shocking and disgusting to him, "But if not, we'll talk about it in the morning."

Opening his door, Jiho found Min-Jung under the covers in one of his hoodies with some candy spread out and Brandon still on the phone. Seeing this funny sight, he broke into a silent fit of giggles, ensuring the other two downstairs didn't hear.

"Don't laugh." Min-Jung pouted, "I wanted to make sure you went to bed okay, and Randy didn't want to leave-"

"I didn't want to leave?" The boy yelled through the phone, utterly shocked at Min-Jung's bold statement.

Rolling her eyes, she huffed, "Okay. I didn't want to hang up until you came to bed. You know, just to be sure."

Giving her brother a big smile, she said goodbye to the Welsh boy. Tossing her phone to the side, holding her arms open. Jiho quickly made it to his sister before engulfing her in a hug.

"I'm glad you are the normal one out of the four of us, Minnie." His words were muffled.

His face was buried on the girl's shoulder. Their hometown always said the first and last born shared a more profound connection than the others-something Jiho would constantly deny, but deep in his heart, he knew it was true.

Min-Jung had never once judged him or anything he had done. Instead, the girl would ask questions and become curious about how her brother's mind works compared to others.

"We both know this family is far from normal, especially the two of us." Min-Jung hums, pulling back before stating seriously, "I didn't know she would say all of that, by the way." Jiho stared intensely at her, confused about why she would make something clear to him. "We had a plan…"

"A plan?" He moved, crawling to the empty side of the bed, now in front of Min-Jung, "What do you mean a plan?"

"You didn't think Eonni really wanted to try French food, right?"

"Then why did she want to go-" The confusion morphed into a state of recognition. Jiho wondered how he could have missed such a change in her behavior. Iseul only ate three food styles, and the French was one.

Nodding, she held her phone up, turning so they could see the screen without trouble, "We found Saoirse online, and with all the media watching her, it wasn't hard to find where she was going to be this week."

The oncoming headache was putting another damper on his mood, "And why did the three of you want to know where she was going to be this week?"

"Well, we wanted to meet her, of course." Swiping her tabs around on her screen, a blog showed a photo of Saoirse, Brandon, and two other men. Zooming in on the faces of each person, Min-Jung introduced them, "This is her brother, Niall Welsh, and brother-in-law, Leo Welsh. Leo is a well-renowned Chef based in France who is opening his second location here."

"According to the blog, Randy will run the place for a few months while they interview and transfer people." She ranted, "That's how we knew Saoirse would be there this week. She's helping with the financial part and the media."

"But how did you know she would be there today?"

Locking her phone, she shook her head, "We didn't; that's why we planned to go there every night until our last day here. We just got lucky on the first try." She shrugged.

Jiho pondered on the sheer luck the youngest always had in her research and timing. It was a little unsettling how much she could know in her short time, "So what was the plan? Was Iseul-ah supposed to act that way?"

True to their nature as sisters, Iseul was tasked with being the 'hard' one in acceptance, but apparently, she took it to heart. Min-Jung, of course, was the translator, and Nari would just sit there taking notes of any sudden behavior she thought to be suspicious or worrisome.

"No." She flung herself back, her head bouncing off the pillow a few times after the impact, "None of us were supposed to act like that. We were just going to give both of you a hard time and tease you with embarrassing stories. But after a few minutes, we would come clean, saying it was a prank before getting to know her."

Copying her movement, Jiho laid on his side. His hands tucked under his head, "So she was just saying whatever was on her mind?"

He asked slowly to process his question in a way that wouldn't downgrade Iseul, no matter how much he wanted to.

"Yep."

"Why didn't you step in after we all sat down?"

Tired after her day of excitement and horror, Min-Jung yawned, rubbing her eyes, "I can't always defend you, Oppa. You usually let us walk all over you, and it was time for you to stop that. It was also a test to see how serious you are about Saoirse."

Suffocating his face into the pillow, his scream of frustration and annoyance was muffled. Raising his head to see his little sister pass out, he sighed.

"What am I going to do with you?" Tucking her in properly, he took off her glasses, placing them on the bedside table.

Gently taking her phone from her grasp, changing it next to his own. Turning off the lamp, the only light source came from the moon, hitting Min-Jung's face and highlighting her features.

Their parents always told them how much they looked identical for being so many years apart, but the two never saw it. There were times when they might have agreed their eyes and nose were the same, thanks to their mother.

"You are too smart for your own good, Minnie."

THE FOLLOWING DAY, Jiho had gotten up early to leave the house. He didn't want to start his day by continuing the argument from yesterday.

Heading to the gym, he had asked Ally if she would like to tag along as hoping to catch up with one another.

Only taking a few minutes, he was under the building, where the parking garage was dedicated to members. Taking the elevator up, he saw Ally already checking in.

"Morning, Al."

"Ji!" Giving him a quick hug, she noticed the difference in his demeanor immediately. Tilting her head to the side, she spoke in a lower voice, trying to ask privately, "What happened?"

"The twins."

"Again?"

She was familiar with his disappointing side. The majority were towards his sisters and their actions. It was never this bad to where it affected him on the outside. Usually, the man buried it deep inside and waited until they were alone to talk about it.

"What did they do?"

"What didn't they do?" He grumbles.

The two began stretching, taking their time to have a safe workout. The gym had been more on the pricey side of things. Their business was held three stories out of the five-story building.

"Well, I have to give you a little backstory." Rotating his neck clockwise, he said, "There is this woman I've…developed feelings for."

"And I'm just finding out now?!"

Wincing at the angry expression on her face, Jiho rubbed his eyes in frustration.

"Yes, because I only met her by chance, and I just recently got her number. Do you want me to continue my dilemma or not?"

He saw Ally zip her lips, just like Min-Jung did when they first talked about Saoirse.

"Anyways, this woman happens to be Eric's cousin. Yes, it's Saoirse." Ally widens her eyes, still quiet to hear the rest of Jiho's life and his problems.

"Well, the girls found out and wanted to meet her. Unfortunately, I didn't have her number, so we couldn't do that yet. But you know them, give them a name, and they'll find you." Jiho inhaled.

"They set up this little plan, one they only knew, and found where she would be. Fast forward to seeing Saoirse, Iseul is just extremely mean to her. Making Saoirse feel like shit, but of course, Iseul only speaks Korean, so she doesn't truly know what is being said."

"Why would she do that?" Ally leaned forward, placing her chin on the palm of her hands as the model did a split, stretching her inner legs and hips.

"This is where I was shocked." Jiho's voice was shaky. He didn't know how she would handle the information, "Iseul doesn't believe I should be romantically involved with someone who isn't Korean..."

Pulling her head back, Ally looked in disbelief, "What...?"

"Iseul thinks foreigners are good friends but not for relationships. And I think Nari also believes that with how quiet she was during the conversation."

"That's such bullshit, Ji."

"I know Ally." He was so conflicted; how was he supposed to view his sister now after her thinking, "God, I know. I don't know what to do. I won't have her dictate my love life or push Saoirse away from me, but she is my sister. They both are."

"What about Minnie?"

"She doesn't understand how the two could think that either," he said. "She's the one who told me about their little plan and why she didn't jump into the conversation. She wanted me to finally defend myself and see how serious I am about Saoirse."

Scooting over, Ally put a hand in the middle of Jiho's back. "Are you serious about her, Ji? She's a bold person, and Eric respects her a lot and would probably try to beat you up if you did anything to hurt her."

He thought about it; to his knowledge, Eric didn't know his pursuit of the woman, but the others around the woman did.

"Ally." He paused, straightened up, "I've never wanted to be with someone like this. I want to spend my days with her and my nights. Since we first met, Saoirse has occupied my mind, and I have not been able to erase her from my memories. If I weren't serious about her, I would have never come clean about her existence to the three of them. I would still be holding her a secret, way from all of you."

"Why didn't you tell me…?" The hurt was there.

Scoffing dryly, Jiho rolled his eyes playfully, "Because I still haven't taken her on a date or even had her number till last night." Softening his features, he said, "Otherwise, I would have."

The two sat in silence.

"What are you going to do with the twins?"

"What can I do…?" The desperation was evident.

Taking another few moments to ponder on the solution to Jiho's sticky situation, Ally thought of it.

The only problem is that he might never have the same relations with the two girls at the end of all this. But it was the only option if he was serious and willing to take the chance on Saoirse.

Chapter Twenty-Seven

No Longer

HAVING SOME TIME TO think about Ally's idea and solution to the ordeal, his ride back home was full of possibilities.

He was scared, not wanting things to be forever changed within his family, but there had to be some repercussions to Nari's and Iseul's behavior, especially Iseul. He had messaged Min-Jung about his talk, asking if she had agreed to his friend's idea-which of course, she did.

Wanting to get rid of all the animosity within the household, he asked every one of the siblings to meet in the living room within the next hour so he could freshen up, going over his key points.

"You ready?" Min-Jung asked, hopping on his bed. He had just finished placing his clothing in the dirty hamper. She had never been one to knock or ask to enter places, which Jiho scolded her for multiple times, "You're going to be okay, right? I mean with whatever decision they pick."

He paused at the question.

It never occurred to him about what he would do or if he could accept the one possible outcome, he hoped they would not choose. This might be one of the last conversations the four have, which scared Jiho. The nervous feeling was seen through his failed attempts to stay calm.

"I'll be fine-"

"Liar." She could see from the other side of the world that her brother would break down today. It was just a matter of how severe it would be, "You do not have to do this if you aren't ready, you know. But you know as well as I do that if you don't, you can never truly be happy later in life."

Letting air out through his nose, he sat next to her. "Yeah," nodding his head, "I know. I have to, for me and my future."

She would never lie if asked what she admires so much about her brother. She would go into detail if able to, but there was one reason that places first every time, no matter who or when asked.

Min-Jung will always acknowledge the strength he had to have in being utterly loyal to his goals and promises. Not just the one to Eun-Ya. Or the one to Taeyoung. But the one to Kyong; to live for himself in this life. Jiho took his promise seriously, to the point where even his sisters could not interfere, even if it killed him to set that boundary and enforce it so harshly.

"Let's do this then."

Patting his back encouragingly. The two stood up; before Jiho could place his hand on the rustic knob, she gripped his wrist.

"I will support your decision no matter what. Even if I, too, have to be on the sidelines."

Jiho's heart felt heavy; the sorrow of his following actions, ones he had to come to terms quickly and painfully with, ultimately determined their relationship for life.

What he wanted to happen was for all of them to respect his decision and let him be with their support. But that was too much to ask for. The world had no room for such luxuries. No, the only thing the world could give was ache, sorrows, and unimaginable pain to those he had thought to be beacons of light.

He had witnessed loss too early in life. There was no child-like innocence within his body, as the only absolute purity was in horror. The carefree turned to fear after that day.

And now, if Jiho did not do this, he would see the plains of green wilt away, deprived, desperately wanting the tender, gentle care of a loving being.

"You will never have to be on the sidelines, Minnie. Not if I can have it my way." He hugged her, tightening his hold at the thought of her leaving him alone.

"I will if it is what needs to be done." Patting his back once more to soothe him, "I need you to be happy, Oppa. You've been pleasing others all my life, but never once did you think of yourself. Not until you spoke of Saoirse. So don't feel bad or regret if it comes down to choosing between us, okay?"

Pulling apart from the embrace, his eyes held conflict. "Why?"

Ghostly holding his face, Min-Jung flicked his forehead. It was his punishment for being so oblivious to the easy answer.

"Because a family you were born in is not necessarily more important than a family you find and make yourself. You need to follow what your gut and heart want, and this family, our family, is not what it should be. Not for you."

Jiho's bitter smile was paired with the airy scoff, "When did you get so wise?"

"When you spend most of your childhood and teen years socializing with others during your time abroad, you tend to hear a lot of lifetimes in one."

She looked down, recalling the places she had traveled so far. The girl was lucky–she knew it too–with all the experiences she could have with the help of her brother and parents.

Her time was not wasted as her studies were held at the top just like Jiho's, but the difference was that Min-Jung cared for her academics and exploration on the same level of importance.

She always needed to immerse herself in the community of the country she was studying in. Talk with older adults, hear their stories, and play with the young to relive her inner child. To take time to find peace with being alone, in her own company.

These were the things she learned, the things she loved. All Min-Jung wanted was the same for her older brother; she wanted him to be at peace, and for her, that was taking a chance with Saoirse.

"Let's do this?" She perked.

Laughing at the sudden change in mood, Jiho nodded. The man let her go first as he held the door open. He inhaled, descending the stairs where the other two were already waiting.

Nari and Iseul both had been in a panic since last night's argument, and their brother had been avoiding them until now. Iseul had no idea why he couldn't see things from her perspective; she was saving his reputation.

Not wanting to leave her twin alone, Nari was conflicted about what to think. On the one hand, she knew her sister's view was old-fashioned and downright prejudiced. On the other hand, she agreed to some extent with her little sister; it would be hard for her family to accept and communicate with a foreigner.

Nari wanted things to return to before they all split up in different directions. She wanted them to stay young and be the family they were before all this happened.

The twins were sitting beside each other on the love seat, while Min-Jung quickly took her spot on the single sofa-which she was grateful for as it was on the other side of the living room.

Jiho thought it was best for him to stand, not to be intimidating but to bring a sense of security where he could quickly get away if he needed to escape.

Clearing his throat, he took this last second to give himself an out, but the stern look on Min-Jung's face told him there was no going back.

"Okay, well, I've umm…" The man thought all the dragging out would happen at the middle or end, where the two would argue with him not as soon as he spoke.

"Oppa," Min-Jung hissed, "just tell them you'll be okay. I promise."

Eagerly, he nods. She was right; he'll be fine, "After thinking about all the 'fighting' that's been happening recently, I have two solutions." He frantically moved his eyes side-to-side, watching the two before him.

"And what are these solutions?" Nari spoke for them. Iseul's stoic face created an unreadable situation for Jiho.

"Well…You either apologize to Saoirse and her brother for the rude behavior and leave me to deal with my love life with the person of *my* choosing." He had emphasized, raising his voice on the word, to give them a clear understanding that he would not deal with their ideals and views.

"And the other option?" Iseul gritted, hating the underlying message between his words.

Glazing back at the youngest, looking for more encouragement, Jiho was granted a small smile telling him to continue.

"Or leave tonight. Go back home and never talk to me again until you can admit you both are wrong with how you handled things and what you have said…"

Iseul was enraged with her brother, and everyone saw that part. She could not believe what he was saying, picking between admitting she was wrong about something she wholeheartedly believed in or leaving and never speaking to her brother again.

Nari was still processing his second option.

Her body felt heavy, uncomfortable, and she wanted the couch to consume her whole to take her away from all this arguing.

She did not think Jiho would make such a massive difference in solution, at most a slap on the wrist, some extra scolding, or a phone call to their parents to complain about their forgotten manners.

Never did she think he would make them leave after only four days of their sibling reunion if they did not apologize to a stranger. A woman their brother had known for less than a year was being placed above them.

It wasn't fair, and it hurt her immensely; she could not find it in her to care about the woman. There were no thoughts about Saoirse; all Nari thought of her was something that would pass, nothing that would destroy her relationship with Jiho, but now she had nothing but hatred for the woman.

Unfortunately, the only one to see this change in behavior was Min-Jung, who watched both of her sisters intensely.

In Iseul's opinion, it was ridiculous to have such solutions when it came down to it, "You would rather side with *that*–" her eyes hardened. Instilling all emotions in her so the only thing you could see was disgust, "-*bitch* than your sisters? How could you put your family aside like this? I'm your sister, she's nobody. If you wanted to fuck her, that's fine but do not entertain this as a possible relationship. I won't let you!"

Jiho's mouth was ajar, stunned with the response to some degree. He did not think Iseul would be so straightforward with her words.

"I did not pick between you. That will be in your hands, not mine, Iseul-ah." Jiho spoke softly.

"You just declared that I am to say sorry to *her*," the word left out Iseul's mouth like venom, "or leave and never talk to you again. What would you call that besides picking that *woman* over your sisters?" She mocked.

"I call it taking responsibility for your actions and respecting my life choices. You both," he pointed accusingly at them, "were extremely rude, making disgusting comments about a person you both never met before. That was childish and immensely uncalled for."

Nari sprung up, her face contorted in a sneer, "Only because her attitude was rude."

"All three of you made her feel uneasy. How else was she supposed to respond? Besides, she apologized already."

"I don't care for her apology," Nari scoffed.

"You cannot have a romantic relationship with her, Oppa." Iseul moved closer to Nari, standing between them, "She will never understand our culture. Our customs-"

"When it gets to that point, I will teach her." Jiho cuts Iseul off.

"We are keeping your best interest at heart." Nari counters, aggression in her tone.

"I am old enough to make that decision." Jiho pleads, "She is worth me trying. I know I don't know her very well, but she occupies my mind every morning, day, evening, night: I see her in my dreams and always want to be near her."

"She will break your heart-"

"Then let her!" Jiho shouts, his neck muscles flexed from the intensity before calming back into its original state, "I will let her break my heart as many times as she wants. Why can't you understand that? I don't care if I am being unreasonable with my feelings; I want to be Saoirse's. I want to take control over who I pursue in life."

The atmosphere held tension unlike they'd ever known. It was suffocating, to say the least; its haunting hands gripped the air, cutting any oxygen they had left.

Sitting the entire time, Min-Jung approached Jiho and placed her hands tentatively on his forearm. The indication of a support system was there for Jiho, making him put his on top of hers, fumbling to hold her hand, a tight squeeze to ensure she was here for him.

"Eomma and Appa will be disappointed in you..." Nari breaks the silence.

Before Jiho could yell in retaliation, Min-Jung's voice held an eerie feeling as she spoke loudly and clearly, "That is not for you to decide, Yoo Nari."

The three were shocked at the youngest. No matter the culture, the full name was always terrifying to hear from a family member.

"Eomma and Appa will be told about what happens in Oppa's life when he wants to tell them. It is not for you to snitch on him whenever you can. Let him live his life the way he wants to."

"Of course, you side with him." Iseul mutters.

"I side with him because we've, all of us, at some point, taken advantage of him." She hung her head low.

She was never proud of how she used her brother in the past while she was just a child.

"He's kept his promise to help others and make something of himself. Now, it's time for Oppa to control his life and live for himself. And if that means chasing after a woman who might leave him broken…Then we have to be there to help pick up the pieces, not fight with him."

Jiho could cry at her small confession and reasoning. He was glad to see his sister grow so much; the little girl who clung to him had grown wise over the years and experiences that she had.

"You are no better than him." Iseul glared, "Fine if we have to decide…" Looking at her twin, Nari nodded, "We'll leave after packing, and don't bother driving us or getting a ticket. We'll call a cab." Scurrying off to their suitcase, Nari and Iseul did not spare another glance.

Jiho, feeling dizzy by the end, raced to sit, Min-Jung on his tail, "You did well, Oppa. I'm very proud of you." Her face showed sincerity.

After all the stress of trying to save their relationship, he was glad that one of the bonds with his sisters was saved. It would have broken him to have lost all three of them in one night.

"Thank you, Minnie." Resting his head on her shoulder, she ran her fingers through his hair, giving a subtle massage to help relax the stressed man, "You've grown."

Chuckling at his words slurring, Min-Jung did not fully understand them, "Of course, I've grown. We all grow from being children."

He pouted at her, moving his head side-to-side.

"No." Staring at the photo directly across from him. It was taken when he first held Min-Jung at their home, feeding her a bottle. "You've grown. You are no longer the little kid who followed me everywhere, wanting me to read or play with you. You don't need me to help you with difficult situations anymore. Instead, I need you to help me."

His voice began drawing out as the exhaustion of emotions hit him, "You are now a young woman. Someone who others can depend on. Someone people will trust more. You are wise. Minnie, you've grown…"

The soft snores were left in place of his words. Min-Jung's face was streaked with tears, and a sad smile accompanied them. She had seen her brother as a role model she looked up to her whole life. Being recognized openly by him warmed her heart, especially where such words were uncommon in their upbringing.

"Thank you, Oppa." Placing one of the throw blankets on top of both, not glancing over, she heard Nari and Iseul leave out the front door.

That night, Jiho and Min-Jung fell asleep on the sofa, both aware that they most likely had damaged their relationship with their family in Korea, but now, they did not have the mind to care.

Knowing they had each other, a robust support system, was all that mattered. An older brother and his younger sister–both allowing the other to live as they wanted: to make mistakes, get hurt, have friends, and love. They had each other, and Jiho could now move forward freely for his feelings.

No regrets where there about what might have been if he had to cave in.

Chapter Twenty-Eight

Family Chats

THE CONSTANT DINGING OF his phone woke Jiho up from his eighteen-hour sleep, something the man had never done before. Some are from Iseul, others from Nari. Many are from his mother, and a few are from his father. One that stood out from the rest was one from Saoirse.

Just the one.

An unread text was at the top of his notification list.

Joy shot through his body as Jiho smiled. But happiness quickly became dread as he saw the names of the Yoo family take over his screen once again, each member taking it upon themselves to ask question after question.

The view of his sister brought a small smile on his face. She was still asleep, her mouth open and saliva coming out. She was a mouth breather when it came to sleeping, but the drool was new to him as he glanced to his side.

Jiho reached over to see her phone light up with notifications. Silencing her phone, he placed it on the coffee table before returning to his device.

His little app had over seventy new messages and was growing. Taking a deep breath, he knew he had to at least see what they were sending him. Even if it left him feeling empty afterward.

Opening Nari's private messages first, hers would be less hostile than the others. Skimming through some of the older messages and the newer ones coming in.

Nari: Not that you care
Nari: But we made it home
Nari: Don't you feel bad?
Nari: You picked some stranger over your family
Nari: I used to look up to you
Nari: But now
Nari: You're just a big letdown
Nari: I can't believe you did this
Nari: Eomma is crying
Nari: She's asking what she did so wrong to have an ungrateful son
Nari: You are the cause of her pain
Nari: Hurry up and come back to your senses and apologize
Nari: You really should just ask for our forgiveness

Her words hurt, though he was glad she told him they made it home safely. They may have been on the out, but he still cared for them and their wellbeing. The twins were his sisters, he would always worry for them.

As she had stopped texting at that last message, Jiho went to his father's.

Unlike the rest of the family, he had only sent a few messages, though they were in complete sentences, as Yu-Jun liked correct punctuation.

Appa: Jiho-yah. I don't know what is happening, but your sisters have come home angrily.
Appa: I want to know what has caused such distress between my children.
Appa: I love you all, but the twins say some foreigner has made you forsake our culture and family.
Appa: Is that true? Have you tossed us aside?
Appa: I don't understand what is happening.
Appa: You all were so happy to see each other again, and only five days after leaving home, they returned.
Appa: What happened? Did something more happen?
Appa: Son. Please answer me. I just want to know what is going on. Everyone is worried.

This was the most his father had ever shown concern towards anything since the murders. His father had been a shell of a man since Jiho's childhood, and to see him like this was strange for him.

He didn't know how to respond.

His attention went to Min-Jung as she moved around, trying to get in a better sleeping position.

Her legs had been placed over his lap; arms moved above her head instead of crossed.

Her face turned towards the cushions and not the open space. Hearing her sudden sharp inhale, he waited a few seconds before returning to his phone. Taking this opportunity to see what Iseul had sent him.

Iseul: Oppa
Iseul: Apologize to me and Eomma

Iseul: She's crying because of you

Iseul: I told them all about that bitch you like so much

Iseul: It's disgusting

Iseul: A foreigner as a potential wife

Iseul: Eomma agrees with me

Iseul: She is disappointed in you, just like the rest of us are

Iseul: Eun-Ya would be disappointed in you

Iseul: How could you turn your back on our family's principles?

Iseul: You are nothing to us now

Iseul: If you come to your senses, then maybe we will forgive you

Iseul: So hurry and apologize

Iseul: You are a disgrace to our family name

Iseul: You are not my Oppa anymore

Iseul: I will hate you forever

Iscul: And your foreigner whore

Iseul: I bet if I tell Taeyoung-seonbae

Iseul: She would be disappointed in you

Iseul: And Kyong-seonbae

Iseul: You are nothing to me

Her words brought sorrow to his heart; afraid she voiced some truth to it. He was at a standstill with his hand hovering over his mother's unread messages.

Closing his eyes, he felt a hand squeeze his shoulder. Min-Jung had been awake by the time he was halfway through Iseul's text.

Seeing the words her older sister sent Jiho, she assumed their mother would be the most difficult for him to accept.

Eomma: Yoo Jiho.

Eomma: How dare you make your sisters cry!

Eomma: I never raised you to be so harsh and ungrateful.

Eomma: You are not my little Jiho-yah.

Eomma: How could you pick some foreigner over your sisters?

Eomma: Is family so easily replaceable?

Eomma: I blame Ally.

Eomma: You replace poor Eun-Ya so effortlessly with that brat.

Eomma: You have basically spit on her grave.

Eomma: She would have been disappointed in you like I am.

Eomma: What happened to my little Jiho-yah, who wanted to marry someone like Eun-Ya?

Eomma: What happened to that sweet, understanding boy?

Eomma: You are no son of mine.

Eomma: Apologizes to your sisters for hurting them so harshly!

Eomma: You've hurt us all with your idiotic decision.

Eomma: I want you to come home as soon as you can.

Eomma: You need to bring Min-Jung-ah as well.

Eomma: You've manipulated her to think you are right.

Eomma: I knew she shouldn't have gone overseas for schooling.

Eomma: Come home and make things right, or don't ever come home again.

Eomma: This may as well not be your home, and we are no longer your family.

The tears poured over, reading his mother's words. *How could things go this downhill,* the man thought as Min-Jung hugged him. At the very least, Jiho thought his mother would stay by his side as he had done everything, she asked of him.

Watching over his sisters, becoming the top student at the academy, taking his extracurricular activities seriously, and helping around the neighborhood to keep their family image alive.

"It's okay, Oppa." Min-Jung soothed, running her hand up and down his arm, "I believe you did the right thing, and I'll stand by you no matter what."

"I just want to be happy." Jiho mutters in between his cries, slightly muffled by his hand.

He had been destroyed by the words and claims of his family.

His blood.

Jiho wanted to reverse time and try to make them see why he stood up for this woman. He didn't regret his desire for Saoirse, but Jiho did with how things were handled.

He thought of all the interactions he had with the twins to find any indication, any sign, that they had opposing views on foreigners.

Many people in his neighborhood had been judgmental of each other, and it only amplified with those non-Koreans. He didn't understand how his family, especially his younger sisters, could feel the same way.

"I know, Oppa." Min-Jung whispered as he cried to sleep. Once again, becoming emotionally exhausted from their families' views and morals, "I know."

Chapter Twenty-Nine

Sweet Dreams

AFTER A FEW MORE HOURS, Jiho had woken alone on the couch, seeing the pitch-black darkness out the window.

Feeling an ache in his throat and stomach, he went to the kitchen to warm leftovers as he chugged two glasses full of water.

Checking the clock hanging by the arch opening, he realized it was almost four in the morning. Looking back into the living room, he rushed upstairs as quietly as possible to see if Min-Jung had gone up.

Sure enough, she was tucked in his bed holding the stuffed animal he'd had for twenty years, with his laptop propped up and hooked to the charger.

Looking closer, Jiho could see Brandon on the screen, sleeping peacefully, his face halfway covered by blankets.

Closing the door softly, he returned to the living room, where his phone was lying on the ground. Seeing the screen light up, Jiho's eyes scanned more messages his family had sent him, scrolling to see only brief snippets of what each one contained. He had stumbled across Saoirse's message once more.

Still the one message.

Only that one.

Saoirse: Mon amour, how are you doing?
Saoirse: Are you okay after the incident?

It was short but meaningful to him. She was asking if he was alright when she was the one to hear such rude comments. Granted, he did have a panic attack, but still, it was thoughtful for her to ask him.

Jiho: I didn't expect you to be the first to message me.
Jiho: I'm doing okay…
Jiho: How about you?

Putting his phone down, Jiho started to stand when he heard a ding come from it. Confused about who was texting him back as he had muted his family, and clearly, it was relatively early, he picked it back up. To his surprise, she messaged instantly.

Saoirse: What can I say? I tend to surprise others.
Saoirse: What happened after you left the restaurant?
Saoirse: I'm currently struggling through paperwork that's slowly drowning me.

He was a little apprehensive in telling Saoirse the truth of the matter.

It was a rather frustrating situation with a disheartening result, one that was based off her race rather than her as a person.

It was best to hide the truth a little if she were to ask, as he did not want to keep things from her, but still, he did not want to hurt her.

Jiho: Nothing you should worry about. Thank you again for helping me.

Jiho: I am genuinely sorry about my sisters.

Jiho: Are you usually up so early?

Saoirse: You do not need to apologize for actions that weren't yours, mon amour.

Saoirse: I would love to hear your sisters admit their wrongdoings in person, as I admitted mine already.

Jiho: The girls had to return home. They have exams that they couldn't reschedule.

Saoirse: That's a shame.

Saoirse: Maybe next time?

Jiho: Possibly.

Saoirse: I've not gone to sleep. To answer your earlier question.

Jiho: You've been working throughout the night?

Jiho: What could possibly be so important that it risks your health?

Jiho: Is there someone there to help you?

Jiho: Surely people will understand if you cannot finish it tonight.

Saoirse: Awe, mon amour. It is cute when you worry.

Saoirse: There is no time for rest now. Not when I have people depending on me.

Jiho: What is it that you do?

Jiho: I mean, I know Lisa and Dmitry work for you, and Daniella helps from time to time.

Jiho: From what I know, at least.

Jiho: I just don't understand how or why one of your workers needs a weapon or to follow me.

Saoirse: Somethings are better a secret, waiting for you to uncover it, mon amour.

Saoirse: Besides, where is the fun in it if I were to tell you everything so openly.

Staring at his screen, Jiho had been left even more confused by her answers. He was trying to get to know Saoirse and the reasoning behind the actions of her workers.

Remembering some words, Dmitry told the abusive man, 'I wouldn't do that if I were you. Someone would be rather angry, and believe me, she's not forgiving.'

Clearly, it must have been Saoirse.

But why?

Jiho: When can I see you again?

Saoirse: Miss me already, mon amour? You flatter me.

Jiho: I do.

Jiho: Miss you, that is. I want to see you again, and not just by coincidence.

Saoirse: What makes you think it was all coincidence? Maybe it's fate.

Jiho: Is that a, no?

Saoirse: It's a 'we'll see.'

Saoirse: I must go now. I will speak to you soon, mon amour.

Saoirse: Fais de beaux rêves.

Jiho: Sweet dreams.

Shutting his phone off, Jiho let out a small scream as Min-Jung sat beside him, a bowl of food in her hand and mouth stuffed.

Giving him a small smile at his reaction, she quickly swallowed before beginning her interrogation.

"So…how long have you been smiling at that phone?"

"What are you doing up? It's four in the morning," Jiho huffed in protest, trying to switch topics. His ears fell on fire as he shifted his eyes downwards, glancing at the phone.

Min-Jung widens her eyes at the information, "You've been talking to her for two hours?"

"Two hours?" He tilted his head, "No, it's only been ten minutes…"

Looking out the window, Jiho saw the sun starting to come up. Checking the time, Jiho was perplexed to read six-twenty-four.

"But it felt like ten minutes…"

"Oppa."

Min-Jung placed her hand on his shoulder, setting the dish on the table. Smiling at her brother, she couldn't help but squeal at the confusion on his face.

"You got it bad for her."

Chapter Thirty

Lake

THE LAST FEW DAYS have been a mix of emotions for Jiho and Min-Jung

Both had been bombarded with threats from the women in their family while their father had been trying to understand their side of the story.

The two never had a full conversation with their father, especially Min-Jung. However, they decided to tell him their side of the story if he was to keep it to himself until Jiho was comfortable speaking to the others the reasoning behind his actions.

The call took almost two hours as Yu-Jun had many questions, ultimately ending with his approval of Jiho's wishes.

It was a tearful ending as he had told Jiho that many people would not like his choice, but if he was ready to proceed with his decision–it was finally time for Jiho to be free from his past and look at the future.

The rest of the family had sent the same painful messages to him and Min-Jung. The only difference was the wording.

Jiho advised her to either mute them or shut off the phone as he could see the 'tasteful' words were affecting her just as much as it was him. Listening, she had opted to mute them.

One upside to the shit show was Brandon. He talked a lot with her; whether by call or text, the two youngest had quickly befriended one another.

That was another upside to the whole debacle: her father thanking her for standing with Jiho and making a friend who understood the feeling of being cast aside the majority of their lives.

Jiho's mood changed after his father's approval.

Saoirse also contributed to his happy mood, having texted at odd hours of the day, constantly worrying about her health while she teased him for doing the same, a little hypocritical on his part.

Due to her busy scheduling, they had not been able to set a time to officially meet one another, despite Jiho's efforts to have just a short lunch if possible.

True to his nature, he asked if she was uncomfortable with him, which she denied entirely, reassuring him that she had missed their little talks truthfully.

Even with this, he was anxious, believing he'd missed his chance with the woman as their messages slowly became longer and longer apart in response time, but held onto the little hope he had, praying that luck was on his side.

With the sudden connection between Min-Jung and Brandon, they shared almost every detail of their day, even when nothing was going on.

But she may have let it slip on why her sisters had to leave after agreeing with Jiho not to tell anyone the whole truth after only day three of the now one-on-one vacation that had occurred.

She'd seen her brother mope around because of his lack of response, causing her to ask Brandon if he knew anything.

He was hesitant as his loyalties did lie with his sister, but because Min-Jung told him the truth about Nari and Iseul, he agreed.

She left the country which led to spotty cell service, to the point where even he couldn't always get through to her.

With the days meshing as one, the brother-sister duo had not left the comfort of home, ordering takeout, watching movies, and comparing their latest reading endeavors, which they were sickly similar in their preference.

They both had an undying hunger for the compelling stories of authors such as Jane Austen, Kazuo Ishiguro, and Han Kang, annotating books before sending them to the other in a way to communicate their thoughts while reading.

It was a tradition they started when Min-Jung had asked for his copy of a book for one of her literary classes five years ago, where she discovered Jiho's chaotic thoughts scattered within the pages and its margins.

While she was reading, her own thinking would sometimes contrast with what Jiho had initially interpreted, responding in her own words to what the author really meant.

After that year, she returned the book, instructing him to reread it. Jiho was pleased, and they began exchanging books every month or so.

Min-Jung mentioned the fact the two hadn't left the house since the restaurant, offering that they should take a walk by the lake, like they had back home.

Jiho drove for only ten minutes before they had reached their destination. Buttoned up for their long outing; Min-Jung held a more soft-colorful palette with floral designs, contrasting with Jiho's neutral monochrome taste. It was an odd sight for passersby to witness.

"You've been chattering wildly with a particular Welsh boy." He emitted a smug look on his face.

"Just because I have a better texting relationship with a Welsh member doesn't mean you have to show your envy so outwardly." Min-Jung counters without a second thought, "Honestly, if you want, I can tell you what Saoirse has been up to."

Grumbling at the poor execution of his attempts to reveal information without asking directly, Jiho's face and neck had taken a lovely red mix of embarrassment and anger.

"I don't envy you…Not really."

She raised an eyebrow at the blatant denial. It was evident that he was striking out in a proper meeting with the woman, but she did not think it was terrible to this degree.

"…What has she been up to?"

Giggling at the stages of grief Jiho had just run through, Min-Jung opened her phone, ensuring she summarized correctly.

"She's been in meetings all day. Literally, taking calls from abroad and going to them in person." Giving him a sympathetic look as she read the recent message that had just come in. "Randy said she went on a blind date with another person their father set up…I'm sorry, Oppa."

Tucking his chin in, Jiho sighs and shuts his eyes tightly before throwing his head back. He was met with a light breeze hitting his face, shaking his head.

"There's nothing to be sorry about, Minnie. She's a beautiful, brilliant woman who can make the room her own, just by walking in. I knew she would have another pinning after her."

Kicking the pebbles in front of them, Jiho loosely hugged himself, placing his hands under his arms.

"I just didn't think things would be moving so quickly."

"What are you going to do?"

"What I told everyone." Smirking at the confused girl. "I will pursue her no matter what. After all, my heart is Saoirse's to break, and only hers."

"You were serious?"

"Entirely."

Breaking out in an excited squeal, Min-Jung clapped. Unknownst to the man, she had made a bet with Brandon on whether Jiho would back down, ultimately giving up after the 'sudden' disappearance from Saoirse. Brandon stated that only a madman would chase after a girl who willingly or not went away.

"Enough about my life for now." Jiho slugged his arm around her shoulder. Leaning so they were the same height before changing his voice, high-pitched, "Tell me about Brandon. Are you two like a thing?"

Shoving him off, she started to hit him with the ends of her scarf, which had a little ball of fuzz, pausing between each word, "We. Are. Not. A. Thing."

She ended with one more hit before straightening her wild hair. Huffing, she spun back around before walking again. Jiho chuckled at his sister's antics, catching up to her with a slight jog.

"He is very well, my brother-in-law at this point. So, if we were to have any feelings of that kind, it would be bizarre and gross."

Jiho choked on his raised laugh, peering down at her to see the disgusted look.

"You are right about that. So, are you two just friends then? Or do you bicker with him like me?"

"I think it might be the same friendship you and Allyria have, but it's too early to tell. We are just close acquaintances who want the same things in life."

"And what's that?" He inquires, an eyebrow raised.

Min-Jung held a wicked grin that made his expression fall, "To see a little Yoo-Welsh baby running around." She shrugged.

In truth, that was the goal she wanted to achieve; Brandon only wanted his sister to be happy and at peace. Much like the life events Jiho grew up in, Saoirse held similarities to hers—at least, that is what Brandon had told her.

But he did not go into too much detail as it wasn't his story, which she respected and understood as she would not tell her brother's story to him no matter the person or situation.

From what Min-Jung had gathered over their long chats, Brandon was at a loss regarding his sister. He usually ranted about things such as her tendency to shove her problems deep down within herself that, for some reason, he was the only one to see.

It caused some fights here and there between the two Welsh siblings, but he would always be the one to hold her as she wept in desperation.

Min-Jung knew it wasn't in her place to tell Jiho about this; he had to find out for himself, and all she could do was wait.

His eyes had widened ten-folds at his sister's bluntness, something he was aware of but tended to forget at times, "I will not have a child if she doesn't want it…"

Min-Jung halted, her tilted and bewildered look as places, "What do you mean? Don't you want children?"

"Yes, very much." He paused, "But that is not my decision." Jiho continued to walk before speaking again, "It's not my body that has to carry that child. And if we both want one, but she doesn't want to go through labor or birth, we will simply adopt."

"Don't you want one with your own genetics?"

He pondered.

Deep down a child that came from him was appealing, but he did not want to put someone, more specifically Saoirse (as he was holding on to hope in having her as his partner), through the pain he witnessed his mother in.

Since being a doctor himself, Jiho had been through the 'Labor and Delivery' unit to talk with other workers on cases that crossed paths; that is where the horror of childbirth really instilled in him.

"It would be nice, but I have no say over someone else, especially their body." Tugging on Min-Jung's sleeve, he hurled the girl into his side, "You promise me that if you get a boyfriend-"

"If?" Offense was in her posture.

"Hey, you might like girls and haven't told me yet; you did kiss a girl." Jiho clarified. She recalled telling him about the kiss and nodded for him to continue.

"If you get a boyfriend, and he wants a baby, but you decide not to go through with getting pregnant and giving birth, promise me to speak up for yourself. Promise you won't go through with it unless you are over a hundred percent sure that's what *you* want."

Min-Jung never really thought of what she wanted in the future regarding children. The whole concept was embedded in her mind from infancy that she would have no choice but to get pregnant once she married.

Her parents were the 'perfect' family within the town. Their father worked long hours to support them, while the mother stayed home mostly and only worked when she was hired for gigs as she is a well-known dancer and instructor.

Their mother had not worked when she had the children. All her efforts were placed into raising them and doing stay-at-home mom duties: cleaning, cooking, and raising them. It was an endless cycle that didn't end till Min-Jung was off to study abroad.

"I promise, Oppa." Leaning on his shoulder, the two had finished the walk quicker than anticipated.

Chapter Thirty-One

At a Lost

THEIR TIME TOGETHER CAME and went as Min-Jung gave a last wave to Jiho from the precheck line.

He was sad to see his sister go, but it was bound to happen whether he liked it. The last few days together consist of what she would do at the end of her last school exam.

She had to check in with the abroad student counselor and finish the short summer volunteer work in Italy she had agreed to do, but Min-Jung did not want to return home to South Korea.

The rest of their family was still harassing them both to take back what they had said, agree with their views, and apologize to the twins–something they would never do.

Sensing distress, he had told her to stay with him until she knew what she wanted in life, for which he would help pay.

Jiho had seen and heard her conversation with Brandon multiple times during her stay here. The two had talked about their future travel plans and even listed where they would go together and explore.

Leaping into her brother's arms at his offer, she was relieved to have some sort of safety net after going against her elders back home. She knew that after arguing with the twins and ignoring the rest of the families' attempts to contact them, Min-Jung would be in a new level of trouble.

Once she was out of sight, Jiho waited a few more minutes to ensure there wasn't anything for which she would return. Though feeling worried, he remained in his car till her plane departed.

Sending a quick 'safe travels' and 'call me when you land,' he made his way to Ally's place as he promised her last time at the gym to talk about Saoirse.

He continuously apologized for not telling the woman about his love life, saying that it was simply due to their busy schedules and that it was too important to just tell her over the phone.

Although Ally could not ask everything, she wanted to know during their gym time, the woman had been keeping tabs through said sister, which, funny enough, she, Min-Jung, Brandon, and Eric had made a group chat dedicated to the two love birds.

When Eric first heard of this, he was rather angry, thinking it was a tactic for being in a relationship with Ally. Still, after the clarification from all three on what happened at the restaurant and the aftermath once the Yoo siblings were alone made him see Jiho in a new, respectable way.

He never saw a man, besides the brothers of Saoirse, some of the in-laws, and himself, stick up for her in that way.

Used to people walking all over her and the reputation she held only behind her back, as she was more than capable of handling herself in those situations up front.

He did hate how the two sisters, from what he understood, spoke in their own language while insulting his little cousin, a more cowardly thing to do, in his opinion.

Jiho, of course, did not know of this sudden unified group, an odd one at that, thinking that his sister was only talking to Brandon the entire time.

On his way to Ally's, he began to ponder where exactly Saoirse had disappeared too. The woman had stopped all forms of contact with Jiho once he asked about her date, only to get a short answer.

Saoirse: Okay.

It's a relatively simple response but not a clear one. He waited and waited, and waited, for her to go more in-depth.

As the seconds turned to minutes–minutes turned to hours; Jiho had sent two more messages stating that he was only curious and not angry at her.

Which he had no right to be if he was, and that he did not mean to overstep the boundaries if he had. Still, she didn't respond, making him send another reply, wanting at least one outing together; he had every intention to pursue her if she would only let him.

Once he arrived there was no need to be buzzed in as he had the second key to her place. Already announcing that he was stopping by to talk to her the day before, he unlocked and opened the door to her loft without much thought, only to wish he knocked.

There his friend was, tangled in pillows and sheets, her naked body fully on display.

Eric, who Jiho had no idea would be there, had his hand gripping her breast with one hand while the other was circling her clit; they did not notice him in the doorway. Otherwise Jiho was certain Eric would have slowed his pace down from the rapid speed he was going at, and Ally would be pale as a ghost.

The couple stopped as a loud, high-pitched shriek was heard. Looking to the left of them, Jiho was standing there, covering his eyes with his hand, while the he tried to locate the door to spare others from the view.

Horrified, Ally pushed Eric off her, fumbling to put on some cover-up. Eric was annoyed by the interruption; he had just flown back a few hours ago, and it was his first-time seeing Ally in five days. He was deprived of his girlfriend and wanted nothing more than to ravish her.

"...Are you decent yet?" Jiho shouted, still uncomfortable by the scene he witnessed.

He never actually saw someone have sex, raised to believe it was a taboo topic for the family. It was to only be spoken about with the person you were in a relationship with. True, there was other means in watching but the discomfort in doing so after all this time of restricting himself, he couldn't boldly look at such a thing.

But he was a man, with needs. Luckly his mind held enough imagination and scenes placed in books help to keep himself satisfied in some self-pleasure.

He felt guilty for walking in during an intimate and vulnerable moment.

"Yeah, we're decent," Eric replies. He had only put on his pants, as Ally had his shirt on and a pair of boxers, "How did you even get in?"

It wasn't in a rude manner; he was genuinely interested in the issue. To his understanding, the only ones with keys were Ally and himself.

He did not know how deep the trust ran between the two friends; his disarray only added when Ally pulled Jiho's hand off his eyes, steering him to a chair before running to shut the door.

"Not that I'm not happy to see you, Ji, but what are you doing here so late?" Ally hesitantly asked.

Clearing his throat, Jiho's eyes darted anywhere other than the two. "Well, we did agree to talk about it," he said, wincing at the point that Eric was here, "Saoirse–that is."

Ally had still frowned in conflict, taking a minute before actuality dawned on her. Her face crumpled in sympathy as she had overlooked it.

"I thought Minnie's flight left tomorrow night...I'm sorry. Ricky just got back in, and I was so focused on that. I totally spaced out."

"It's okay." Jiho finally made eye contact with her, "Just wished I knocked this time."

Eric had gotten up during their little chat, getting them all something to drink. Offering a cup of water, Jiho thanked the man who was, not even a few minutes ago, balls deep in his best friend.

"So," Eric started, "you want to date my little cousin?"

He choked on the water, spitting some on Ally in response. Eric could only grin at the action before getting a towel for Ally to wipe her face.

"I didn't know you were part fountain."

"How did you-" Jiho snapped his head towards the only person that could have told him. It was then that Ally rapidly shook her head.

"Don't look at me; I didn't tell him first."

"Then who?"

"Brandon and Minnie"

"Minnie?" Hearing his little sister had something to do with the information caused a headache. Jiho groaned in frustration, "How does she even know you?"

"Brandon met me in Canada a few days after the restaurant thing and told me while he was on the phone with your sister." He shrugged, "Sweet girl. She would be a good friend to him."

"I think so too…"

There was a pause in the conversation, "So what is it you were going to talk about regarding Erin with Ally?"

"Erin?"

"I mean Saoirse." Eric waved off, "It's one of the nicknames the family calls her."

The familiarity in the name sends Jiho to a realization. It had been a while since he had heard one of those alternative names, "Viktor did say you had two nicknames for her."

"How did you know my brother-in-law?" Eric inquired. It was sudden and weird to hear Viktor's name from the mouth of a man he hardly knew.

Rubbing the back of his neck, Jiho flustered, "Well, I work with Viktor, and I've spent time with their family."

Eric was lost.

How had most of the family met Jiho before him? Was there something going on of which he wasn't aware of? Did that mean the new doctor under his brother-in-law, who praised countless times, was Jiho? Eric scratched his head.

"So, you've met my sister and their children?"

"Yes, Emilia is very kind. Nikolia and Anya, both call me Dyadya sometimes." Jiho confirmed. Seeing the annoyance on the man's face, Jiho backpedaled, "Of course, they always talk about you; I just didn't know your name. Or at least your real name; they only ever call you Dyadya Okean, so I assumed that was your name until Viktor told me it was your nickname."

Narrowing his eyes, Eric battled internally with the explanation. Of course, his family wouldn't use his given name; it was just weird Emilia never said anything about Jiho. Then again, she never said anything about those she views as family.

He couldn't lie to himself; the thought of being outshined and wanted by the children as their favorite uncle was always something he feared.

Although Emilia gave the children a godmother, they did not give him the title of godfather. Which hurt him tremendously, but he didn't hold that against the children.

She later revealed that with Eric traveling so much for his job, it would be too difficult to place the children in his care if something happened to them, which he understood.

Saoirse could stay in one place for extended periods; she could give the stability the other family members could not.

"Never mind that." Eric sat before Jiho, pulling Ally's hand into his, "What will you talk about with Ally?"

"Umm." Jiho shifted his eyes nervously to hers.

"It's okay, Ji," she reassured, "Ricky will promise not to let Saoirse know, right?" She nudged his shoulder, gaining a grunt of acceptance.

"Right."

Clearing his throat before starting. Jiho let everything out; where he first met Saoirse, the time she saved him from an unwanted advancement, the company party (not telling the graphic details of the kiss), and finally, the restaurant run in.

He was undoubtedly smitten with her as he recalls everything she does in her mannerisms.

Remembering her clothing and how it complemented her differently; some gave her a bold, confident, assertive demeanor, and others would play with the softer, free, easy-going side.

He remembered the nose scrunches, the small dimples in her lower back, which he had been lucky to touch two times.

The gleam of mischief in her eyes when she ran him in circles trying to think of words. He loved the laugh she gave; it was enchanting and contagious.

Jiho went on about how she had been so detailed in her appearance, mainly her hair, as the way she had done it looked time-consuming.

Ally and Eric were both stunned at the soft smile held on his face; he was completely unaware of the light behind not only his smile but his eyes as well.

It was a whole new side to him that Ally had never seen before. Sometimes, she thought he would always be alone or never understood the appeal of being with someone who makes you feel completely, utterly loved, and cared for.

But the way he speaks so flawlessly about Saoirse, proved her wrong.

Eric was astonished by Jiho's passion. How he had spoken so sweetly about his little cousin was almost sickening.

Over three years, Eric has had to help his uncle, Saoirse's father, Cain Welsh, find a suitable match for the heiress. In his opinion, Cain could drop dead and wouldn't feel sorry about it.

As soon as she turned seventeen, the legal age in Ireland, Cain started to set up blind dates to have his daughter settled and married as soon as possible. Eric knew why his uncle was hellbent on marrying her off, but it pissed him off and made him guilt ridden for her.

After hearing the sickening, twisted details of what had happened during her first setup, Eric had asked to help see over her dates, a way to protect and postpone till his cousin was ready for such a commitment.

As Jiho continued his little rant about how effortlessly Saoirse had gained his attention and the respect he had given her in response, Eric realized that Saoirse might be in good hands if he did not interfere as well as Cain. He was still wary of Jiho due to the attempts and advantage taken from some of the men in the past, but he was willing to let Jiho have a chance to win Saoirse's heart.

"I just don't know what to do now. She's stopped all contact with me." He slouched in the chair, wanting to be consumed by it, "Did I say anything wrong?"

Ally, who had been listening intensely, disagreed with him. The friend knew a little more than him regarding some information about the blind date she had, thanks to Brandon.

"You did nothing wrong, Ji. Maybe she's too busy to get to her phone for personal stuff, right Ricky?"

"She did have to fly back to France for our grandparents. She gets awful with responding during times like these since she's usually helping them around the house most of the time. So don't think bad about it." He sends a small, sympathetic smile, patting Jiho's knee.

"So I just have to wait for her?" He raised an eyebrow, frowning.

Eric felt sorry and offered help, something he'd never done before, "What if I tell her to reach out to you? When she gets service again, of course."

Jiho instantly perked up, straightening in his chair, "Really?!" The grin he had was almost as wide as a child in a candy store.

"Really."

"Why?"

Eric shrugged, "Because no one said anything bad about you. Also, you paint my cousin sweetly and genuinely makes me believe you only hold good intentions."

"I do."

"Let's hope so." He chuckles, tension in his hand as he squeezed Jiho's shoulder. With a weak smile, he stood up with the help of Eric.

"Now, since we have that in order, do you think you can leave so I can finish show how much I've miss my girlfriend?" Eric deadpans.

He's had a hard-on ever since Jiho got here, and unfortunately, it wasn't going away anytime soon.

Grimacing, Jiho did not reply. Instead, he walked to the door, yelling out for Ally not to get pregnant too soon as he wasn't ready to be an uncle again before shutting the door.

All he could hear as he stepped into the elevator was the start of his friend's bed creaking.

Chapter Thirty-Two

Reunions

VIKTOR INVITED JIHO FOR a nice late lunch/early dinner before they both went to their respectable homes.

In passing, during their morning rounds, the two had discussed when they would be off, excitement pulsing through them at the hour difference.

They rarely got off around the same time from their long shifts, often missing each other by a day or two. Jiho had agreed to wait for Viktor to pick him up at the end of his shift.

He was a bit nervous about their one-on-one outing as they had not found time to talk since he began pursuing Saoirse so outwardly.

He'd been trying to think of the right words to say. Looking at his screen again, Jiho scrolled through the messages between Saoirse, where only he was contributing and trying anything to get a response.

Jiho: Good morning. How did you sleep?
Jiho: I hope you've been eating well. Make sure to look after yourself…
Jiho: The flowers are blooming nicely here.
Jiho: Past a floral shop the other day.

Jiho: They didn't have the color I was looking for, but they had some pale blue ones that I thought you would like.
Jiho: They're called bellflowers. The man there said it had a good meaning…
Jiho: I grabbed a bunch.
Jiho: Please make sure you sleep at a responsible time…

Hearing a knock, Jiho quickly shut his phone off before seeing Viktor poking his head in, a sly grin dancing on his lips.

"You ready?"

Sending a small smile to the impatient man, he grabbed his belongings before stuffing them in his backpack, locking his office, and walking beside Viktor.

The two had fallen into a comfortable silence, taking in the peacefulness they had been unable to have during work.

Entering the restaurant, the two had been led towards the back, where a large window was in front of them, looking at city life as they dined on the fifth floor.

The place was empty, with only a handful of customers. Quickly thanking the host for escorting them over, Jiho had tipped them.

It was something he would not have done in the past, but after seeing and asking Ally why she had handed the person money during one of their vacations, he had found it astonishing that it was considered a norm in some places.

"I'm starving," Viktor quietly said, "I wonder what's here."

Chuckling at the overly excited man, he couldn't help but compare Viktor to a child. There was one thing that Jiho had come to find rather quickly during his first few months in the States.

Viktor loved food.

The man could inhale all kinds and still be left hungry. It was a funny sight when they first had an outing together.

"How can you still be hungry after the lunch Emilia made you?" Jiho asked, never taking his eyes off the menu, "She packed you three big containers of food."

With a long sigh, he looked to see Viktors stuck in a dreamy haze.

"I love that woman. She knows how to make a man full." Chuckling at himself, Viktor held some seriousness.

"I can only last so long without a snack, which I usually get, but the little demons left a note in my bag saying sorry for eating all of them." He grumbled, pulling his lips into a playful sneer, "I swear, they all have me wrapped around their fingers."

"But you enjoy it." Jiho mockingly stated.

"I do."

They two smiled at each other before a waiter took their orders and placed some drinks in front of them. Viktor had stunned the worker with the amount of food he wanted, five dishes worth.

The younger did not have such an appetite, ordering two things before thanking the staff member.

They had fallen into a smooth conversation over different cases they had, trying to see if the other was able to find a better solution to the problem they were faced with.

One of the cases regarded a man in his twenties with brain trauma who was in a coma for the past six months. The patient had woken up not even a few days ago, unable to speak. It was a rather interesting case as the man could do everything else just fine, but his brain charts indicated that talking was useless.

As soon as they began talking, Viktor could see the discomfort swirling in Jiho's eyes. Wanting to ask what was on his mind, Viktor's words caught in his throat as a woman threw herself onto Jiho.

Before the woman had collided with the man, Jiho was about to put his glass down when brown hair took his vision, spilling a little on the tablecloth.

He could feel the tight squeeze come from her as she uttered a quiet apology before pulling back.

"Dani?"

"Hi, Jiji!" She smiled brightly before pulling out a chair and sitting close to the man, "I've missed you. It's been too long."

"Yes." Jiho mused, "It's been some time. How is school?" He looked over Daniella, a hidden meaning between his words.

Waving the man off, she smiled widely, "I am fine now. He's not bothering me anymore. He moved schools a week after your *talk*."

Playing with the hem of her tattered shirt, Daniella turned to see Viktor, whose mouth hung ajar, tears welling in his eyes.

"Hi Vikky."

"*Malysha*." His voice croaked, "What are you doing here?"

"Do you mean at the restaurant or the country?"

"...Both." He hesitantly asked.

His eyes darted over her face, going over to Jiho and back, trying to figure out the relationship between the two.

He didn't understand how his little sister could know Jiho or how they were so comfortable with one another. The last Viktor saw Daniella was when she was still a small child; she was sitting before him as a teenager.

The style of clothing had changed dramatically in his eyes. No longer wearing overalls, long sleeves, and a pair of sneakers. She now wore oversized pants and a tight-fitting tank top underneath a shirt that swallowed her with holes and tears. Viktor felt weird knowing his *Malysha* was growing up without him.

"Well, I finished my studies early this year without any distractions, thanks to my Jiji." Daniella proudly announced, grabbing Jiho's arm and hugging it. "But I wanted to see some people over here." Losing her grip as a man moves towards them from behind Viktor, "And the reason why I'm here is-"

"Because we have a dinner reservation." An angered voice cut her off, "Which is where we were going until you left my side, *Pcholka*."

"Well, I want to talk with Jiji." She pouted, walking over to her irritated brother. Tugging on his sleeve, using her favoritism card to gain sympathy, "Please, Dima. Can we eat with them?"

Looking over at his sister, Dmitry's eyes soften at her request. Turning to Jiho, he asked if that would work for the two doctors. Giving a quick nod, the standing Petrov's sat down, Daniella retaking her seat next to Jiho and Dmitry hesitantly sitting next to Viktor.

"How have you been, Dmitry?"

"Could be better at this moment." He spoke with some strain as if he could not talk without raising his voice in a repulsive tone while glancing over at Viktor, "No need for me to ask how you've been."

The two had begun a harsh whisper to one another, not wanting to raise attention to their conversation.

At the same time, Jiho and Daniella went over how her school year has been treating her and talked about her favorite courses, comparing them to his past experiences.

"Do not do this, Mitry."

"Do what, doctor?" Forging confusion, "I know how good your life is treating you. It would be a waste of breath to ask you a stupid question."

"Please," Viktor pleaded, gripping his glass tightly, "I need you to understand why I did what I did. I had no choice-"

"*Yerunda.*" Dmitry turned his head to meet Viktor with a glare, "You knew how I would feel if you followed through. You knew and still did it. I will never forgive or forget."

The server walked up to the table, ending the discussion between the two groups, placing down each dish.

"I see your appetite never went away, Vikky." After a few seconds of awkward silence, Daniella jokes, trying to lift the tension between her brothers. "I don't know how Emilia can keep up with you."

"You remember Lia?" His voice didn't hold the confidence he usually had, scared that his siblings would leave.

"Of course I do." Swallowing her food, "She would always bring me cookies in secret when allowed over."

Chuckling at the memories, he commented, "I forgot she did that. It was nice of her, huh?" His smile died as Dmitry let out a scoff through his nose, finding this thing ridiculous. Not wanting the argument to continue, Jiho let out a tiny cough, gaining their attention from the intense glares.

"Um, I know it may not be my business, but what is happening between you?" Pointing his knife at both Petrov men, "I know I don't know you very well, Dmitry, but you are scoffing at a topic Emilia is in. And that is something I can't allow around me. Not when I see her as a close friend-as an older sister. And Dani is only trying to lighten the mood by conversing, so do not let your petty feelings make her feel bad for talking with Viktor."

Seeing the blushes in embarrassment caused Daniella to let out a small sounds of giggles, trying her hardest to muffle them in her napkin. She knew this could be a possible outcome of sitting her brothers together after years of not seeing each other.

It might not have been the best, but Daniella did miss the times when her brothers would come into her room to help make a fort and tell her stories.

"Jiji really let you have it!" Grinning at the glares the two gave her, both empty of negative feelings, "So you going to tell him? Or do I have to?"

The little mischievous played throughout Daniella's body, ready to spill everything to the man she now looked up to.

There were pieces she didn't know as she was still a child when everything had happened, but she knew the main things that pushed everything over the edge.

The two looked once more at each other before Dmitry just shrugged, placing a piece of meat in his mouth, laying his head on his hand as his elbow was on the table, turning to the oldest.

Indicating that Viktor would start.

Taking a long sip of the wine before him, Viktor built up the courage to tell another person about his past, something of which he was not proud.

Exhaling through his nose, he proceeded, glad that there was no one around them to overhear, "I used to do something I regret now-"

"If you are going to tell him, tell him the whole truth, Viktor." Dmitry spat. His anger was starting to boil at his brother dancing around the truth.

"Fine."

Scratching the back of his head, Viktor looked to see Jiho giving his undivided attention, eager to know.

"I used to be an enforcer for my family."

"Enforcer?"

Jiho turned to Daniella in hopes she would further explain the meaning, as he had no idea what it truly meant.

She did explain, but not through words.

Daniella had made a gun out of her hand before putting it underneath her chin, mouthing 'boom' as she pulled the trigger. Widening his eyes, Jiho looked back at Viktor only to see his head down in shame.

"Enforcer," he whispered back.

"And that's not the best part," Dmitry smirked, smacking his hand on Viktor's back, putting pressure on it. Viktor let out a hiss in pain, "He abandoned the family. Right, *Viktor.*"

The man in question was stiff at the pronunciation. It was uncannily the same as their parents bringing back memories of his past. Nodding his head, Dmitry grinned at the silence. Turning to Jiho, he continued his little game.

"But that's okay. Because we are all fine now, our *brother*," mocking the word with resentment, "will always show the hurt we felt by his actions. You want to know why?"

Jiho tilted his head, hesitantly eager to know.

"Because we are all alive and healthy, but Viktor here," a fake look of concern, "our big brother is the only one to bear any scars of that day."

He had pulled Viktor's shirt collar down, revealing a scar that looks to be still healing to this day.

It was a pinkish color, the end of it was white. Jiho knew from looking at it that the cut was deep; you would need to nurse it longer than usual for survival.

Taking a sharp inhale, he wondered just how much he really knew about the world and what lives in it.

But the question that stuck in his head the most was–*how Saoirse and the Petrov family is really connected if Viktor used to be an enforcer.*

Chapter Thirty-Three

Petrov Business

AFTER HEARING THE WORDS, he couldn't breathe.

Unsure how to process the information, as his mentor had been kind to him throughout his time here. It was hard to digest that his past was so violent and vicious.

"Don't worry, Jiji." Daniella poked his arm, gaining his attention. "Vikky hasn't done anything like that since he left the family, and Dima is the only one still holding a grudge."

"I have a good reason," Dmitry mutters. "I don't know how you all got over it so easily."

Rolling her eyes, Daniella throws one of the cutting knife, impaling it to the table and landing a few centimeters away from his pinky. Dmitry looks unfazed by the action, only giving her a little scoff in response.

"He was under orders." She narrowed her eyes and gritted her teeth, "Get off your high horse, Dima. You all got the same order." She said, leaning back into her chair. Resting her head on Jiho's shoulder, "You're just mad by his end choice."

In truth, Viktor had missed his youngest siblings terribly. Their little bickering amused him, always bringing a smile to his face and letting the time slip by with joy. He had been following orders, but it pained him deep down. All Viktor could do was follow the instructions, just like they were raised.

No questions.

No hesitation.

No feelings.

No way for a task to go wrong.

That was how he was raised, how they were all raised, especially the boys.

Looking down at the young girl, Jiho frowned, his eyebrows together, "What do you mean by orders? From Saoirse?"

Viktor shot his head up, his eyes calculating Jiho, "How do you know her?"

He never introduced them directly. He was hesitant to talk about her as both families had always been intertwined for better or worse.

"Eric is dating my friend, Ally...I met her when Ally introduced me to him."

Deciding to leave out some things from Viktor as he held a bit of fear. Hearing the man you called your mentor, an older brother who helped him 'rejoin' society in a way–was an enforcer before was nerve-wracking.

Dmitry and Daniella made eye contact, silently telling each other to stay quiet as they had been told not to reveal anything regarding the two's relationship.

Dmitry knew of Jiho's liking towards his boss, as the man told him, himself. Daniella was suspicious about Jiho's fondness for Saoirse as he always lit up when she was brought into the conversation.

Granted, he did help her with her little boy problem, so she would help with his; by not saying anything.

There was a moment of pause as Viktor tried to decipher if Jiho was telling the truth, only to accept it after his blank stare did not break.

"Saoirse only recently inherited the family business from what I remember. Her father, Cain Welsh, was in charge when the order was placed…I was hired under his grandfather's order, Muiris Welsh, as a favor for helping Cain's sister, Rois, when we were in school together."

Nodding at the information, he acted like it was all new, seeing as Saoirse had told him about Viktor's past with her aunt.

"If you were hired, then how come Dani said you all got the same order?"

"The Petrov family will forever work for the Welsh family. It has been set in stone for the past five generations." Dmitry cuts in, taking the last bit of his main course, "The only reason there was a favor in place was because Cain did not trust Viktor as he was only loyal to Muiris even after his retirement."

Viktor nodded, picking up where Dmitry ended, "Which is why there was an order set in place for the sons of the Petrov family's head, our father Akim Petrov, to take him out."

Daniella stepped in, looking at her nails to see if they needed a touch-up, "Vikky had to fight, almost to his death, for Cain's entertainment."

"Why would you all do that?" Jiho questioned, still not understanding the purpose of such violent acts.

He was scared sitting around the family now. Jiho was told their family had been enforcers indirectly, even Daniella with her attack earlier.

"Our family prides itself in taking whatever orders, no matter what, with full dedication. That is how we were raised." The girl shrugged her shoulders before reaching for a piece of the dessert Jiho had ordered during their silence.

"We are usually lent out to others worldwide." Dmitry reveals, "If they pay both the Welsh and the Petrov head a good amount, then we are sent to do the bidding with no questions asked."

"I believe our grandfather on Papa's side was sent overseas to stop a killer before." Daniella recalled, "He stopped a woman from killing any more children. However, he took almost a year to get her as she was moving faster than he anticipated. She was rather gruesome, but he did say she was on a psychotic break."

Kill any more children? Jiho thought. Shaking his head, Jiho brought his attention back to the topic, asking his question.

"So, when asked to handle Viktor….?"

Nodding, Viktor clarified, "It was going to happen at some point. The family had to follow through with the order. So, I went into hiding."

Thinking over the words, Jiho had a sudden question puzzling him, "What about Emilia?"

Sending a soft smile, Viktor looks at his ring, twirling it around, "She's the one who helped me plan my attack."

"Which is why she is one of my favorites," Daniella said, words muffled by the cake. "She is one badass woman when tempted."

The table chuckled at Daniella's bluntness and the fact that they all knew the woman in question had a few tricks up her sleeve that had still not been shown yet.

"The order had taken over six months to take action as everyone had other things they were dealing with personally."

Viktor continued. "Although our family will always work for theirs, there have been rules to help the Petrov family from dying out as our work is deadly."

Leaning back, Dmitry took over the conversation. At the same time, Viktor had paused to replenish his thirst, his finger tapping the table in a rhythm.

"The family needed to grow, and our two older brothers and older sister were all starting their own families, something we pride ourselves in as well."

Their older brother, Maxim Petrov, was on his third child and wanted to be there for the family more. The man had told the rest of the family his plan, which they had agreed to as the second son Ivan Petrov was expecting his second.

Towards the middle of the in-law's pregnancy, Vera, the first daughter of the Petrov siblings, announced her first pregnancy.

It was somewhat chaotic, but even the wrath of Cain's tempter did not budge their own rules with the Petrov family.

"What was the real reason for the order? Why was Viktor the only one to have a scar, and how come he hasn't seen you all? His reaction tells me that it's been a while."

"Jumping straight to the burning questions, huh?" Dmitry teases, leaning forward, hiding his smirk behind his hands, "Cain, as you know now, did not trust Viktor to the point he was ready to risk the rest of us to kill him."

"Although it was an order by a Welsh head, once Muiris got there in time, he stop the said attack, but only after Dima stuck a knife deep in Vikky's shoulder."

She remembered the screams of her brothers' struggles against each other, "It was then that Vikky had decided to leave the family under the agreement that he would not see our parents again for as long as he lives."

"Why would you agree to that, Viktor?

"Because I was going to be a father myself..." He quietly muttered, "I could not stay in a place where I would be ordered to my death. Not when I have a wife and child to look after. So, I agreed to the terms only if there would be no targets on my family's back once we left."

"But if you couldn't have seen your parents, what about the others?" Jiho turned to Dmitry, waiting for his answer as Viktor had just shrugged, not knowing himself.

"...Why would I want to have a relationship with someone who doesn't value me as much as I do them?" The pure hatred in his voice told everyone how hurt he was by the decision to leave the family.

"Dima, you must realize that he would have died one way or another with Cain still in charge." Daniella said, "Think for once instead of being so selfish."

"How was I selfish? I just wanted my brother to stay with us. You know as well as I do that there was too big of an age gap with the other three. They might as well be our uncles and aunt. There was no connection of an older sibling with them, only Viktor." He seethe.

"I know." Daniella mutters, "But he had a child to think of. We were getting old enough to fend for ourselves, so stop."

Shaking his head, Dmitry stood up, placing some money on the table, before grabbing Daniella by her hand, leaving the other two seated.

Waving goodbye to them, Daniella said that she would be okay and that they would see them soon.

Once again, the two were alone with just each other. Knowing this was hard for Viktor, Jiho stood up and walked over to the teary-eyed man, bringing him into a hug, where the two embraced till Viktor felt better. The rest of the walk back to their cars was quiet, not wanting to disperse the peacefulness in the night sky.

Bidding each other a good night, Jiho had felt his knees buckle once he was alone. He had been terrified of the meal as the tension between the brothers was noticed.

He was sure to have dropped dead at Daniella's knife throw if it wasn't for the fact he was already sitting.

"What the hell am I getting myself into with you, Saoirse?"

Chapter Thirty-Four

Two Months

TWO MONTHS.

It had been two months since Jiho had seen or spoken to her. Within that, all his patience had withered away. He hoped to see her in person soon, having her near him again, to touch her-feeling her under him.

A sane person would tell him to stop waiting, but he could not. Even if she were to send a text in a year, he would be grateful.

He became insufferable to those around him. Of course, he was still respectful and kind to people when needed, but the man had built himself a short temper.

Raising his voice at another doctor, calling him an idiot, which led to an insult or two about the coworker's upbringing, all because the other doctor had shared about his little getaway with his girlfriend, only reminding Jiho of his loneliness.

Viktor had witnessed all this, utterly confused by the younger's behavior. He had half a mind to scold Jiho until he saw Eric come in one day, asking where his office was.

At that moment, Eric had told Viktor what was going on. Baffled by the new information, he brought his brother-in-law to Jiho's office–where the man was muttering under his breath.

Jiho had lit up as Eric walked in. He was the only one who could contact Saoirse while she was still in France.

Why only Eric?

He didn't know or care now. He was only interested in any updates. Hearing that Saoirse would return to the States within the next two days made his mood flip.

The sudden personality change stunned everyone as they had gotten used to the snappy man.

During this joyful news, Viktor called Emilia to ask if she knew. Surprisingly, his wife had confirmed she knew about Jiho and Saoirse. Wondering why she said nothing to him, Viktor began asking questions. Emilia revealed that Saoirse was the one to tell her about a man she met at the bar. After every encounter, Saoirse would call her cousin for advice.

He did not know if he should feel angry or excited after the news. It had been some years since there was this much happening in the joint families, something that would only occur again once his own children got older.

Viktor had now called Brandon to see if he knew anything else. Thus began a black hole of needing any information about Jiho and Saoirse. A reason why both Viktor and Emilia were added to the group chat with Ally, Min-Jung, Eric, and Brandon.

The group of four increased to six.

THE DAY HAD BEEN busy with paperwork for Jiho.

Most of his time was spent at his desk, the downside of his practice. He wasn't halfway through his stack when Beth knocked on his door before poking her head through the frame.

"There's someone here to see you."

"Who?" Jiho asked, not looking up from his work.

Not gaining a response for a few moments, Jiho picked his head up. His pen had dropped with his grip loosened, his mouth parted, and eyes widened.

He stood up, knocking some papers and items off his desk. Quickly, he took off his glasses before rushing around his desk a few meters away from the visitor.

"You're back."

"And you were crabby, apparently." Saoirse teased, striding to the chairs that were facing him.

When he kept his head down, Saoirse let herself in, thanking the nurse for showing her the way. Under Viktor's permission, she was allowed in his office whenever she came, giving Jiho a pleasant surprise.

"It's been a while."

"It's been two months." Jiho quickly corrects, leaning back against his desk and taking all of her in as if it had been years since they had seen each other. He wanted to see how much the woman–who occupied his head and corrupted his heart–had changed.

He could see she had gotten a haircut since he'd last seen her; the brunette locks had been worn down today, only reaching the lower parts of her shoulder blades.

A few short strands framed her face, which was slightly tanned, and two braids on each side that had been started at the base of her neck.

Saoirse's bare face showed her freckles, something he had not seen before. They scattered all around, and they formed a heart on the right side–it was small but there; almost acted like a beauty mark. Another feature Jiho would surely think about later.

The elegant silhouettes Saoirse usually wore were in place of a pale blue turtleneck, which is only seen in the V-neckline of a white sweater. Which was accompanied by worn-out jeans and boots. Jiho found it rather endearing to see her like this.

"You've been counting? That's very sweet, *mon amour*."

Tucking her leg behind her, Saoirse had made herself comfortable in her seat. The happiness bubbled in Jiho; he wanted her to stay as long as possible, which was a good sign of that happening.

"How have you been *mon amour*?"

Moving the other chair closer to the woman, Jiho sat down, holding his hand out hesitantly at the bold move. He was silently asking to see her hand, which she allowed with a gentle smile to his request.

"Restless if I am telling the truth."

Playing with her fingers, giving a slow massage, he noticed calluses that were not there before her trip.

"I've had a lot occupying my mind as of recently." Looking up to catch her eye.

"And what had been occupying your mind, *mon amour*?"

Leaning closer towards the man. With each moment, Saoirse shortened the distance, Jiho's mind fogged more.

"You." He whispers, feeling her breath hit his lips. "You are the only thing that has occupied my mind since I met you."

Never could she admit it out loud, but she had missed him dearly while she was away. Seeing his messages and choosing not to respond hurt her.

Desperate to talk to Jiho, she was still afraid that it was all a game for him. On top of the fear, her father had been pushing her to marry within the next year to keep her in the family.

Otherwise, she would be disowned.

She could never speak to her brothers and other family members again, which broke her heart.

Pulling back, Saoirse remembered why she was here in the first place. Scolding herself for getting distracted.

Jiho started to panic; he didn't know what he had done wrong. Standing as well, he apologized, "I-I'm sorry. Did I...Was I making you uncomfortable?"

"No, *mon amour*. You did nothing." Turning her head to the side, "That's the problem." She mutters under her breath.

"Then...what is it?" Stepping closer.

Placing a facade, she spoke in a manner that he was unfamiliar with: "We cannot see each other until you get over this silly little crush."

Jiho paused, "What?"

He was confused.

Did she not feel the same way? Was all this a game for her? Those questions of self-doubt were pushed to the side after a moment. *It doesn't matter*, he thought. *I've already given her my heart. She can break it as many times as she likes.*

"I can't entertain this anymore." Saoirse declares, as her inner self breaks. "We cannot see each other until you stop whatever feelings you have. That is why I came today. To tell you to stop."

The man was floored by her statements. It didn't make any sense to him. After all this time, she wanted nothing to do with him.

He didn't believe it.

She could have told him at any point that it wasn't something she wanted, but this Saoirse was not the same one he fell for. This was the Saoirse he saw when her worker came to tell her news she did not like.

Jiho shook his head, "No."

"No?"

"No." He voiced his reasoning, "I need a reason on why I must stop my feelings? Why do I have to stay away? I am perfectly okay with being in a one-sided affection with you."

She was stunned as he confessed. She had never been confronted this harshly before. Usually, men would only need to be told once by her and Eric to leave and find an easier person. *So why does this man not accept her rejection without reason? Why is he content with just himself being hurt*? She thought.

"Do you not feel the same as I do?" Jiho asked after she fails to respond, "Did that moment on the balcony mean nothing to you?"

With each word, Jiho took a step closer, daring himself to confess to the woman before him, "You cannot tell me that you felt nothing. In any of our moments. Not when you have been the one to make the moves, the one to enchant me with one look, one word. With just your very being."

He tugs her closer with her hips. Eyes darted everywhere in search of some emotion. Something to confirm his gut feeling about them.

"I have and will always be at your mercy. You have complete control over me. All that I am is yours. The only price for that is to allow me to stay by your side. You can have me any way you like." Gripping her chin between his fingers, their eyes bound to each other, "Give me a good reason why I need to stop."

Saoirse had been hooked on the first question. Her mask slowly faded as she thought about her time with the man. Although they had only met in person a few times, each moment was remarkable for her.

To have someone be utterly devoted to her, as Jiho had shown, was something she dreamt about. The woman had talked about him to Emilia, asking if she was crazy for having thoughts about a man she'd only just met.

She was surprised when she learned that Emilia had known Jiho for a while, confirming and answering any questions the woman might have. Saoirse discovered that Jiho was truly genuine; he was a caring and loving man, but his past was difficult.

"Please tell me." He pleaded.

His desperation was there for everyone to see, with no amount of shame in his body. There was no doubt that Saoirse was the one he wanted.

All he could do was think of her day and night. Of course, he thought of the sinful activities, but he also thought of the mundane things.

He wondered what she would look like in his arms after a night of rest. The simple outings they would have or new activities to try.

All the small gestures he had prepared for her: flowers every week, mastering her favorite foods, taking her godchildren on outings together. Jiho had envisioned them sitting in a home together, just talking with one another, laughing, dancing.

Saoirse's eyes searched for any possible lie, anything to tell herself he was tricking her. But she couldn't.

All that was there was hope.

She didn't want to hurt him, but she had to tell the truth, something that would kill the both them. Jiho's words rang in her ear: *Have me any way you like*. She wanted one last kiss before breaking his heart.

Saoirse held onto Jiho's white coat, parting her mouth, smashing their lips together. The kiss was not delicate but rushed, passionate, and painful. There were so many emotions running through her, and Jiho could feel it. Wanting to help her forget, at least for this moment, he grabbed the back of her neck.

His thumb rested on her cheek, taking control of the sloppy kiss she had begun. Wrapping his arm around her waist as he gained the upper hand, pulling her closer to him, if possible. Jiho had waited for this, and he would take the given opportunity to devour her in such a way.

With the need to breathe, the two parted, leaning their foreheads together, an endearing affection he had grown to love.

With the two breathing heavily, Jiho opened his eyes to see tears come from hers. In a panic, Jiho started to blame himself for being too rough on her.

His apologies fell on deaf ears as Saoirse vigorously shook her head, pushing them apart.

Tilting his head at the confusing signals his siren was giving him. He wanted to ask what was happening to her, but Saoirse beat him.

"I am getting married."

Acknowledgement

I want to thank my family for their undying support on my journey. My mother always encouraged me to have creative outlets and endless praise for the different stages of writing. My brother, who is not a reader of any sort, took the time to read my work. It brings me joy to know he did something he does not particularly like, for my sake, considering my dreams and showing interest. Lastly, I thank my partner for his sacrifice in taking over our shared responsibility to ensure the book release happened to my liking. I could not have done this without you! Thank you, and I love you!

I also want to thank another aspiring author whose book I had the privilege of beta reading, Ash, books_and.dragons on Instagram. Without our formed friendship and constant support from one another, as well as the editing tips, I would still be in the process of drafting.